THE TIME
OF FRIENDSHIP

Paul Bowles

THE TIME OF

By Paul Bowles

FRIENDSHIP

A volume of short stories

Holt,
Rinehart and
Winston

New York   Chicago
San Francisco

Designer: Ernst Reichl
8646457
Printed in the United States of America

CONTENTS

THE TIME
OF FRIENDSHIP

T HE trouble had been growing bigger each year, ever since the end of the war. From the beginning, although aware of its existence, Fräulein Windling had determined to pay it no attention. At first there were only whispered reports of mass arrests. People said: "Many thousands of Moslems have been sent to prison in France." Soon some of her own friends had begun to disappear, like young Bachir and Omar ben Lakhdar, the postmaster of Timimoun, who suddenly one morning were gone, or so she was told, for when she returned the following winter they were not there, and she never had seen them since. The people simply made their faces blank when she tried to talk about it. After the hostilities had begun in earnest, even though the nationalists had derailed the trains and disrupted the trans-Saharan truck service on several occasions, still it was possible to get beyond the disturbed region to her oasis. There in the south the fighting was far away, and the long hours of empty desert that lay between made it seem much farther, almost as though it had been across the sea. If the men of her oasis should ever be infected by the virus of discontent from the far-off north—and this seemed to her almost inconceivable —then in spite of the fact that she was certain that war could bring them nothing but unhappiness, she would have no re- course but to hope for their victory. It was their own land they would be fighting for, their own lives they would be losing in

1

order to win the fight. In the meantime people did not talk; life was hard but peaceful. Each one was aware of the war that was going on in the north, and each one was glad it was far away.

Summers, Fräulein Windling taught in the Freiluftschule in Bern, where she entertained her pupils with tales of the life led by the people in the great desert in Africa. In the village where she lived, she told them, everything was made by the people themselves out of what the desert had to offer. They lived in a world of objects fashioned out of baked earth, woven grass, palmwood and animal skins. There was no metal. Although she did not admit it to the children, this was no longer wholly true, since recently the women had taken to using empty oil tins for carrying water, instead of the goathide bags of a few years before. She had tried to discourage her friends among the village women from this innovation, telling them that the tins could poison the water; they had agreed, and gone on using them. "They are lazy," she decided. "The oil tins are easier to carry."

When the sun went down and the cool air from the oasis below with its sting of woodsmoke rose to the level of the hotel, she would smell it inside her room and stop whatever she was doing. Then she would put on her burnoose and climb the stairs to the roof. The blanket she lay on while she sunbathed each morning would be there, and she would stretch out on it facing the western sky, and feel the departed sun's heat still strong underneath her body. It was one of the great pleasures of the day, to watch the light changing in the oasis below, when dusk and the smoke from the evening fires slowly blotted out the valley. There always came a moment when all that was left was the faint outline, geometric and precise, of the mass of mud prisms that was the village, and a certain clump of high date palms that stood outside its entrance. The houses themselves were no longer there, and eventually the highest palm disappeared; and unless there was a moon all

2

that remained to be seen was the dying sky, the sharp edges of the rocks on the hammada, and a blank expanse of mist that lay over the valley but did not reach as far up the cliffs as the hotel.

Perhaps twice each winter a group of the village women would invite Fräulein Windling to go with them up into the vast land of the dunes to look for firewood. The glare here was cruel. There was not even the trace of a twig or a stem anywhere on the sand, yet as they wandered along the crests barefoot the women could spot the places where roots lay buried beneath the surface, and then they would stoop, uncover them, and dig them up. "The wind leaves a sign," they told her, but she was never certain of being able to identify the sign, nor could she understand how there might be a connection between the invisible roots in the sand and the wind in the air above. "What we have lost, they still possess," she thought.

Her first sight of the desert and its people had been a transfiguring experience; indeed, it seemed to her now that before coming here she had never been in touch with life at all. She believed firmly that each day she spent here increased the aggregate of her resistance. She coveted the rugged health of the natives, when her own was equally strong, but because she was white and educated, she was convinced that her body was intrinsically inferior.

All the work in the hotel was done by one quiet, sad-faced man named Boufelja. He had been there when she had first arrived many years ago; for Fräulein Windling he had come to be as much a part of the place as the cliffs across the valley. She often sat on at her table by the fireplace after lunch, playing cards by herself, until the logs no longer gave out heat. There were two very young French soldiers from the fort opposite, who ate in the hotel dining-room. They drank a great amount of wine, and it annoyed her to see their faces slowly turning red as they sat there. At first the soldiers had tipped their caps

3

to her as they went out, and they had stopped their laughing long enough to say, *"Bonjour, madame,"* to her, but now they no longer did. She was happy when they had left, and savored the moment before the fire burned out, while it still glowed under the gusts of wind that wandered down the wide chimney.

Almost always the wind sprang up early in the afternoon, a steady, powerful blowing that roared through the thousands of palms in the oasis below and howled under each door in the hotel, covering the more distant village sounds. This was the hour when she played solitaire, or merely sat, watching the burnt-out logs as they fell to pieces before her eyes. Later she would go along the terrace, a high, bright place like the deck of a great ship sailing through the desert afternoon, hurrying into her room for an instant to get her sweater and cane, and start out on a walk. Sometimes she went southward following the river valley, along the foot of the silent cliffs and through the crooked gorges, to an abandoned village built in a very hot place at a turn in the canyon. The sheer walls of rock behind it sent back the heat, so that the air burned her throat as she breathed it in. Or she went farther, to where the cliff dwellings were, with their animals and symbols incised in the rock.

Returning along the road that led to the village, deep in the green shade of the thickest part of the palm forest, she was regularly aware of the same group of boys sitting at the turn of the road, at a place just before it led up the hill to the shops and the village. They squatted on the sand behind the feathery branches of a giant tamarisk, quietly talking. When she came up to them she greeted them, and they always replied, remained silent a moment until she had passed by, and then resumed their conversation. As far as she could tell, there was never any reference to her by word, and yet this year it sometimes seemed to her that once she had gone by, their inflection had subtly altered, as though there had been a modulation into another key. Did their attitude border on derision?

She did not know, but since this was the first time during all her years in the desert that the idea had ever suggested itself to her, she put it resolutely out of her mind. "A new generation requires a new technique if one is to establish contact," she thought. "It is for me to find it." Nevertheless she was sorry that there was no other way of getting into the village save along this main road where they invariably gathered. Even the slight tension caused by having to go past them marred the pleasure of her walks.

One day she realized with a slight shock of shame that she did not even know what the boys looked like. She had seen them only as a group from a distance; when she drew near enough to say good-day to them, she always had her head down, watching the road. The fact that she had been afraid to look at them was unacceptable; now, as she came up to them, she stared into the eyes of one after the other, carefully. Nodding gravely, she went on. Yes, they were insolent faces, she thought—not at all like the faces of their elders. The respectful attitudes into which they had been startled were the crudest sort of shamming. But the important thing to her was that she had won: she was no longer preoccupied with having to pass by them every day. Slowly she even grew to recognize each boy.

There was one, she noted, younger than the others, who always sat a little apart from them, and it was this shy one who stood talking to Boufelja in the hotel kitchen early one morning when she went in. She pretended not to notice him. "I am going to my room to work on the machine for about an hour," she told Boufelja. "You can come then to make up the room," and she turned to go out. As she went through the doorway she glanced at the boy's face. He was looking at her, and he did not turn away when his eyes met hers. "How are you?" she said. Perhaps half an hour later, when she was typing her second letter, she raised her head. The boy was standing on the

5

terrace looking at her through the open door. He squinted, for the wind was strong; behind his head she saw the tops of the palms bending.

"If he wants to watch, let him watch," she said to herself, deciding to pay him no attention. After a while he went away. While Boufelja served her lunch, she questioned him about the boy. "Like an old man," said Boufelja. "Twelve years old but very serious. Like some old, old man." He smiled, then shrugged. "It's the way God wanted him to be."

"Of course," she said, remembering the boy's alert, unhappy face. "A young dog that everyone has kicked," she thought, "but he hasn't given up."

In the days that followed, he came often to the terrace and stood watching her while she typed. Sometimes she waved to him, or said: "Good morning." Without answering he would take a step backward, so that he was out of her range. Then he would continue to stand where he was. His behavior irked her, and one day when he had done this, she quickly got up and went to the door. "What is it?" she asked him, trying to smile as she spoke.

"I didn't do anything," he said, his eyes reproachful.

"I know," she answered. "Why don't you come in?"

The boy looked swiftly around the terrace as if for help; then he bowed his head and stepped inside the door. Here he stood waiting, his head down, looking miserable. From her luggage she brought out a bag of hard candy, and handed him a piece. Then she put a few simple questions to him, and found that his French was much better than she had expected. "Do the other boys know French as well as you?" she asked him.

"Non, madame," he said, shaking his head slowly. "My father used to be a soldier. Soldiers speak good French."

She tried to keep her face from expressing the disapproval she felt, for she despised everything military. "I see," she said with some asperity, turning back to her table and shuffling the papers. "Now I must work," she told him, immediately adding in a warmer voice, "but you come back tomorrow, if you like." He waited an instant, looking at her with unchanged wistfulness. Then slowly he smiled, and laid the candy wrapper, folded into a tiny square, on the corner of her table. "*Au revoir, madame*," he said, and went out of the door. In the silence she heard the scarcely audible thud of his bare heels on the earth floor of the terrace. "In this cold," she thought. "Poor child! If I ever buy anything for him it will be a pair of sandals."

Each day thereafter, when the sun was high enough to give substance to the still morning air, the boy would come stealthily along the terrace to her door, stand a few seconds, and then say in a lost voice that was all the smaller and more hushed for the great silence outside: "*Bonjour, madame*." She would tell him to come in, and they would shake hands gravely, he afterward raising the backs of his fingers to his lips, always with the same slow ceremoniousness. She sometimes tried to fathom his countenance as he went through this ritual, to see if by any chance she could detect a shade of mockery there; instead she saw an expression of devotion so convincing that it startled her, and she looked away quickly. She always kept a bit of bread or some biscuits in a drawer of the wardrobe; when she had brought the food out and he was eating it, she would ask him for news about the families in his quarter of the village. For discipline's sake she offered him a piece of candy only every other day. He sat on the floor by the doorway, on a torn old camel blanket, and he watched her constantly, never turning his head away from her.

She wanted to know what he was called, but she was aware of how secretive the inhabitants of the region were about names, seldom giving their true ones to strangers; this was a peculiarity she respected because she knew it had its roots in their own prehistoric religion. So she forbore asking him, sure that the time would come when he trusted her enough to give it of his own volition. And the moment happened one morning unexpectedly, when he had just recounted several legends involving the great Moslem king of long ago, whose name was Solomon. Suddenly he stopped, and forcing himself to gaze steadily at her without blinking, he said: "And my name too is Slimane, the same as the king."

She tried to teach him to read, but he did not seem able to learn. Often just as she felt he was about to connect two loose ends of ideas and perhaps at last make a contact which would enable him to understand the principle, a look of resignation and passivity would appear in his face, and he would willfully cut off the stream of effort from its source, and remain sitting, merely looking at her, shaking his head from side to side to show that it was useless. It was hard not to lose patience with him at such moments.

The following year she decided not to go on with the lessons, and to use Slimane instead as a guide, bearer and companion, a role which she immediately saw was more suited to his nature than that of pupil. He did not mind how far they went or how much equipment he had to carry; on the contrary, to him a long excursion was that much more of an event, and whatever she loaded onto him he bore with the air of one upon whom an honor is conferred. It was probably her happiest season in the desert, that winter of comradeship when together they made the countless pilgrimages down the valley. As the weeks passed the trips grew in scope, and the hour of departure was brought forward until it came directly after she had finished her breakfast. All day long, trudging in the open sun and in the occasional shade of the broken fringe of palms that skirted the river-bed, she conversed passionately with him. Sometimes she could see that he felt like telling her what was in his head, and she let him speak for as long as his enthusiasm lasted, often reviving it at the end with carefully chosen questions. But usually it was she who did the speaking as she walked behind him. Pounding the stony ground with her steel-tipped stick each time her right foot went down, she told him in great detail the story of the life of Hitler, showing why he was hated by the Christians. This she thought necessary since Slimane had been under a different impression, and indeed had imagined that the Europeans thought as highly of the vanished leader as did he and the rest of the people in the village. She talked a good deal about Switzerland, casually stressing the cleanliness, honesty and good health of her countrymen in short parables of daily life. She told him about Jesus, Martin Luther and Garibaldi, taking care to keep Jesus distinct from the Moslem prophet Sidna Aissa, since even for the sake of argument she could not agree for an instant with the Islamic doctrine according to which the Savior was a Moslem. Slimane's attitude of respect bordering on adoration with regard to her never altered unless she inadvertently tangled with the subject of Islam; then, no matter what she said (for at that point it seemed that automatically he was no longer within hearing) he would shake his head interminably and cry: "No, no, no, no! Nazarenes know nothing about Islam. Don't talk, madame, I beg you, because you don't know what you're saying. No, no, no!"

Long ago she had kept the initial promise to herself that she would buy him sandals; this purchase had been followed by others. At fairly regular intervals she had taken him to Benaissa's store to buy a shirt, a pair of baggy black cotton trousers of the kind worn by the Chaamba camel-drivers, and ultimately a new white burnoose, despite the fact that she knew the entire village would discuss the giving of so valuable an object. She also knew that it was only the frequent bestowing of such gifts that kept Slimane's father from forbidding him to spend his time with her. Even so, according to reports brought by Slimane, he sometimes objected. But Slimane himself, she was sure, wanted nothing, expected nothing.

9

Paul Bowles

It was each year when March was drawing to a close that the days began to be painfully hot and even the nights grew breathless; then, although it always required a strenuous effort of the will to make herself take the step which would bring about renewed contact with the outside world, she would devote two or three days to washing her clothing and preparing for the journey. When the week set for her departure had come, she went over to the fort and put in a call to the café at Kerzaz, asking the proprietor to tell the driver of the next northbound truck to take the detour that would enable her to catch him at a point only about three kilometers from the village.

She and Slimane had come back to the hotel on the afternoon of their last excursion down the valley; Fräulein Windling stood on the terrace looking out at the orange mountains of sand behind the fort. Slimane had taken the packs into the room and put them down. She turned and said: "Bring the big tin box." When he had pulled it out from under the bed he carried it to her, dusting it off with the sleeve of his shirt, and she led the way up the stairs to the roof. They sat down on the blanket; the glow of the vanished sun's furnace heated their faces. A few flies still hovered, now and then attacking their necks. Slimane handed her the biscuit tin and she gave him a fistful of chocolate-covered cakes. "So many all at once?"

"Yes," she said. "You know I'm going home in four days."

He looked down at the blanket a moment before replying. "I know," he murmured. He was silent again. Then he cried out aggrievedly: "Boufelja says it's hot here in the summer. It's not hot! In our house it's cool. It's like the oasis where the big pool is. You would never be hot there."

"I have to earn money. You know that. I want to come back next year."

He said sadly: "Next year, madame! Only Moulana knows how next year will be."

Some camels growled as they rolled in the sand at the foot of the fort; the light was receding swiftly. "Eat your biscuits,"

10

she told him, and she ate one herself. "Next year we'll go to Abadla with the caid, *incha'Allah.*"

He sighed deeply. "Ah, madame!" he said. She noted, at first with a pang of sympathy and then, reconsidering, with disapproval, the anguish that lent his voice its unaccustomed intensity. It was the quality she least liked in him, this faintly theatrical self-pity. "Next year you'll be a man," she told him firmly. Her voice grew less sure, assumed a hopeful tone. "You'll remember all the things we talked about?"

She sent him a postcard from Marseille, and showed her classes photographs they had taken of one another, and of the caid. The children were impressed by the caid's voluminous turban. "Is he a Bedouin?" asked one.

When she left the embassy office she knew that this was the last year she would be returning to the desert. There was not only the official's clearly expressed unfriendliness and suspicion: for the first time he had made her answer a list of questions which she found alarming. He wanted to know what subjects she taught in the Freiluftschüle, whether she had ever been a journalist, and exactly where she proposed to be each day after arriving in the Sahara. She had almost retorted: I go where I feel like going. I don't make plans. But she had merely named the oasis. She knew that Frenchmen had no respect for elderly Swiss ladies who wore woolen stockings; this simply made them more contemptible in her eyes. However, it was they who controlled the Sahara.

The day the ship put into the African port it was raining. She knew the gray terraced ramps of the city were there in the gloom ahead, but they were invisible. The ragged European garments of the dock workers were soaked with rain. Later, the whole rain-sodden city struck her as grim, and the people passing along the streets looked unhappy. The change, even from the preceding year, was enormous; it made her sad to sit in the big, cold café where she went for coffee after dinner, and so she returned to her hotel and slept. The next day she

11

got on the train for Perrégaux. The rain fell most of the day. In Perrégaux she took a room in a hotel near the station, and stayed in it, listening to the rain rattle down the gutter by her window. "This place would be a convenient model for Hell," she wrote to a friend in Basel before going to sleep that night. "A full-blown example of the social degeneracy achieved by forced cultural hybridism. Populace debased and made hostile by generations of merciless exploitation. I take the southbound narrow-gauge train tomorrow morning for a happier land, and trust that my friend the sun will appear at some point during the day. *Seien Sie herzlich gegrüsst von Ihrer Maria.*"

As the train crawled southward, up over the high plateau land, the clouds were left behind and the sun took charge of the countryside. Fräulein Windling sat attentively by the smeared window, enveloped in an increasing sadness. As long as it had been raining, she had imagined the rain as the cause of her depression: the gray cloud light gave an unaccustomed meaning to the landscape by altering forms and distances. Now she understood that the more familiar and recognizable the contours of the desert were to become, the more conscious she would be of having no reason to be in it, because it was her last visit.

Two days later, when the truck stopped to let her out, Boufelja stood in the sun beside the boulders waving; one of the men of the village was with him to help carry the luggage. Once the truck had gone and its cloud of yellow dust had fled across the hammada, the silence was there; it seemed that no sound could be louder than the crunch of their shoes on the ground.

"How is Slimane?" she asked. Boufelja was noncommittal. "He's all right," he said. "They say he tried to run away. But he didn't get very far." The report might be true, or it might be false; in any case she determined not to allude to it unless Slimane himself mentioned it first.

She felt an absurd relief when they came to the edge of the cliffs and she saw the village across the valley. Not until she had made the rounds of the houses where her friends lived, discussed their troubles with them and left some pills here and some candy there, was she convinced that no important change had come to the oasis during her absence. She went to the house of Slimane's parents: he was not there. "Tell him to come and see me," she said to his father as she left the house.

On the third morning after her arrival Slimane appeared, and stood there in the doorway smiling. Once she had greeted him and made him sit down and have coffee with her, she plied him with questions about life in the village while she had been in Europe. Some of his friends had gone to become patriots, he said, and they were killing the French like flies. Her heart sank, but she said nothing. As she watched him smiling she was able to exult in the reflection that Slimane had been reachable, after all; she had proved that it was possible to make true friends of the younger people. But even while she was saying, "How happy I am to see you, Slimane," she remembered that their time together was now limited, and an expression of pain passed over her face as she finished the phrase. "I shall not say a word to him about it," she decided. If he, at least, still had the illusion of unbounded time lying ahead, he would somehow retain his aura of purity and innocence, and she would feel less anguish during the time they spent together.

One day they went down the valley to see the caid, and discussed the long-planned trip to Abadla. Another day they started out at dawn to visit the tomb of Moulay Ali ben Said, where there was a spring of hot water. It was a tiny spot of oasis at the edge of a ridge of high dunes; perhaps fifty palms were there around the decayed shrine. In the shade of the rocks below the walls there was a ruined cistern into which the steaming water dribbled. They spread blankets on the sand nearby, at the foot of a small tamarisk, and took out their

13

lunch. Before starting to eat, they drank handfuls of the water, which Slimane said was famed for its holiness. The palms rattled and hissed in the wind overhead.

"Allah has sent us the wind to make us cool while we eat," Slimane said when he had finished his bread and dates.

"The wind has always been here," she answered carelessly, "and it always will be here."

He sat up straight. "No, no!" he cried. "When Sidna Aissa has returned for forty days there will be no more Moslems and the world will end. Everything, the sky and the sun and the moon. And the wind too. Everything." He looked at her with an expression of such satisfaction that she felt one of her occasional surges of anger against him.

"I see," she said. "Stand over by the spring a minute. I want to take your picture." She had never understood why it was that the Moslems had conceded Jesus even this Pyrrhic victory, the coda to all creation: its inconsistency embarrassed her. Across the decayed tank she watched Slimane assume the traditional stiff attitude of a person about to be photographed, and an idea came into her head. For Christmas Eve, which would come within two weeks, she would make a crèche. She would invite Slimane to eat with her by the fireplace, and when midnight came she would take him in to see it.

She finished photographing Slimane; they gathered up the equipment and set out against the hot afternoon wind for the village. The sand sometimes swept by, stinging their faces with its invisible fringe. Fräulein Windling led the way this time, and they walked fast. The image of the crèche, illumined by candles, occurred to her several times on the way back over the rocky erg; it made her feel inexpressibly sad, for she could not help connecting it with the fact that everything was ending. They came to the point north of the village where the empty erg was cut across by the wandering river valley. As they climbed slowly upward over the fine sand, she found herself whispering:

"It's the right thing to do." "*Right* is not the word," she thought, without being able to find a better one. She was going to make a crèche because she loved Christmas and wanted to share it with Slimane. They reached the hotel shortly after sunset, and she sent Slimane home in order to sit and plan her project on paper.

It was only when she began actually to put the crèche together that she realized how much work it was going to be. Early the next morning she asked Boufelja to find her an old wooden crate. Before she had been busy even a half-hour, she heard Slimane talking in the kitchen. Quickly she pushed everything under the bed and went out onto the terrace.

"Slimane," she said. "I'm very busy. Come in the afternoon." And that afternoon she told him that since she was going to be working every morning until after the day of the Christ Child, they would not be making any more long trips during that time. He received the information glumly. "I know," he said. "You are getting ready for the holy day. I understand."

"When the holy day comes, we will have a feast," she assured him.

"If Allah wills."

"I'm sorry," she said, smiling.

He shrugged. "Good-by," he told her.

Afternoons they still walked in the oasis or had tea on the roof, but her mornings she spent in her room sewing, hammering and sculpting. Once she had the platform constructed, she had to model the figures. She carried up a great mass of wet clay from the river to her room. It was two days before she managed to make a Virgin whose form pleased her. From an old strip of muslin she fashioned a convincing tent to house the Mother and the Child in its nest of tiny white chicken feathers. Shredded tamarisk needles made a fine carpet for the interior of the tent. Outside she poured sand, and then pushed the clay camels' long legs deep into it; one animal walked behind

15

the other over the dune, and a Wise Man sat straight on top of each, his white *djellaba* falling in long pointed folds to either side of the camel's flanks. The Wise Men would come carrying sacks of almonds and very small liqueur chocolates wrapped in colored tinfoil. When she had the crèche finished, she put it on the floor in the middle of the room and piled tangerines and dates in front of it. With a row of candles burning behind it, and one candle on each side in front, it would look like a Moslem religious chromolithograph. She hoped the scene would be recognizable to Slimane; he might then be more easily persuaded of its poetic truth. She wanted only to suggest to him that the god with whom he was on such intimate terms was the god worshipped by the Nazarenes. It was not an idea she would ever try to express in words.

An additional surprise for the evening would be the new flash-bulb attachment to her camera, which Slimane had not yet seen. She intended to take a good many pictures of the crèche and of Slimane looking at it; these she would enlarge to show her pupils. She went and bought a new turban for Slimane; he had been wearing none for more than a year now. This was a man's turban, and very fine: ten meters of the softest Egyptian cotton.

The day before Christmas she overslept, duped by the heavy sky. Each winter the oasis had a few dark days; they were rare, but this was one of them. While she still lay there in bed, she heard the roar of the wind, and when she got up to look out of the window she found no world outside—only a dim rose-gray fog that hid everything. The swirling sand sprayed ceaselessly against the glass; it had formed in long drifts on the floor of the terrace. When she went for breakfast, she wore her burnoose with the hood up around her face. The blast of the wind as she stepped out onto the terrace struck her with the impact of a solid object, and the sand gritted on the concrete floor under her shoes. In the dining-room Boufelja had bolted the shutters; he greeted her enthusiastically from the gloom inside, glad of her presence.

"A very bad day for your festival, alas, mademoiselle!" he observed as he set her coffee pot on the table.

"Tomorrow's the festival," she said. "It begins tonight."

"I know. I know." He was impatient with Nazarene feasts because the hours of their beginnings and ends were observed in so slipshod a manner. Moslem feasts began precisely, either at sundown or an hour before sunup, or when the new moon was first visible in the western sky at twilight. But the Nazarenes began their feasts whenever they felt like it.

She spent the morning in her room writing letters. By noon the air outside was darker with still more sand; the wind shook the hotel atop its rock as if it would hurl it over the tips of the palms below into the river-bed. Several times she rose and went to the window to stare out at the pink emptiness beyond the terrace. Storms made her happy, although she wished this one could have come after Christmas. She had imagined a pure desert night—cold, alive with stars, and the dogs yapping from the oasis. It might yet be that; there was still time, she thought, as she slipped her burnoose over her head to go in to lunch.

With the wind, the fireplace was an unsure blessing: besides the heat it gave, it provided the only light in the dining-room, but the smoke that belched from it burned her eyes and throat. The shutters at the windows rattled and pounded, covering the noise of the wind itself.

She got out of the dining-room as soon as she had finished eating, and hurried back to her room to sit through the slowly darkening afternoon, as she continued with her letter-writing and waited for the total extinction of daylight. Slimane was coming at eight. There would be enough time to carry everything into the dining-room before that, and to set the crèche up in the dark unused wing into which Boufelja was unlikely

17

to go. But when she came to do it, she found that the wind's force was even greater than she had imagined. Again and again she made the trip between her room and the dining-room, carrying each object carefully wrapped in her burnoose. Each time she passed in front of the kitchen door she expected Boufelja to open it and discover her. She did not want him there when she showed the crèche to Slimane; he could see it tomorrow at breakfast.

Protected by the noise of the gale she succeeded in transporting all the parts to the far dark corner of the dining-room without alerting Boufelja. Long before dinner time the crèche was in readiness, awaiting only the lighting of the candles to be brought alive. She left a box of matches on the table beside it, and hurried back to her room to arrange her hair and change her clothing. The sand had sifted through her garments and was now everywhere; it showered from her underwear and stuck like sugar to her skin. Her watch showed a few minutes after eight when she went out.

Only one place had been laid at table. She waited, while the blinds chattered and banged, until Boufelja appeared carrying the soup tureen.

"What a bad night," he said.

"You forgot to prepare for Slimane," she told him. But he was not paying attention. "He's stupid!" he exclaimed, beginning to ladle out the soup.

"Wait!" she cried. "Slimane's coming. I mustn't eat until he comes."

Still Boufelja misunderstood. "He wanted to come into the dining-room," he said. "And he knows it's forbidden at dinner time."

"But I invited him!" She looked at the lone soup plate on the table. "Tell him to come in, and set another place."

Boufelja was silent. He put the ladle back into the tureen. "Where is he?" she demanded, and without waiting for him to reply she went on. "Didn't I tell you he was going to have dinner with me tonight?" For suddenly she suspected that in her desire for secrecy she might indeed have neglected to mention the invitation to Boufelja.

"You didn't say anything," he told her. "I didn't know. I sent him home. But he'll be back after dinner."

"Oh, Boufelja!" she cried. "You know Slimane never lies."

He looked down at her with reproach on his face. "I didn't know anything about mademoiselle's plans," he said aggrievedly. This made her think for a swift instant that he had discovered the crèche, but she decided that if he had he would have spoken of it.

"Yes, yes, I know. I should have told you. It's my fault."

"That's true, mademoiselle," he said. And he served the remaining courses observing a dignified silence which she, still feeling some displeasure with him, did not urge him to break. Only at the end of the meal, when she had pushed back her chair from the table and sat studying the pattern of the flames in the fireplace, did he decide to speak. "Mademoiselle will take coffee?"

"I do want some," she said, trying to bring a note of enthusiasm into her voice. "*Bien,*" murmured Boufelja, and he left her alone in the room. When he returned carrying the coffee, Slimane was with him, and they were laughing, she noted, quite as though there had been no misunderstanding about dinner. Slimane stood by the door an instant, stamping his feet and shaking the sand from his burnoose. As he came forward to take her hand, she cried: "Oh, Slimane, it's my fault! I forgot to tell Boufelja. It's terrible!"

"There is no fault, madame," he said gravely. "This is a festival."

"Yes, this is a festival," she echoed. "And the wind's still blowing. Listen!"

Slimane would not take coffee, but Boufelja, ceding to her pressure, let her pour him out a cup, which he drank standing by the fireplace. She suspected him of being secretly pleased that Slimane had not managed to eat with her. When he had finished his coffee, he wished them good-night and went off to bed in his little room next to the kitchen.

They sat a while watching the fire, without talking. The wind rushed past in the emptiness outside, the blinds hammered. Fräulein Windling was content. Even if the first part of the celebration had gone wrong, the rest of the evening could still be pleasant.

She waited until she was sure that Boufelja had really gone to bed, and then she reached into her bag and brought out a small plastic sack full of chocolate creams, which she placed on the table.

"Eat," she said carelessly, and she took a piece of candy herself. With some hesitation Slimane put out his hand to take the sack. When he had a chocolate in his mouth, she began to speak. She intended to tell him the story of the Nativity, a subject she already had touched upon many times during their excursions, but only in passing. This time she felt she should tell him the entire tale. She expected him to interrupt when he discovered that it was a religious story, but he merely kept his noncommittal eyes on her and chewed mechanically, showing that he followed her by occasionally nodding his head. She became engrossed in what she was saying, and began to use her arms in wide gestures. Slimane reached for another chocolate and went on listening.

She talked for an hour or more, aware as from a distance of her own eloquence. When she told him about Bethlehem she was really describing Slimane's own village, and the house of Joseph and Mary was the house down in the *ksar* where Slimane had been born. The night sky arched above the Oued Zousfana and its stars glared down upon the cold hammada. Across the erg on their camels came the Wise Men in their burnooses and turbans, pausing at the crest of the last great dune to look ahead at the valley where the dark village lay. When she had finished, she blew her nose.

Slimane appeared to be in a state bordering on trance. She glanced at him, expected him to speak, but as he did not, she looked more closely at him. His eyes had an obsessed, vacant expression, and although they were still fixed on her face, she would have said that he was seeing something much farther away than she. She sighed, not wanting to make the decision to rouse him. The possibility she would have liked to entertain, had she not been so conscious of its unlikelihood, was that the boy somehow had been captivated by the poetic truth of the story, and was reviewing it in his imagination. "Certainly it could not be the case," she decided; it was more likely that he had ceased some time back to listen to her words, and was merely sitting there, only vaguely aware that she had come to the end of her story.

Then he spoke. "You're right. He was the King of Men."

Fräulein Windling caught her breath and leaned forward, but he went on. "And later Satan sent a snake with two heads. And Jesus killed it. Satan was angry with Him. He said: 'Why did you kill my friend? Did it hurt you, perhaps?' And Jesus said: 'I knew where it came from.' And Satan put on a black burnoose. That's true," he added, as he saw the expression of what he took to be simple disbelief on her face.

She sat up very straight and said: "Slimane, what are you talking about? There are no such stories about Jesus. Nor about Sidna Aissa either." She was not sure of the accuracy of this last statement; it was possible, she supposed, that such legends did exist among these people. "You know those are just stories that have nothing to do with the truth."

He did not hear her because he had already begun to talk. "I'm not speaking of Sidna Aissa," he said firmly. "He was a Moslem prophet. I'm talking about Jesus, the prophet of the Nazarenes. Everyone knows that Satan sent Him a snake with two heads."

She listened to the wind for an instant. "Ah," she said, and took another chocolate; she did not intend to carry the argument further. Soon she dug into her bag again and pulled out the turban, wrapped in red and white tissue paper.

"A present for you," she said, holding it out to him. He seized it mechanically, placed it on his lap and remained staring down at it. "Aren't you going to open it?" she demanded.

He nodded his head twice and tore open the paper. When he saw the pile of white cotton he smiled. Seeing his face at last come to life, she jumped up. "Let's put it on you!" she exclaimed. He gave her one end, which she pulled taut by walking all the way to the door. Then with his hand holding the other end to his forehead, he turned slowly round and round, going toward her all the time, arranging the form of the turban as it wound itself about his head. "Magnificent!" she cried. He went over to the row of black windows to look at himself.

"Can you see?" she asked.

"Yes, I can see the sides of it," he told her. "It's very beautiful."

She walked back toward the center of the room. "I'd like to take your picture, Slimane," she said, seeing an immediate look of puzzlement appear in his face. "Would you do me a favor? Go to my room and get the camera."

"At night? You can take a picture at night?"

She nodded, smiling mysteriously. "And bring me the yellow box on the bed."

Keeping the turban on his head, he got into his burnoose, took her flashlight and went out, letting the wind slam the door. She hoped the sound had not wakened Boufelja; for an instant she listened while there was no sound but the roar of air rushing through the corridor outside. Then she ran to the dark wing of the room and struck a match. Quickly she lighted all the candles around the crèche, straightened a camel in the sand, and walked back around the corner to the fireplace. She would not have thought the candles could give so much light. The other end of the room was now brighter than the end where she stood. In a moment the door burst open and Slimane came back in, carrying the camera slung over his shoulder. He put it down carefully on the table. "There was no yellow box on the bed," he told her. Then his glance caught the further walls flickering with the unfamiliar light, and he began to walk toward the center of the room. She saw that this was the moment. "Come," she said, taking his arm and pulling him gently around the corner to where the crèche was finally visible, bright with its multiple shuddering points of light. Slimane said nothing; he stopped walking and stood completely still. After a moment of silence, she plucked tentatively at his arm. "Come and see," she urged him. They continued to walk toward the crèche; as they came up to it she had the impression that if she had not been there he would have reached out his hand and touched it, perhaps would have lifted the tiny gold-clad infant Jesus out of His bed of feathers. But he stood quietly, looking at it. Finally he said: "You brought all that from Switzerland?"

"Of course not!" It was a little disappointing that he should not have recognized the presence of the desert in the picture, should not have sensed that the thing was of his place, and not an importation. "I made it all here," she said. She waited an instant. "Do you like it?"

"Ah, yes," he said with feeling. "It's beautiful. I thought it came from Switzerland."

To be certain that he understood the subject-matter, she began to identify the figures one by one, her voice taking on such an unaccustomed inflection of respect that he glanced up at her once in surprise. It was almost as if she too were seeing it for the first time. "And the Wise Men are coming down out of the erg to see the child."

"Why did you put all those almonds there?" asked Slimane, touching some with his forefinger.

"They're gifts for the little Jesus."

"But what are you going to do with them?" he pursued.

"Eat them, probably, later," she said shortly. "Take one if

you like. You say there was no yellow box on the bed?" She wanted to take the photographs while the candles were still of equal height.

"There was nothing but a sweater and some papers, madame."

She left him there by the crèche, crossed the room and put on her burnoose. The darkness in the corridor was complete; there was no sign that Boufelja had awakened. She knew her room was in great disorder, and she played the beam of the flashlight around the floor before entering. In the welter of displaced things that strewed the little room there seemed small chance of finding anything. The feeble ray illumined one by one the meaningless forms made by the piling of disparate objects one on the other; the light moved over the floor, along the bed, behind the flimsy curtain of the armoire. Suddenly she stopped and turned the beam under the bed. The box was in front of her face; she had put it with the crèche.

"I mustn't fall," she thought, running along the corridor. She forced herself to slow her pace to a walk, entered the dining room and shut the door after her carefully. Slimane was on his knees in the middle of the room, a small object of some sort in his hand. She noted with relief that he was amusing himself. "I'm sorry it took me so long," she exclaimed. "I'd forgotten where I'd put it." She was pulling her burnoose off over her heard; now she hung it on a nail by the fireplace, and taking up the camera and the yellow box, she walked over to join him.

Perhaps a faint glimmer of guilt in his expression as he glanced up made her eyes stray along the floor toward another object lying nearby, similar to the one he held in his hand. It was one of the Wise Men, severed at the hips from his mount. The Wise Man in Slimane's hand was intact, but the camel had lost its head and most of its neck.

"Slimane! What are you doing?" she cried with undisguised anger. "What have you done to the crèche?" She advanced around the corner and looked in its direction. There was not really much more than a row of candles and a pile of sand that had been strewn with tangerine peel and date stones; here and there a carefully folded square of lavender or pink tinfoil had been planted in the sand. All three of the Wise Men had been enlisted in Slimane's battle on the floor, the tent ravaged in the campaign to extricate the almonds piled inside, and the treasure sacks looted of their cholocate liqueurs. There was no sign anywhere of the infant Jesus or of his gold-lamé garment. She felt tears come into her eyes. Then she laughed shortly, and said: "Well, it's finished. Yes?"

"Yes, madame," he said calmly. "Are you going to make the photograph now?" He got to his feet and laid the broken camel on the platform in the sand with the other debris.

Fräulein Windling spoke evenly. "I wanted to take a picture of the crèche."

He waited an instant, as if he were listening to a distant sound. Then he said: "Should I put on my burnoose?"

"No." She began to take out the flash-bulb attachment. When she had it ready, she took the picture before he had time to strike a pose. She saw his astonishment at the sudden bright light prolong itself into surprise that the thing was already done, and then become resentment at having been caught off his guard; but pretending to have seen nothing, she went on snapping covers shut. He watched her as she gathered up her things. "Is it finished?" he said, disappointed. "Yes," she replied. "It will be a very good picture."

"Incha 'Allah."

She did not echo his piety. "I hope you've enjoyed the festival," she told him.

Slimane smiled widely. "Ah yes, madame. Very much. Thank you."

She let him out into the camel-square and turned the lock in the door. Quickly she went back into her room, wishing it were a clear night like other nights, when she could stand out

25

on the terrace and look at the dunes and stars, or sit on the roof and hear the dogs, for in spite of the hour she was not sleepy. She cleared her bed of all the things that lay on top of it, and got in, certain that she was going to lie awake for a long time. For it had shaken her, the chaos Slimane had made in those few minutes of her absence. Across the seasons of their friendship she had come to think of him as being very nearly like herself, even though she knew he had not been that way when she first had met him. Now she saw the dangerous vanity at the core of that fantasy: she had assumed that somehow his association with her had automatically been for his ultimate good, that inevitably he had been undergoing a process of improvement as a result of knowing her. In her desire to see him change, she had begun to forget what Slimane was really like. "I shall never understand him," she thought helplessly, sure that just because she felt so close to him she would never be able to observe him dispassionately.

"This is the desert," she told herself. Here food is not an adornment; it is meant to be eaten. She had spread out food and he had eaten it. Any argument which attached blame to that could only be false. And so she lay there accusing herself. "It has been too much head and high ideals," she reflected, "and not enough heart." Finally she traveled on the sound of the wind into sleep.

At dawn when she awoke she saw that the day was going to be another dark one. The wind had dropped. She got up and shut the window. The early morning sky was heavy with cloud. She sank back into bed and fell asleep. It was later than usual when she rose, dressed, and went into the dining-room. Boufelja's face was strangely expressionless as he wished her good-morning. She supposed it was the memory of last night's misunderstanding, still with him—or possibly he was annoyed at having had to clean up the remains of the crèche. Once she had sat down and spread her napkin across her lap, he unbent sufficiently to say to her: "Happy festival."

"Thank you. Tell me, Boufelja," she went on, changing her inflection. "When you brought Slimane back in after dinner last night, do you know where he had been? Did he tell you?"

"He's a stupid boy," said Boufelja. "I told him to go home and eat and come back later. You think he did that? Never. He walked the whole time up and down in the courtyard here, outside the kitchen door, in the dark."

"I understand!" exclaimed Fräulein Windling triumphantly. "So he had no dinner at all."

"I had nothing to give him," he began, on the defensive.

"Of course not," she said sternly. "He should have gone home and eaten."

"Ah, you see?" grinned Boufelja. "That's what I told him to do."

In her mind she watched the whole story being enacted: Slimane aloofly informing his father that he would be eating at the hotel with the Swiss lady, the old man doubtless making some scornful reference to her, and Slimane going out. Unthinkable, once he had been refused admittance to the dining-room, for him to go back and face the family's ridicule. "Poor boy," she murmured.

"The commandant wants to see you," said Boufelja, making one of his abrupt conversational changes. She was surprised, since from one year to the next the captain never gave any sign of being aware of her existence; the hotel and the fort were like two separate countries. "Perhaps for the festival," Boufelja suggested, his face a mask. "Perhaps," she said uneasily.

When she had finished her breakfast, she walked across to the gates of the fort. The sentry seemed to be expecting her. One of the two young French soldiers was in the compound painting a chair. He greeted her, saying that the captain was in his office. She went up the long flight of stairs and paused an instant at the top, looking down at the valley in the unaccustomed gray light, noting how totally different it looked from its usual self, on this dim day.

27

A voice from inside called out: *"Entrez, s'il vous plaît!"* She opened the door and stepped in. The captain sat behind his desk; she had the unwelcome sensation of having played this same scene on another occasion, in another place. And she was suddenly convinced that she knew what he was going to say. She seized the back of the empty chair facing his desk. "Sit down, Mademoiselle Windling," he said, rising halfway out of his seat, waving his arm, and sitting again quickly.

There were several topographical maps on the wall behind him, marked with lavender and green chalk. The captain looked at his desk and then at her, and said in a clear voice: "It is an unfortunate stroke of chance that I should have to call you here on this holiday." Fräulein Windling sat down in the chair; leaning forward, she seemed about to rest her elbow on his desk, but instead crossed her legs and folded her arms tight. "Yes?" she said, tense, waiting for the message. It came immediately, for which she was conscious, even then, of being grateful to him. He told her simply that the entire area had been closed to civilians; this order applied to French nationals as well as to foreigners, so she must not feel discriminated against. The last was said with a wry attempt at a smile. "This means that you will have to take tomorrow morning's truck," he continued. "The driver has already been advised of your journey. Perhaps another year, when the disturbances are over. . ." ("Why does he say that?" she thought, "when he knows it's the end, and the time of friendship is finished?") He rose and extended his hand.

She could not remember going out of the room and down the long stairway into the compound, but now she was standing outside the sentry gate beside the wall of the fort, with her hand on her forehead. "Already," she thought. "It came so soon." And it occurred to her that she was not going to be given the time to make amends to Slimane, so that it was really true she was never going to understand him. She walked up to the parapet to look down at the edge of the oasis for a moment, and then went back to her room to start packing. All day long she worked in her room, pulling out boxes, forcing herself to be aware only of the decisions she was making as to what was to be taken and what was to be left behind once and for all.

At lunchtime Boufelja hovered near her chair. "Ah, mademoiselle, how many years we have been together, and now it is finished!" "Yes," she thought, but there was nothing to do about it. His lamentations made her nervous and she was short with him. Then she felt guilt-stricken and said slowly, looking directly at him: "I am very sad, Boufelja." He sighed "Ay, mademoiselle, I know!"

By nightfall the pall of clouds had been blown away across the desert, and the western sky was partly clear. Fräulein Windling had finished all her packing. She went out onto the terrace, saw the dunes pink and glowing, and climbed the steps to the roof to look at the sunset. Great skeins of fiery storm-cloud streaked the sky. Mechanically she let her gaze follow the meanders of the river valley as it lost itself in the darkening hammada to the south. "It is in the past," she reminded herself; this was already the new era. The desert out there looked the same as it always had looked. But the sky, ragged, red and black, was like a handbill that had just been posted above it, announcing the arrival of war.

It was a betrayal, she was thinking, going back down the steep stairs, running her hand along the familar rough mud wall to steady herself, and the French of course were the culprits. But beyond that she had the irrational and disagreeable conviction that the countryside itself had connived in the betrayal, that it was waiting to be transformed by the struggle. She went into her room and lit the small oil lamp; sitting down, she held her hands over it to warm them. At some point there had been a change: the people no longer wanted to go on living in the world they knew. The pressure of the past had become too great, and its shell had broken.

In the afternoon she had sent Boufelja to tell Slimane the news, and to ask him to be at the hotel at daybreak. During dinner she discussed only the details of departure and travel; when Boufelja tried to pull the talk in emotional directions, she did not reply. His commiseration was intolerable; she was not used to giving voice to her despair. When she got to her room she went directly to bed. The dogs barked half the night.

It was cold in the morning. Her hands ached as she gathered up the wet objects from around the washbowl on the table, and somehow she drove a sliver deep under the nail of her thumb. She picked some of it out with a needle, but the greater part remained. Before breakfast she stepped outside.

Standing in the waste-land between the hotel and the fort, she looked down at the countryside's innocent face. The padlocked gasoline pump, triumphant in fresh red and orange paint, caught the pure early sunlight. For a moment it seemed the only living thing in the landscape. She turned around. Above the dark irregular mass of palm trees rose the terraced village, calm under its morning veil of woodsmoke. She shut her eyes for an instant, and then went into the hotel.

She could feel herself sitting stiffly in her chair while she drank her coffee, and she knew she was being distant and formal with Boufelja, but it was the only way she could be certain of being able to keep going. Once he came to tell her that Slimane had arrived bringing the donkey and its master for her luggage. She thanked him and set down her coffee cup. "More?" said Boufelja. "No," she answered. "Drink another, mademoiselle," he urged her. "It's good on a cold morning." He poured it out and she drank part of it. There was a knocking at the gate. One of the young soldiers had been sent with a jeep to carry her out to the truck-stop on the trail.

"I can't!" she cried, thinking of Slimane and the donkey. The young soldier made it clear that he was not making an offer, but giving an order. Slimane stood beside the donkey outside the gate. While she began to speak with him the soldier shouted: "does he want to come, the *gosse?* He can come too, if he likes." Slimane ran to get the luggage and Fräulein Windling rushed inside to settle her bill. "Don't hurry," the soldier called after her. "There's plenty of time."

Boufelja stood in the kitchen doorway. Now for the first time it occurred to her to wonder what was going to become of him. With the hotel shut he would have no work. When she had settled her account and given him a tip which was much larger than she could afford, she took both his hands in hers and said: "*Mon cher* Boufelja, we shall see one another very soon."

"Ah, yes," he cried, trying to smile. "Very soon, mademoiselle."

She gave the donkey-driver some money, and got into the jeep beside the soldier. Slimane had finished bringing out the luggage and stood behind the jeep, kicking the tires. "Have you got everything?" she called to him. "Everything?" She would have liked to see for herself, but she was loath to go back into the room. Boufelja had disappeared; now he came hurrying out, breathless, carrying a pile of old magazines. "It's all right," she said. "No, no! I don't want them." The jeep was already moving ahead down the hill. In what seemed to her an unreasonably short time they had reached the boulders. When Fräulein Windling tried to lift out her briefcase the pain of the sliver under her nail made the tears start to her eyes, and she let go with a cry. Slimane glanced at her, surprised. "I hurt my hand," she explained. "It's nothing."

The bags had been piled in the shade. Sitting on a rock near the jeep, the soldier faced Fräulein Windling; from time to time he scanned the horizon behind her for a sign of the truck. Slimane examined the jeep from all sides; eventually he came to sit nearby. They did not say very much to one another. She was not sure whether it was because the soldier was with them, or because her thumb ached so constantly, but she sat quietly waiting, not wanting to talk.

It was a long time before the far-off motor made itself heard. When the truck was still no more than a puff of dust between sky and earth, the soldier was on his feet watching; an instant later Slimane jumped up. "It is coming, madame," he said. Then he bent over, putting his face very close to hers. "I want to go with you to Colomb-Bechar," he whispered. When she did not respond, because she was seeing the whole story of their friendship unrolled before her, from its end back to its beginning, he said louder, with great urgency: "Please, madame."

Fräulein Windling hesitated only an instant. She raised her head and looked carefully at the smooth brown face that was so near. "Of course, Slimane," she said. It was clear that he had not expected to hear this; his delight was infectious, and she smiled as she watched him run to the pile of bags and begin carrying them out into the sunlight to align them in the dust beside the edge of the trail.

Later, when they were rattling along the hammada, she in front beside the driver and Slimane squatting in the back with a dozen men and a sheep, she considered her irresponsible action in allowing him to make this absurd trip with her all the way to Colomb-Bechar. Still, she knew she wanted to give this ending to their story. A few times she turned partially around in her seat to glance at him through the dirty glass. He sat there in the smoke and dust, laughing like the others, with the hood of his burnoose hiding most of his face.

It had been raining in Colomb-Bechar; the streets were great puddles to reflect the clouded sky. At the garage they found a surly Negro boy to help them carry the luggage to the railway station. Her thumb hurt a little less.

"It's a cold town," Slimane said to her as they went down the main street. At the station they checked the bags and then went outside to stand and watch a car being unloaded from an open freight train: the roof of the automobile was still white with snow from the high steppes. The day was dark, and the wind rippled the surface of the water in the flooded empty lots. Fräulein Windling's train would not be leaving until late in the afternoon. They went to a restaurant and ate a long lunch. "You really will go back home tomorrow?" she asked him anxiously at one point, while they were having fruit. "You know we have done a very wicked thing to your father and mother. They will never forgive me." A curtain seemed to draw across Slimane's face. "It doesn't matter," he said shortly.

After lunch they walked in the public garden and looked at the eagles in their cages. A fine rain had begun to be carried on the wind. The mud of the paths grew deeper. They went back to the center of the town and sat down on the terrace of a large, shabby modern café. The table at the end was partly sheltered from the wet wind; they faced an empty lot strewn with refuse. Nearby, spread out like the bones of a camel fallen on the trail, were the rusted remains of an ancient bus. A long, newly-felled date palm lay diagonally across the greater part of the lot. Fräulein Windling turned to look at the wet orange fiber of the stump, and felt an idle pity for the tree. "I'm going to have a Coca Cola," she declared. Slimane said he, too, would like one.

They sat there a long time. The fine rain slanted through the air outside the arcades and hit the ground silently. She had expected to be approached by beggars, but none arrived, and now that the time had come to leave the café and go to the station she was thankful to see that the day had passed so easily. She opened her pocket-book, took out three thousand francs, and handed them to Slimane, saying: "This will be enough for everything. But you must buy your ticket back home today. When you leave the railway station. Be very careful of it."

Slimane put the money inside his garments, rearranged his burnoose, and thanked her. "You understand, Slimane," she said, detaining him with her hand, for he seemed about to rise from the table. "I'm not giving you any money now, because

33

I need what I have for my journey. But when I get to Switzerland I shall send you a little, now and then. Not much. A little."

His face was swept by panic; she was perplexed.

"You haven't got my address," he told her.

"No, but I shall send it to Boufelja's house," she said, thinking that would satisfy him. He leaned toward her, his eyes intense. "No, madame," he said with finality. "No. I have your address, and I shall send you mine. Then you will have it, and you can write to me."

It did not seem worth arguing about. For most of the afternoon her thumb had not hurt too much; now, as the day waned, it had begun to ache again. She wanted to get up, find the waiter, and pay him. The fine rain still blew; the station was fairly far. But she saw that Slimane had something more to say. He leaned forward in his chair and looked down at the floor. "Madame," he began.

"Yes?" she said.

"When you are in your country and you think of me you will not be happy. It's true, no?"

"I shall be very sad," she answered, rising.

Slimane got slowly to his feet and was quiet for an instant before going on. "Sad because I ate the food out of the picture. That was very bad. Forgive me."

The shrill sound of her own voice exclaiming, "No!" startled her. "No!" she cried. "That was good!" She felt the muscles of her cheeks and lips twisting themselves into grimaces of weeping; fiercely she seized his arm and looked down into his face. "Oh, *mon pauvre petit!*" she sobbed, and then covered her face with both hands. She felt him gently touching her sleeve. A truck went by in the main street, shaking the floor.

With an effort she turned away and scratched in her bag for a handkerchief. "Come," she said, clearing her throat. "Call the waiter."

They arrived at the station cold and wet. The train was being assembled; passengers were not allowed to go out onto the platform and were sitting on the floor inside. While Fräulein Windling bought her ticket Slimane went to get the bags from the checkroom. He was gone for a long time. When he arrived he came with his burnoose thrown back over his shoulders, grinning triumphantly, with three valises piled on his head. A man in ragged European jacket and trousers followed behind carrying the rest. As he came nearer she saw that the man held a slip of paper between his teeth.

The ancient compartment smelled of varnish. Through the window she could see, above some remote western reach of waste-land, a few strips of watery white sky. Slimane wanted to cover the seats with the luggage, so that no one would come into the compartment. "No," she said. "Put them in the racks." There were very few passengers in the coach. When everything was in place, the porter stood outside in the corridor and she noticed that he still held the slip of paper between his teeth. He counted the coins she gave him and pocketed them. Then quickly he handed the paper to Slimane, and was gone.

Fräulein Windling bent down a bit, to try and see her face in the narrow mirror than ran along the back of the seat. There was not enough light; the oil lantern above illumined only the ceiling, its base casting a leaden shadow over everything beneath. Suddenly the train jolted and made a series of crashing sounds. She took Slimane's head between her hands and kissed the middle of his forehead. "Please get down from the train," she told him. "We can talk here." She pointed to the window and began to pull on the torn leather strap that lowered it.

Slimane looked small on the dark platform, staring up at her as she leaned out. Then the train started to move. She thought surely it would go only a few feet and then stop, but it continued ahead, slowly. Slimane walked with it, keeping abreast

35

of her window. In his hand was the paper the porter had given him. He held it up to her, crying: "Here is my address! Send it here!"

She took it, and kept waving as the train went faster, kept calling: "Good-by!" He continued to walk quickly along beside the window, increasing his gait until he was running, until all at once there was no more platform. She leaned far out, looking backward, waving; straightway he was lost in the darkness and rain. A bonfire blazed orange by the track, and the smoke stung in her nostrils. She pulled up the window, glanced at the slip of paper she had in her hand, and sat down. The train jolted her this way and that; she went on staring at the paper, although now it was in shadow; and she remembered the first day, long ago, when the child Slimane had stood outside the door watching her, stepping back out of her range of vision each time she turned to look at him. The words hastily printed for him on the scrap of paper by the porter were indeed an address, but the address was in Colomb-Bechar. "They said he tried to run away. But he didn't get very far." Each detail of his behavior as she went back over it clarified the pattern for her. "He's too young to be a soldier," she told herself. "They won't take him." But she knew they would.

Her thumb was hot and swollen; sometimes it seemed almost that its throbbing accompanied the side-to-side jolting of the coach. She looked out at the few remaining patches of colorless light in the sky. Sooner or later, she argued, he would have done it.

"Another year, perhaps," the captain had said. She saw her own crooked, despairing smile in the dark window-glass beside her face. Maybe Slimane would be among the fortunate ones, an early casualty. "If only death were absolutely certain in wartime," she thought wryly, "the waiting would not be so painful." Listing and groaning, the train began its long climb upwards over the plateau.

THE
SUCCESSOR

In THE middle of the afternoon, lying on his mat, Ali sneezed. A hen that had been drowsing near him screeched and rushed out of the room to a circle of bare dusty ground under the fig tree, where she settled. He listened a while to the distant intermittent thunder in the mountains to the south of the town; then, deciding that he would be able to sleep no more until night, he sat up.

Beyond the partition of upright reeds his brother was talking to El Mehdi, one of the drivers of the carriages that brought people up from the town. From the terrace of the café the eye could wander over the tortured red earth with its old olive trees to the dark caves that lay just below the walls of the town.

The view was something visitors usually considered worth seeing. They would take one of the ancient carriages that waited down in the town and be driven up along the winding road that baked all day in the sunlight; it took less than an hour to reach the café. There they would sit under the trellis in the shade of the vines and drink their tea or their beer. The driver would give the horses water and before twilight they would start back.

On Sundays many carriages and cars came; the café was full all day. His brother, who owned the café and kept the accounts and the money, claimed that he made more on a Sunday than during all the rest of the week. Ali was skeptical of that, not because the statement seemed incredible, but simply because his brother had made it. There was the overwhelming fact that his brother was older than he and therefore had inherited the café from their father. In the face of such crushing injustice there was nothing to be done. Nor was anything his brother had to say of interest to him. His brother was like the weather: one watched it and was a victim to its whims. It was written, but that did not mean it could not change.

He leaned against the wall matting and stretched. His brother and El Mehdi were drinking beer; he was certain of it by the way their voices died down when there was any sound outside the room. They wanted to be able to hide the glasses swiftly if someone should come near the door, so they were listening as they talked. The idea of this childish secrecy disgusted him; he spat on the floor by his feet, and began to rub his bare toe back and forth in the little white mass of saliva.

The thunder rolled in the south mountains, no louder but longer than before. It was a little early in the season for rain, but the rain might come. He reached for the water jug and drank lengthily. Then he sat quite still for a while, his eyes fixed on the framed portrait of the Sultan that hung on the opposite wall.

The thunder came again, still scarcely any louder, but this time unmistakably nearer, the sound more intimate in its movements. It was like a person taking pains to conceal his approach. There was a clapping of hands on the terrace, and a man's voice called: "*Garçon!*" His brother went out, and he heard El Mehdi gulp the rest of his beer and follow him. Presently a woman's voice remarked that it was going to rain. Then El Mehdi shouted, "*Eeeeee!*" to his horses, and the carriage began to creak as it started down the road.

After the customers had left, his brother remained outside. Ali went silently to the door, saw him standing by the parapet, his hands behind him, looking out over the town. At the other end of the terrace squatted the boy who washed the glasses and swept the floor. His eyes were closed. There was very little sound from the town below. Occasionally a bird flew out from the hill behind and let itself drop down toward the lower land. The sky was dark. His brother turned and saw him standing in the doorway.

"You slept?"

"Yes."

"It's going to rain."

"*Incha' Allah*."

"Listen." His brother's hand went up and he turned his face sideways. Very faintly from the town came the sound of the small boys' voices as they ran through the streets chanting the song to Sidi Bou Chta, the song they always sang just before the rain.

"Yes."

Now the thunder was over the nearest mountains. His brother came toward the door and Ali stepped aside to let him pass.

"We'll close up," said his brother. He called to the boy, who began to carry the chairs and tables into the room where they were kept piled. Ali and his brother sat on the mattress and yawned. When the boy had finished he closed the door, snapped the padlock and came into the front part of the room, where he set to fanning the fire with the bellows. Presently he brought them each a glass of tea.

"Go to the house. We'll eat early," said his brother. The boy went out.

A crash of thunder directly above them made them look at each other. Ali said: "I'll close the house. The boy is an idiot."

The little house was behind the café, built against the low cliff, just beneath the road. When he got to the fig tree he heard his brother talking to someone. Surprised, he stopped and listened. Great drops of rain began to fall here and there on to the dust. It was hard to hear what his brother was saying. He went on to the house.

No one lived there but the two of them and the boy, who

39

slept outside. It was never very clean. If only his brother had been willing to get married, Ali would have had an excuse for going away. Until then, it would be impossible, because his father had told him to stay and help his brother with the café. All he got for staying was a dirty room and the bad food the boy cooked for them.

On the other hand, when his brother walked through the Moulay Abdallah *quartier* he was greeted by the women of every house. The money went on bracelets for them, and on wine and beer for his friends. Besides these women, with whom he spent most of his nights, there was always a young girl of good reputation whom he had hopes of seducing; usually he failed in these endeavors, but his setbacks only increased his interest.

At the moment it was Kinza, the daughter of a shopkeeper from Taza, whose favors he sought. She had granted him short conversations in unfrequented alleys, with a maidservant standing a few feet away; he had met her one twilight outside Bab Segma and put his arm around her (after persuading the servant to stand facing in the other direction), and he even had had a *tête-à-tête* alone with her in a room behind a café, when he had lifted her veil and kissed her. But she had refused any further intimacies, threatening, if he used force, to call the servant who was outside the door. After accepting a good many gifts she had promised him another such rendezvous, so he still had hopes.

Ali knew all about his brother's life and about Kinza, since, in spite of the fact that such subjects cannot be discussed between brothers, it is perfectly proper to talk about them with anyone and everyone else. He knew all about Kinza and he hoped his brother would have no luck with her.

The rain was falling more heavily now. He closed the windows so it would not come in. Then, out of boredom and because he was curious to know who had arrived at the café, he went across the open space between the two establishments, taking long strides, and re-entered the back room. Behind the partition the fire was being fanned again, this time by his brother.

"I'm very fond of your tea here in Morocco," a man's voice was saying; they were speaking French.

His brother said: "Me, I like beer best."

"Have another bottle," said the stranger magnanimously. "Drink to the end of this damned rain. If it keeps up I won't get back to town before dark."

Ali tried to look through the cracks to see what sort of person it was who would walk all the way up to the café, but the man was seated in the doorway looking out at the rain and he could see nothing but his back.

"We are glad to have the rain," said his brother. "Each drop is money. The *fellahin* give thanks."

"*Oui, bien sûr*," said the stranger without interest.

The thunder had passed over, but the rain was roaring; soon a stream of water burst through the ceiling in a corner of the room and spattered on to the earthen floor. The added noise made it more difficult to hear their talk. He put his ear close to the reeds.

"Isn't Belgium near France?" his brother asked.

"Next door."

"It's a good country?"

"Oh, yes."

His brother handed the stranger a glass of tea.

"Have another bottle of beer," the stranger suggested.

Ali heard the bottle being opened and the cap fall on to the stone door-sill.

"What's that?" said his brother, his voice bright with interest.

"Just a pill. If I'm nervous I take one. It makes me feel better. If I can't sleep I take two."

41

"And then you sleep?"

"Like a child."

There was a pause. Then his brother asked: "And would they do that to anyone?"

The stranger laughed. "Of course," he said. "Some people might have to take three, some only one."

"And how long does it make you sleep?"

"All night."

"If someone touched you, you'd wake up?"

"Why, yes,"

"But if you took four or five?"

"*Oh, là, là!* You could ride a horse over me then, and I wouldn't know it. That's too many."

This time there was a long silence, and Ali heard only the noise of the rain all around. The water leaking through the roof had made a channel in the mud to the back door. Now and then a distant growl of thunder came from the hills on the north. The air that moved in through the door was cold and smelled of earth.

Presently his brother said: "It's getting dark."

"I suppose you want to close."

"*Oh, ne t'en fais pas!*" said his brother cordially. "Stay until it stops raining."

The stranger laughed. "It's very kind of you, but I'm afraid I'm going to get wet anyway, because it's not going to stop."

"No, no!" his brother cried, an anxious note creeping into his voice. "Wait a few minutes. Soon it will stop. Besides, I enjoy talking with you. You aren't like a Frenchman."

The man laughed again; he sounded pleased and flattered.

Then Ali heard his brother saying timidly: "Those pills. Where could I buy a bottle?"

"My doctor in Belgium gave them to me, but I imagine you could get a doctor here to prescribe some."

"No," said his brother hopelessly.

"Why do you want them? You don't look as though you had trouble sleeping."

His brother squatted down beside the stranger. "It's not that," he said, almost whispering.

Ali peered intently between the reeds, making an effort to follow the movements of his brother's lips. *"C'est une fille.* I give her everything. She always says no. I was thinking, if just once I could——"

The man interrupted him. "You give her enough of these and she won't be able to say anything." He chuckled maliciously. "Here. Hold out your hand."

With a few inarticulate phrases of thanks, his brother rose to his feet, probably to get a box or an envelope for the pills.

Quickly Ali went out of the door through the rain to the house, where he changed his shirt and spread the wet one over the pillows, and lighted the lamp. Then he sat reading, with some difficulty, a newspaper that a customer had left behind the day before. A few minutes later his brother came in, looking pleased and a little mysterious.

It rained most of the night. At dawn, however, when they got up, the sky was clear. His brother drank his coffee hurriedly and went out, saying he would be back about noon.

Two couples came to the café during the morning, but since they took beer the boy did not have to light the fire.

Somewhat later than twelve his brother returned. Ali looked up at his face as he came in the door, and said to himself: "Something has happened." But he pretended to have noticed nothing and turned away unconcernedly after greeting him. Whatever it might be, he knew his brother would never tell him anything.

The afternoon was exceptionally fine. A good many visitors came, as they always did when the weather was clear and the view good. His brother's face did not change. He carried the trays of tea glasses out to the tables like a man walking in his sleep, and he kept his eyes averted from the customers' faces. Each time someone arrived and walked under the arbor onto the terrace, Ali's brother looked as though he were about to run and jump off the edge of the parapet. Once when Ali saw him smoking, he noticed his hand trembling so violently that he had difficulty in getting the cigarette to his lips, and he looked away quickly so his brother would not see him watching.

When the evening call to prayer was over and the last carriage had rattled away down the road, the boy brought the tables and chairs in and swept the floor of the terrace. Ali stood in the doorway. His brother sat on the parapet, looking down over the olive trees in the dimming light, while the town below sank deeper into the gulf of shadow between the hills. An automobile came along the road, stopped. Against the sky Ali saw his brother's head jerk upward. There were the two sounds of a car's doors being shut. His brother rose, took two hesitant steps, and sat down again.

Ali moved backward into the room, away from the door. It was not yet too dark for him to see that the two men walking across the terrace were policemen. Without slipping into his babouches he ran barefoot through the inner room of the café, across the open space to the house. He lay down on his mattress, breathing rapidly. The boy was in the kitchen preparing the evening meal.

For a long time Ali lay there, thinking of nothing, watching the cobwebs that dangled from the ceiling move slowly in the breeze. It seemed so long to him that he thought the two men must have gone away without his having heard them. He tiptoed to the door. The boy was still in the kitchen. Ali stepped outside. The crickets were singing all around and the moonlight looked blue. He heard voices on the terrace. Without making a sound he crept into the café's back room and lay down on the mat.

The policemen were making fun of his brother, but not pleasantly. Their voices were harsh and they laughed too loud.

"A Belgian, no less!" cried one with mock surprise. "He fell out of the sky like an angel, *bien sûr*, with the veronal in one hand. But nobody saw him. Only you."

Ali caught his breath, sprang up. Then very slowly he lay down again, scarcely breathing now, still listening. "Nobody," said his brother, his voice very low. It sounded as though he had his hands over his face. "He said she'd just go to sleep."

They thought this very funny. "She did that, all right," said one at length. Then their speech became abrupt, the tone brutal: "*Allez, assez! On se débine!*" They rose, yanking him up with them.

As they pushed him into the car, his brother was still saying: "I didn't know. He didn't tell me."

The motor started up; they turned the car around and drove down the road. Soon the distant sound of its motor was covered by the song of the crickets.

For a while Ali lay very still. Then, being hungry, he went to the house and had his dinner.

THE HOURS AFTER NOON

"If one could awaken all the echoes of one's memory simulanteously, they would make a music, delightful or sad as the case might be, but logical and without dissonances. No matter how incoherent the existence, the human unity is not affected."

—*Baudelaire*

1

"OH, YOU'RE A *man!* What does a man know about such things? I can tell you how much: absolutely nothing!" When she argued with her husband at mealtimes, Mrs. Callender often sought the support of the other diners in the room. In this instance, however, her appeal was purely formal, since at the moment she was the only woman present, and thus assumed she had their attention anyway. Her bright eyes flashed indignantly from one male diner to the next, and she even turned around in her chair to include old Mr. Richmond, the teller in the Bank of British West Africa. He looked up from his food and said: "Eh? Oh, yes. I dare say."

The Pension Callender was surprisingly empty these days—empty even for the hot season. Besides old Mr. Richmond, who had been with them since they had started eleven years ago, there was Mr. Burton down from London to write a book; he had come last autumn and as yet had given no indication of being ready to leave. Mr. Richmond and Mr. Burton were the only true residents of the pension. The others either came and went irregularly, like Mr. Van Siclen the archeologist and Clyde Brown who was in business in Casablanca, or were merely there for a few days waiting for money or visas before they continued southward or northward, like the two young Belgians who had left that morning.

"A young girl—any young girl—is unbelievably sensitive. Like a thermometer, or a barometer. She catches hold of whatever's in the air. It's true, I tell you." Mrs. Callender looked around at each one defiantly; her black eyes flashed.

Mr. Callender was in a good humor. "That may be," he said indulgently. "But I wouldn't worry about Charlotte. And anyway, we don't even know for sure whether Monsieur Royer's coming or not. You know how he is, always changing his mind. He's probably on his way to Marrakesh right now."

"Oh, he *will* come. You know he will! You simply don't want to face facts." (Sometimes this was true of Mr. Callender. When it was obvious that one of the Moslem servants was systematically stealing foodstuffs from his pantry, he would make no effort to discover who the culprit was, preferring to wait until he might possibly catch him red-handed.) "You hope that somehow he won't get here. But he will, and he's a filthy, horrible man, and he's going to be sitting opposite your own daughter at every meal. I should think that might mean something to you."

Her husband looked around at the other diners, an expression of amusement on his face. "I don't think sitting opposite to him at mealtimes'll bring about her downfall, do you?"

"Abdallah! *Otra taza de café!*" The boy who had been standing by the fireplace trying to follow the conversation stepped forward and filled her cup. "Silly boy!" she cried, sipping the coffee. "It's quite cold." He understood, and lifted the cup to carry it out. "No, no," she said sighing, reaching out for it. "*Déjalo, déjalo.*" And without pausing: "He has a sinister personality. It has an effect on one. Women *feel* those things. I've felt it myself."

Her husband raised his eyebrows. "Aha! So now we come to the meat of the conversation. Gentlemen! Wouldn't you say that my wife is the one to watch? Don't you think *she* should be kept from Monsieur Royer?"

Mrs. Callender simpered. "Bob! You're positively appalling!" At the same time Mr. Richmond raised his head in a startled fashion and said: "Monsieur Royer? Oh?"

Clyde Brown was the only one of the four guests who had been following the conversation from the beginning. His watery blue eyes stared with interest. "Who is this Monsieur Royer? A Latin Quarter Don Juan?"

There was a slight silence. The wind was blowing a blind outside the dining-room window back and forth; the distant sound of heavy waves pounding against the cliffs came up from below. "Don Juan?" echoed Mrs. Callender, laughing thinly. "My dear, I wish you could see him! He looks like a furious lobster, one that's just been cooked. Absolutely hideous! And he's at least fifty."

"You're treading on delicate ground," said Mr. Callender into his plate.

"I know, darling, but you don't go about annoying young girls and getting into messes. He gets into the most frightful messes. You haven't forgotten Señora Coelho's niece last year, when he. . ."

Mr. Callender pushed back his chair; the scraping sound it made on the tile floor was very loud in the room. "Probably does, and probably richly deserves whatever trouble he gets into," he announced. Then impatiently, quickly, to his wife: "I know all about him. What do you want me to do—wire him we're full up?" He knew she would say no, and she did. There was always something in one of the stores in town which she coveted at the time: a silk scarf, a pair of shoes or gloves, and the only money which came in was that paid by the guests who stayed at the pension. "But I should think you'd show more interest where your own daughter is concerned," she added.

Mr. Burton, who had just become aware that a discussion

was in progress, raised his head from the book he had been reading and smiled affably at Mrs. Callender. Old Mr. Richmond folded his napkin, stuffed it into its aluminum ring, and said: "I expect it's time to be getting back into town." Mr. Callender announced that he was going to his cottage to take his afternoon siesta. Soon only Mr. Van Siclen remained at his table by the window, sipping his coffee and looking distractedly out at the windblown landscape. He was a young man who had let his beard grow during the war when he had been stationed on some distant island in the Pacific; now finding that he looked more impressive with it (he was very young to be an archeologist, people told him), he still wore it. Mrs. Callender found herself watching him, wondering whether or not he would be better-looking without its black decoration: he would be less romantic, she decided, perhaps even a little frail of face. As he turned to look at her she felt a tiny thrill of excitement, but his expression swiftly effaced it. He always seemed pleasantly preoccupied; the cynical smile that flickered about his lips made him more remote than if there had been no smile at all. His way of being friendly was to look up from his book and say: "Good morning. How are you today?" in a very firm voice; then by the time you had replied he would be buried again in the book. She considered his behavior insufferably rude, but then, she never had met an American who did not impress her as wanting in courtesy. It was more their attitude than it was anything they did or failed to do. She herself had been born in Gibraltar of an English father and a Spanish mother, her school days had been passed in Kent, and, although Mr. Callender was an American, she considered herself English through and through. And Charlotte was going to be a typical English girl, a wholesome, simple lass without the ridiculous attitudes and featherbrained preoccupations of most American girls. Nor would she be granted the freedom so many American mothers allowed their daughters. Mrs. Callender had enough of the Mediterranean in her to believe that while a boy should have complete liberty, a girl should have none at all. The wind continued to bang the shutter.

"I see. Trying to get rid of old Royer," said Mr. Van Siclen lazily, shaking his head with mock disapproval. "Poor old Royer who never did any harm except ruin a girl's life here and there."

"Oh, I'm so glad!" she cried; the force of her emotion startled him. He glanced at her suspiciously.

"Glad about what?"

"Glad that you agree with me about Monsieur Royer."

"That he's a useless old rake who'll be up to no good until the day he dies? Sure I agree."

"Of course you do," she assured him; she did not see that he was baiting her.

"But I don't agree with you about keeping him away from anybody. Why? *Sauve qui peut*, I always say. And the devil take the hindmost."

She was genuinely indignant. "How can you talk that way? I'm being perfectly serious, even if you're not."

"I'm perfectly serious, too. After all, a girl's education has to start somewhere, some time."

"I think you're quite revolting. Education, indeed!" Her eyes looked beyond his face, through the window, to the stunted cypresses below, at the top of the cliff. She could remember some experiences she would have liked to avoid, or at least have put off until later, when she might have been ready for them. Her aunt in Málaga had been far too lenient, otherwise it never would have been possible for her to meet the sailor from the *Jaime II*, much less to have made an appointment with him in the Alameda for the following day. And the two students she had gone on the picnic with to Antequera, who had thought they could take advantage of her because she was not Spanish. "I must still have had a slight accent," she thought. She was sure it was because of such memories as these that she now had "sad days," when she felt that life would never be right again. There were many things a girl should not know until she was married, and they were the very things it seemed every man was determined to impart to her. Once she was married and it all mattered so much less, precisely then the opportunities for learning were cut down to a minimum. But of course it was better that way.

Slowly her expression was changing from indignation to wistfulness. Voluptuous memories burned in the mind like fire in a tree stump: they were impossible to put out, and they consumed from within, until suddenly nothing was left. If she had a great many memories instead of only a few, she reflected, she would surely be lost.

"You wouldn't talk that way, so playfully, if you knew the hazards of bringing up a girl in this place," she said wearily. "With these Moors all about, and strange new people coming to the pension every day. Of course, we try to get the good Moors, but you know how they are—utterly undependable and mad as hatters, every one of them. One never knows what any of them will take it into his head to do next. Thank God we can afford to send Charlotte to school in England."

"I'm chilly," said Mr. Van Siclen. He rose from the table rubbing his hands together.

"Yes, it's cool. It's the wind. Mind, I have absolutely nothing personal against Monsieur Royer. He's always been a model of fine behavior with me. It isn't that at all. If he were a young man" (she almost added: "like you"), "I'd think it was amusing. I don't object to a young man who's sowing his wild oats. That's to be expected. But Monsieur Royer is at least fifty. And he goes after such mere children. A young man is more likely to be interested in older women, don't you think? That isn't nearly so dangerous." She followed him with her gaze, turning her head as he went toward the door. "Not nearly."

He paused in the doorway, the same inexpressive smile on his lips. "Send him out to El Menar." He had a little native house at El Menar, where he was digging through the Roman

51

and Carthaginian layers of rubble, trying to get at the earlier material. "If he chases the girls around out there they'll find him in a couple of days behind a rock with a coil of wire around his neck."

"Such brutes!" she cried. "How can you stay out there all alone with those wild men?"

"They're fine people," he said, going out.

She looked around the empty room, shivered, and went out on to the terrace, feeling unpleasantly nervous. The wind was near to being a gale, but the clouds, which until now had covered the sky, were breaking up, letting the hard blue backdrop of the sky show through in places. In the cypresses the wind whistled and hissed, and when it hit her face it took her breath away. The air was sharp with the odor of eucalyptus, and damp from the fine spray of the breaking waves below. Then, when the landscape was least prepared for such a change, the sun came out. In all these years of living in Morocco she never had ceased wondering at the astonishing difference made by the sun. Immediately she felt the heat seeping in through her pores, the wind was warm, no longer hostile; the countryside became greener, smiled, and slowly the water down there turned to a brilliant blue. She breathed deeply and said tentatively to herself that she was happy. She was not sure it was true, for it seldom happened, but sometimes she could bring it about in this way. It seemed to her that long ago she had known happiness, and that the brief moments of it she found now were only faint memories of the original state. Now, she always felt surrounded by the ugliness of humanity; the scheming little human mind was always present. A certain awareness of what went on around her was essential if she were to find even normal contentment.

She saw a Moroccan coming towards her from the driveway. Vaguely she knew that his arrival would entail something unpleasant, but for the moment she refused to think about it. She ran her hand through her hair which the wind had blown

awry, and tried to bring her mind back to the pension. There
was Mr. Richmond's mirror which was broken, Brahim needed
a new electric bulb in the pantry, she had to look in the laundry
for an undershirt of Bob's that was missing, she must catch
Pedro before he drove the station wagon into town, to remind
him to stop at the Consulate and pick up Miss Peters whom
she had invited for tea.

The Moroccan, his ragged *djellaba* whipping in the wind,
emerged from the shadows of the nearest eucalyptus. She exclaimed with annoyance and turned to face him. He was old
and he carried a basket. Suddenly she remembered him from
last year: she had bought mushrooms from him. And as she
remembered, she glanced involuntarily at the withered hand
holding the basket and saw the six dark fingers that she knew
would be there. "Go away!" she cried passionately. "*Cir f'halak!*"
She wheeled about and began to run down the path to her cottage in the garden below. Without looking behind she went in
and slammed the door behind her. The room smelled of damp
plaster and insecticide. She stood a moment at the window
looking apprehensively up the path through the bushes. Then,
feeling slightly absurd, she drew the curtains across and began
to remove her make-up. As a rule the mornings took care of
themselves; it was the hours after noon that she had to beware
of, when the day had begun to go toward the night, and she no
longer trusted herself to be absolutely certain of what she would
do next, or of what unlikely idea would come into her head.
Once again she peered between the curtains up the sunlit path,
but there was nobody.

2

The months in Spain had been not at all relaxing; he was
fed up with the coy promises of eyes seen above fans, furious
with mantillas, crucifixes and titters. Here in Morocco, if love

lacked finesse, at least it was frank. The veils over the faces did not disturb him; he had learned long ago to decipher the features beneath. Only the teeth remained a hazard. And the eyes he could read as easily as words. When they showed any interest at all, they expressed it clearly, with no hint of the prudishness he so hated.

Above a bank of thick clouds the twilight sky burned with a fierce blueness. He turned into the crowded native quarter. He had sent his luggage to the Pension Callender by taxi and had arranged to take Mr. Callender's station wagon when it started up from the market just before dinner. That left him free to wander a half-hour or so in the Casbah, nothing on his mind, nothing in his hands. He turned into the Rue Abdessadek. The hooded figures in the street moved from stall to stall, their hands making the decorative oriental gestures, their voices strident with disagreement over prices. It was all familiar to Monsieur Royer, and very comforting. He felt he could again breathe easily. Slowly he ascended the hill, trying to recall a passage of something he once had read and loved: *"Le temps qui coule ici n'a plus d'heures, mais—"* He could not get beyond this point into the other thought. Turning into a smaller street, he was suddenly met by an overpowering odor of jasmine; it came from behind the wall beside him. He stood still a moment beneath the overhanging branch of a fig tree on the other side of the wall, and inhaled slowly, deliberately, still hoping to get beyond that part of the thought which had to do with time. The jasmine would help. It was coming to him: *"mais, tant le loisir—"* No.

A child brushed against him, and he had the impression that it had done so purposely. He glanced down: sure enough, it was begging. In a cajoling, unnatural little voice that set his nerves on edge it was asking alms, raising a tiny cupped hand toward him. He began to walk quickly, still sniffing the jasmine, feeling the elusive phrase he sought moving a little further away from him. The child hurried along beside him, continuing its odious chant. "No!" he cried explosively, without looking down at it again, and forcing his legs to take enormous strides in the hope of escaping its singsong voice.

"*Le temps qui coule ici n'a plus d'heures, mais tant—*" he murmured aloud, to cover the sound beside him. It was impossible. Now his mood was irrevocably shattered. The child, growing bolder, touched his leg with a tentative finger. "*Dame una gorda,*" it whined. With a suddenness and ferocity which astonished him even as he acted, he dealt it a savage blow in the face, and a fraction of a second later heard it moan. Then he watched it duck and run to the side of the street where it stood against the wall holding its hand to its face and staring at him with an expression of reproach and shocked disbelief.

Already he was feeling a sharp pang of regret for his behavior. He stepped toward the cowering child, not aware of what he was about to say or do. The child looked up; its pinched face was pale in the light of the arc-lamp that swung above. He heard himself say in a tremulous voice: "*Porqué me molestas así?*" It did not answer, and he felt its silence making an unbridgeable abyss between them. He took hold of its thin arm. Again, without stirring, it made its absurd, animal moan. In a new access of rage he struck it again, much harder. This time it made no sound; it merely stood. Completely unnerved and miserable, Monsieur Royer turned and walked off in the direction from which he had just come, colliding with a shrouded woman who was emptying garbage from a pan into the middle of the street. She called after him angrily, but he paid no attention. The idea that the Moroccan urchin must consider him with the same dread and contempt it felt for any other Christian interloper was intolerable to him, for he considered himself a particularly understanding friend of the Moslems. He hurried back through the town to the market, found the station wagon, and got into it. By the light of the many flares in the vegetable stands opposite, he recognized old Mr. Richmond of the Bank of British West Africa sitting on the seat facing him.

"Good evening," said Monsieur Royer, feeling that any kind of conversation at all would help him to recover from the ill-humor induced by his walk.

Mr. Richmond grunted a reply, and after a pause said: "You're Royer, I believe?"

"Aha, you remember me," smiled Monsieur Royer. But Mr. Richmond said no more.

Presently Pedro arrived, his arms full of bundles which he piled on the floor between them. He greeted Monsieur Royer ceremoniously, and explained that they would not be going directly to the pension because they had to stop by the airport to call for Miss Charlotte, who was coming down from London. As they drove slowly through the crowded market, several times Monsieur Royer saw Mr. Richmond glance across at him was a surreptitiousness which bordered on the theatrical. "*Pauvre vieux*," he thought. "He's losing his grip."

3

It had been a nerve-racking flight down, through clouds most of the way, with sudden terrifying exits into regions of pitiless burning sunlight against which the softness of the clouds seemed a protection. She was not afraid of flying; the uneasiness had begun long before she had left school. Each morning on waking she had smelled the freshly-cut grass, heard the birds' familiar chirping in the bushes, and said to herself that she did not want to leave.

Of course there was no question of her not going home to visit her family; although her mother had come to England the year before to spend the vacation months with her, she had not seen her father for two years, and she really cared more for him than she did for her mother. He was quiet, he looked at her in a strange, appraising manner that enormously flattered her and, above all, he let her alone, refrained from making suggestions for the betterment of her appearance or character, which ostensibly meant that he considered her a fully formed individual. And while she had to admit that her mother was sweet, at the same time she could not help thinking her silly and something of a nuisance: she was so laden with advice and so eternally ready to bestow it. And the more one took, the more of it she attempted to unload upon one. There was no end to the chain of suggestions and admonitions. She told herself that this constant watching was a very common misapplication of maternal love, but that did not make it any easier to bear.

Her last two days at school she had spent packing slowly, automatically; they had been filled with a particular anguish which she finally brought herself to diagnose. It was sheer apprehensiveness at the prospect of being again with her mother. Other years she had prepared to go home without feeling this tremulous dread. It was as they left London Airport and she was bracing herself against the plane's banking that the reason came to her; without realizing it she already had determined to resist. The discovery was a shock. For a moment she felt like a monster. "I can't go home feeling like this," she thought. But as the plane righted itself, and, soaring higher, broke through the pall of fog into the clarity above, she sighed and sat back to read, reflecting that after all the decision was purely private and could scarcely be read in her face. However, throughout the flight, as the plane moved onward from sunlight into shadow and out again, she continued from time to time to be plagued by the feeling that she had become disloyal; and with this suspicion went the fear that in some way she might hurt her mother.

It was a small airport. Before the plane had landed Charlotte had sighted the station wagon, standing in the glare of the floodlights near the shack which served as waiting-room and customs office. She was not surprised to find that her father had not come to meet her; he left the pension only when he was forced to. Pedro piled her luggage on top and helped her into the back of the car.

"Pleasant journey?" Mr. Richmond asked when they had greeted each other and she was seated beside him.

"Yes, thank you," she said, waiting to be presented to the other gentleman sitting opposite them. He was obviously from the Continent and of a rather distinguished appearance, she thought. But Mr. Richmond looked unconcernedly out at the lights of the airport, and so she spoke with the gentleman anyway.

They chatted about the weather and the natives. The car climbed the steep road; at each turn its headlights swept the while walls along the sides, crowned with masses of trailing flowers and vines. High in the dark trees a few cicadas continued to rasp their daytime song. She and the gentleman were still talking when the station wagon pulled into the garage. Mr. Richmond, however, had not said another word.

4

At the pension nothing had changed since her last visit. Her mother looked younger and prettier than ever, and seemed, if possible, still more scatteredbrained and distraught—so much so that she too forgot to introduce her to the French gentleman. However, since he was seated in the farthest corner of the dining-room by the window, and was already finishing when the family sat down to eat, it did not matter much.

Her father looked at her across the table and smiled.

"So there you are," he said with satisfaction. He paused and turned to his wife: "Better get Señorita Marchena busy on a

58

dress." And to Charlotte: "There's a big shindig Saturday night at the Country Club."

"Oh, but I have plenty of things to wear!" she objected.

"Yes, but this is very special. And calls for something very special. Señorita Marchena'll be equal to the occasion." He looked at her carefully. "And all I can say is, the Ramirez girls had better look to their laurels."

She felt herself blushing. The Ramirez girls were three sisters who held the reputation of having a local monopoly on beauty.

"The Ramirez girls!" cried Mrs. Callender, a note of scorn in her voice.

"What's the matter with them?" demanded her husband. "They're nice girls."

"Oh, they're pretty, yes, Bob, but they're scarcely what one would call nice girls." (For Mrs. Callender all Spaniards by definition were inclined to dubious morality.)

"Mother! How can you say that!" Charlotte exclaimed.

Mrs. Callender looked about uneasily; it seemed to her that Monsieur Royer was listening to their conversation. She had purposely delayed sitting down to dinner until she thought he would be finished eating, but he was still toying with his fruit. "I'll tell you about them later," she said *sotto voce* to Charlotte, and changed the subject, fervently hoping that in a moment he would leave and go down to his cottage.

In the middle of the meal the door from the terrace opened and Mr. Van Siclen burst in, fresh from El Menar, dressed in earth-stained overalls. He had a way of appearing unannounced at any hour of the day or night. Sometimes it was inconvenient for the servants, but since he paid full pension and ate few meals there, the Callenders never remarked upon his impromptu arrivals. He shut the door carefully so the wind sweeping through the room from the kitchen would not slam it.

"Hello, everybody!" he said, running his hand through his

Paul Bowles

hair. Mrs. Callender glanced toward the window where Monsieur Royer was slicing an apple into paper-thin sections. "Oh, how terrible! Monsieur Royer has your table! Do sit here with us. Abdallah! *Trae otra silla!*" She moved her own chair up a bit and indicated the space beside her. "Before you sit down, this is my daughter Charlotte." He acknowledged the introduction dryly, with a minimum of civility, and seated himself, sighing mightily.

"What a night!" he exclaimed as his soup was placed before him. "An ocean breeze, a full moon, and big clouds. I just came in from El Menar in my jeep," he told Charlotte. (She had decided he was pretentious, with that beard.)

"How enchanting!" cried Mrs. Callender. "Now, do tell us. Have you stumbled on something fantastic out there? Gold coins? Lapis lazuli cups?"

As he spoke, Charlotte watched his face, complacent and slightly mocking. It summed up all the things she disliked most in men: conceit, brashness, insensitivity. Still, he could not be as bad as he looked, she thought; some of it must be the beard. No one his age had a right to such a decoration.

From time to time she stole a glance at her mother, who was following his dull discourse as if it were of the greatest interest, punctuating it with little cooing sounds and exclamations of rapture. Somehow she had expected to find her less silly this time (perhaps because of her determination to resist) and instead, here she was, worse than ever. "It must be her age," she decided. At some point she would probably change suddenly, overnight. And now, becoming aware that it was precisely this quality of superficiality to which she most objected, she no longer felt even a twinge of guilt at her own rebelliousness. Trying to manage other people's lives was a definite thing. It had its limits. But the kind of irresponsibility she saw in her mother amounted to a denial of all values. There was no beginning and no end; anything was equal to anything else.

Two nurses on leave from the hospital in Gibraltar pushed

back their chairs and walked across the room to the door. "Good nayt," they said. Both wore glasses; both were dressed in execrable taste. Charlotte watched them and thought: "To have reached thirty and to look like that—!"

Someone laid a hand lightly on her shoulder. She twisted her head around. The French gentleman was standing behind her chair, smiling at her mother.

"I wish to compliment you, madam. A lovely girl like this could only be the daughter of so charming a mother as you."

He bowed low, from behind her, so that for a second his head was level with hers; his hand remained on her shoulder. A short silence fell upon the table. To Mr. Van Siclen Monsieur Royer said: "Good evening, my dear fellow! How are you? Have you made any remarkable discoveries recently?"

"Hello, Royer. I was just telling the Callenders a little about the new wall I came to yesterday."

"But it's splendid! Only yesterday! I want to hear about it."

"Sit down," said Mr. Van Siclen. Mrs. Callender flashed him a furious glance.

"I'm afraid it'll be rather crowded," she said, scraping her chair back and forth on the tiles as noisily as possible, and failing to move it an inch.

"Oh, no. There's room," objected Charlotte. "Here beside me."

But Monsieur Royer laughed.

"No, no! You are very kind and I want very much to hear about the latest developments of this prodigious excavating. Perhaps tomorrow, Mr. Van Siclen?" Ceremoniously he kissed the hands of Mrs. Callender and Charlotte, and went out.

Mrs. Callender rolled her eyes at her husband. "One needs the patience of Job," she said. "What an insufferable fool!"

Charlotte hesitated an instant before saying: "Why? I think he's rather sweet."

Her mother gave a little shriek, part giggle, and looked at Mr. Callender as if seeking support. Then she said very seriously:

"I'm sorry to hear it, darling, because if only shows what faulty judgment you have. The man's an utter cad, a complete bounder. They don't come lower."

Charlotte in turn looked at her father. "Is that really true?" she asked.

"He's a bad egg, all right," he said.

They sat a while over coffee exchanging news. The dining-room was empty now save for their table. Abdallah leaned by the fireplace more asleep than awake. Mr. Van Siclen had ceased taking part in the talk, and tilted his chair back, puffing on a pipe. From time to time the wind shook the house. Slowly the conversation had centered itself upon Charlotte. She was telling her parents about school, about her classes and friends; she had almost forgotten Mr. Van Siclen was present. Suddenly she stopped short.

"This must all be the most frightful bore for Mr. Van Siclen," she said apologetically.

"Nonsense; go on," said her father. "If he doesn't like it he can leave."

Mr. Van Siclen smiled sleepily through the smoke. "I'm not bored at all," he assured her. "It's very instructive."

She was convinced he was making fun of her, and she grew hot with anger.

"I'm dreadfully tired. I think I should go to sleep." It was the only way to avoid going on with it; now that she was conscious of his amused eyes she could not possibly continue talking.

Her mother jumped up. "Of course she's tired, poor baby. Come along. You must get to bed immediately." She tried to take her arm, to pull her toward the door, but Charlotte could not allow that. Gently she disengaged herself and went over to kiss her father good night; she took leave of Mr. Van Siclen with more civility than she felt; then, back at the door, she seized her mother's arm and led her down the steps through the garden to the cottages below. Mrs. Callender went in and sat on the bed while she unpacked, gossiping about the servants.

Hassan's eleven-year-old brother had been put in prison for reaching in through the open window into Mr. Burton's room and taking a hundred-peseta note which lay on the table.

"But, mother! that's terribly young to be in prison."

"Darling, I've said for years that the child was a thief. I've told Hassan to watch him, or we should have trouble. Isn't that the bathrobe Mrs. Grey gave you? It's rather pretty, but it seems a bit long." Eventually she went out, leaving Charlotte wide awake in the dark, listening to the rhythmical roar of the waves. They were not very loud tonight; she could remember many nights when they had seemed right in the room. But tonight the wind was from the west.

5

It was not long before she realized how foolish of her it had been to drink coffee after dinner; she would not be sleepy for hours. And since her mother generally read for an hour or so before going to sleep, and could see across to her cottage, she could not very well get up. Directly she turned on her light, her mother would be over to see what was wrong. She wanted to take a walk—perhaps down on the beach. But it would mean getting dressed in the dark and stealing out quietly at the risk of meeting her father. She had not yet heard him go into his own cottage. If she waited, it would be safer, but she did not feel like waiting. As she groped about cautiously for her skirt she heard him shut his door. She sighed with relief. Now that everyone was in, it would be much easier.

It all went very smoothly; she did not make a sound. Under the grape-arbor, through the vegetable garden, down across the open field towards the promontory where the cypresses and rocks overlooked the water beneath. The low clouds scudding overhead made waves of shadow that moved slowly across the moonlit country. She hummed happily as she walked along. To the right, under the big bent cypress, through the little ravine, up again; she knew the way perfectly. What she had not counted on was meeting Mr. Van Siclen sitting on a rock directly in the path, as she reached the edge of the cliff. He sat there looking out to sea; at her involuntary "Oh!" he turned and smiled at her in the moonlight.

The sight of him there had so thoroughly disrupted her state of mind that she merely stood still and looked at him.

"I *thought* you'd be out," he said with satisfaction.

She could only say, stupidly: "Why?"

"I didn't think you were sleepy."

She said nothing. Her impulse was to be unfriendly, but she decided it would be childish. "I thought I'd go for a walk down on the beach for a bit."

He laughed. "I saw you come sneaking out." (Why did he have to be so objectionable?) "Care to go for a little ride?"

"Oh, I don't think so, thank you," she said politely, conscious at the same time that her voice lacked forcefulness.

"Sure you would. Come on!"

He sprang up, seized her hand, and began to pull her along, back up the path. "No, really! No! Listen to me!" She wanted to resist physically, but she was afraid of seeming a whining creature—a poor sport. Presently she was obliged to stop for a moment. "Please!" she gasped "Not so fast!" This he appeared to construe as a tacit acceptance of his suggestion; he laughed, loosened his grip, and said: "The jeep's in the upper driveway."

And once she was in the car, going up the mountain with the night wind in her face, she thought that perhaps she had meant to accept from the moment he had invited her. There was a sharp, spicy odor in the air: they were in the eucalyptus forest. It was like going through a high dark tunnel. The sound of the motor reverberated overhead. A minute later the walls of Sultan Moulay Hafid's palace loomed, growing higher as they approached the entrance. In another moment there were no walls at all; the car was on the high, flat section of road leading through the olive-grove to Bou Amar. The rolling hills stretched away to the south in a vast misty panorama whitened by the moonlight. Here and there the uncertain shadow of a cloud moved up a slope, assuming a new form as it reached the summit and spread over the valley beyond. The clouds were low and moved swiftly. She wanted to say: "It's lovely." But he had turned the windshield horizontal, and her breath was cut by the onrushing blast of air. The little white native houses of Bou Amar flitted past, and again they were in the country, among the pines now. The road did not deviate from its straight line, but it rose and dipped like a roller-coaster over the hills. He closed the windshield.

"Shall I open her up?" he called.

"Don't go any faster, if that's what you mean."

"That's what I mean."

"No!"

"This thing can't go, anyway!" he yelled.

But it seemed to her he had increased the speed.

Now there were no more trees; it was a high, open, rocky region dotted with clumps of holly and heather that glistened under the moon. Far ahead the lighthouse on the cape sent out its recurrent message. All at once he brought the jeep to a stop. It was absolutely silent up here save for the wind: there were no insects and the sea was too far away to be heard. He lit a cigarette without offering her one, and looked at her sideways.

"Are you what's laughingly called a virtuous young lady?"

Her heart sank.

"What?" (And it was so idiotic, in any case.) She waited, then said: "I expect so. Why?"

"*Very* virtuous?"

"Did you bring me out here to inquire after my morals?"

"They don't mean a damn thing to me, if you want to know. I'm just asking to be polite. You know—how's your lumbago? How's your abscessed tooth?"

65

In spite of herself she said: "You know, I think you're quite disgusting."

He blew some smoke in her face. "All disgust, my dear young lady, is nothing but lack of appetite—desire not to touch with the mouth."

"What?"

"Eating an object. Kissing somebody. Same thing."

"I don't know what you are talking about." She began to be alarmed: it was like conversing with a madman.

"I'm just trying to tell you that I don't really disgust you."

The lighthouse was flashing. "How can I get him to go back?" she thought.

"I should think I'd be the best judge of that," she said a bit shakily.

"And yet you want me to kiss you."

"What?" she cried shrilly. After a moment she said in a low voice: "Why should I want you to kiss me?"

"I'm damned if I know. But you do."

"It's not true. I don't."

He tossed his cigarette away. "I think we've argued enough about this little thing," he said, turning toward her.

She had never been treated this way before. When he seized her, she could do nothing. When with all her might she tried to pull her head away, he caught hold of her lip with his teeth, so that she cried out with pain. After a prolonged struggle he let go and sat grinning at her. She tried to speak, but sobbed and choked.

"Have a handkerchief," he said. Automatically she accepted it and blew her nose. Then she dabbed at her lip and saw the dark blood on the white linen. For some reason this gave her the courage to raise her head and look at him.

"I——"

"Don't try to talk," he said shortly.

She stared at him, overcome by her hatred of him, opened

her mouth to speak, and choked afresh. When she had calmed herself sufficiently to be able to think: "That was beastly," rather than "This is beastly," she handed him his handkerchief and said quietly: "My mother was wrong. She said they don't come lower than Monsieur Royer."

He laughed delightedly. "Oh, he's much worse! *Mu-u-uch* worse!"

"If you don't mind, I'd prefer not to talk about it any more."

"Ah, it wasn't as bad as all that," he said.

She did not answer.

"As a matter of fact," he pursued, "this ride was good for you."

"I don't think my father would agree," she said somewhat primly.

"Probably not. But he'll never be asked his opinion, will he?"

Remembering her sigh of relief when she had heard her father shut the door of his cottage, she was silent. He started up the engine, turned the jeep around, and they went back over the road as quickly as they had come. When they arrived at the garage, she jumped out without speaking again, and hurried to her cottage. All the lights in the other cottages were out. She undressed in the dark, turning on the light over the wash-basin just long enough to put a drop of iodine on her lip. As she got into bed she noticed that she was trembling. Even so, it was not long before the sound of the waves had lulled her to sleep.

6

In the morning she awoke in rather a bad humor. Perhaps the trip was just having its effect, or perhaps the unpleasantness of last night had upset her nerves. Halima, the younger of

Mustapha the cook's two wives, brought her breakfast. When she had finished eating, she got out of bed and looked in the mirror. Her lower lip was still swollen. "Maybe by lunchtime it will be gone," she thought hopefully, and she put on her bathing suit and rushed down to the beach where she spent the whole morning swimming and sunbathing. About noon she caught sight of Monsieur Royer coming around the point at the base of the cliffs. He was in while flannels and flourished a cane. She watched him approach, glad he was not Mr. Van Siclen.

"Aha! A mermaid today!" he cried. "Is the sea comfortable?"

"Oh, yes. It's lovely."

He stood above her, making designs in the sand with the tip of his cane, and they talked. Finally he said: "May I be seated?"

"Oh, please! Of course!" She felt rude for not having suggested it.

When he was beside her he continued to chat and plough up the sand with his cane. After a few minutes he turned and looked into her face, smiling in such a way that his eyes seemed to shine more brightly, and said: "It is not too many times in his life that a man has the privilege of sitting with a real mermaid, you know. So you must forgive me if I enjoy this privilege."

She did not know what she ought to say, but his manner amused her, and so she laughed and said: "Thank you."

He did not seem entirely satisfied. "I don't want to embarrass you, my dear. You must realize that what I say is said quite sincerely. It is not meant to be flattery. If it seems comic, that is merely my English vocabulary."

"But it's not comic at all," she protested. "It's very charming, really. And you speak English beautifully."

His conversation consisted of very little else besides these elaborate compliments, but she found them inoffensive, a little touching, and on the whole enjoyable. As they talked, her sympathy for him increased, and she found herself wishing she could confide in him—not about anything in particular or anything serious, she thought—just about whatever came into her head at the moment. He was friendly, detached, sincere, and, she was sure, very wise. As a little fishing-boat rounded the point, bobbing up and down in the rough water, she suddenly said: "Monsieur Royer, tell me your honest opinion. Do you think it's despicable for a man to kiss a girl against her will?" She was shocked to hear the words coming out; she had not known they would be exactly those words, but apparently she needed to say them, and there was no one else to say them to.

A cloud seemed to spread across Monsieur Royer's sunburned face. Slowly he said: "Ah. I see that people have been talking to you about me."

"No! No!" she cried, startled and then horrified.

"Naturally they have," he said calmly. "We have never even been presented one to the other. Do you realize that? Yes. Of course they have. Why not? They are quite right." He paused. "Luncheon will be ready soon, and I must first prepare. But I want to answer your question. Yes. I think such a thing is despicable. You used the words: 'against her will.' But there are a great many girls who have no will, like the natives here, or even the Spanish girls of the lower class. It is all the same to them, as long as they receive a gift. They have no wish one way or the other. And if they have no will, one can scarcely go against it, can one?"

She was silent. "I wasn't talking about you," she finally said.

He looked at her very seriously; he seemed not to have heard her. "Do you see what I mean to say?"

"I'm not sure," she said, letting the sand run between her fingers. "But I really didn't mean——"

He had risen.

"Good morning, madame."

She looked around: her mother stood there. She greeted Monsieur Royer crisply. Then she looked down.

"Charlotte, it's lunchtime. Come up and dress." There was an edge of fury in her voice that recalled long-forgotten days of childhood misbehavior and recrimination.

The upward climb was steep. Charlotte went first, with her mother panting behind her. "Charlotte, I'm extremely angry with you. You're not a child any more, you know—" Between each sentence she ceased speaking and took a breath. "Your father and I as much as told you to have nothing to do with Monsieur Royer. How explicit must one be? I was going to tell you all about him this morning. But of course you disappeared. I don't know why— I couldn't be more annoyed with you. You're thoroughly throughtless and egotistical—"

Charlotte listened with apathy to the diatribe, walking quickly so that her mother, in attempting to keep up with her, would have the maximum of difficulty in delivering it. At one point she had been about to protest that Monsieur Royer had only happened by a short while ago, and that she had been sitting with him only a few minutes, but she felt that this would seem to put her in the wrong; it would sound like an excuse, and she was determined to admit to no fault. Since she did not answer at all, her mother's voice softened tentatively as she continued: "Don't you think it's time you changed, and thought of others?"

"I expect so," she said vaguely, adding in a louder voice, "But I can't see what you have against poor Monsieur Royer to say such horrid things about him."

Mrs. Callender snorted impatiently.

"Oh, good heavens, Charlotte! I know all about the man. Please believe me, he has a most unsavory reputation. If only for that, he's no one for you to see. But I happen to know as well that his reputation is completely justified. He's a confirmed roué and a scoundrel. In any case, I don't intend to argue the point with you. It's an established fact. But what I do intend to have is your promise—your promise that you won't speak to him again unless either your father or I, one of us is present."

They were at the top of the cliff. Mrs. Callender would have liked to stop a moment and catch her breath, but Charlotte hurried on. The path was less steep here, and her mother quickly caught up with her, breathing heavily. She sounded angrier now.

"I refuse to stand by and watch an old libertine like that try to ruin your life—I won't *have* you seeing him. Do you understand me?"

Charlotte spoke without looking around. "Yes, of course I understand. But I don't agree."

"It's of no interest to me whether you agree or not!" cried Mrs. Callender shrilly. "I expect you think it's brilliant and becoming to show spirit—"

They had reached the vegetable garden. One of the nurses from Gibraltar was sitting on the porch of her cottage sunning herself. Mrs. Callender lowered her voice and became cajoling. "Darling, please don't ruin my pleasure in your stay by being stubborn and belligerent about this."

"Do you want me to be rude to him?"

"It's not necessary. But if you disobey me I shall be the one to be rude. I shall simply ask him to leave. And I've never done that to anyone."

"Then the only thing for me to do is to tell him in front of you that you've forbidden me to speak to him."

They stood in the garden between their respective cottages.

"If that's the pleasantest way you can devise, do so by all means," said her mother acidly. "I'm sure I don't mind." She went into her room and shut the door. Charlotte stood a moment looking after her.

In her mirror she examined her lip; the salt water had brought the swelling down. She dressed quickly and went up to the dining-room, noting to her immense relief that Mr. Van Siclen was not there. During lunch she glanced out of the window and saw Monsieur Royer being served on the terrace in the sun; she wondered if he were eating outside because he liked it, or out of consideration for her. While her parents were still finishing their dessert she excused herself and went out. She paused an instant on the steps, and then walked casually toward the table where Monsieur Royer sat sipping his coffee. He rose and seized a chair from the next table for her. Knowing she was being watched through the window, she sat down with him. Hassan brought her a cup of coffee and they talked brightly for a quarter of an hour or so. She fully expected her mother to appear and precipitate a scene, but nothing happened. When she got up and went down to her cottage she thought, "Now she'll come," but she lay awake a long time listening for her mother's footsteps, and they did not arrive. At last she sank into a heavy slumber.

7

In the rose garden behind the bar Mr. and Mrs. Callender walked back and forth, conversing in low tones.

"You saw it!" exclaimed Mrs. Callender in an intense whisper. "Pure infatuation, nothing else. It's not like Charlotte to behave this way. She'd never defy me like this. I admit it was only a provocation, the whole little act, yes. But she's never been this way before. The man has bewitched her, it's perfectly clear. We must do something. Immediately."

Back and forth along the short, bordered path they walked. "We've got to send him away," she said.

"Impossible," said Mr. Callender.

"Then I shall take Charlotte and go to a hotel until he leaves," she declared.

Mr. Callender grunted.

"All she needs," he said at length, "is to meet some boys her own age. The ones she used to know here are mostly gone. Too bad the dance at the Club isn't tonight or tomorrow night. She'd forget about Royer in short order."

Mrs. Callender sighed. "If he could only be put on ice until the dance," she mused. Then she straightened and tried once more. "Oh, Bob, we *must* get rid of him."

Her husband stood still. "The time to get rid of Monsieur Royer was before he came. You had your chance. I asked you if you wanted me to wire him there was no room, and you said no. It's one thing to tell someone the place is full up. And another to send a man away for no reason at all. You can't do it."

"No reason at all, indeed!" she snorted.

Now she sat in her room on the edge of the bed and fidgeted. The long windswept afternoon depressed her. There was too intimate and mysterious a connection between what she felt, and the aspect of the countryside, now brilliant under the ardent sun, now somber in shadow as the endless procession of separate clouds raced past. It was easy to say, "This is a sad day," and attribute it to the unfortunate coincidence which had brought Charlotte and Monsieur Royer here at the same time. But that did not really explain anything. The aching nostalgia for her own youth remained—the bright Andalusian days when each hour was filled to bursting with the promise of magic, when her life lay ahead of her, inexhaustible, as yet untouched. It was true that she had not always been happy then, but there had been the imminent possibility of it, at every moment. And the people around her had not had the strange faculty they now had of becoming suddenly sinister. Even her husband, when she looked at him quickly, sometimes seemed to be coming hurriedly back from somewhere not in the light. It disconcerted her, and if she ever had dwelt on it for very long at a time, it would have terrified her.

A *rhaïta* was being played fairly far away on the mountain, announcing a wedding. It would probably go on for several days and nights. She put her hands over her ears. As if that could help! Whenever she took them away, the slippery little sound would be there, twisting thinly around itself like a tree-snake. She pressed her palms more tightly against her head, until the vacuum hurt her eardrums. But the images had been awakened: the donkeys laden with blankets and painted wooden chests, the procession of lanterns, the native women in white with their drums. . . . She jumped up, looked at her watch, stepped to the mirror and powdered her face. Then she went down to Mr. Van Siclen's cottage. He had had lunch in town with the American Vice-Consul, saying that he would be back early as he was returning to El Menar before dark. She knocked; there was no answer. She went up to the bar where he often sat thumping out old tunes with one finger on the piano. He was talking with the barman.

"Mr. Van Siclen, I must speak with you."

"Sure." He followed her outside.

"I know all this won't interest you in the least, but it's the only favor I shall ever ask of you. Monsieur Royer has his eye on Charlotte. No, don't laugh. It's most serious. I'm counting on you. You *must* help me."

"Well, well!" he said. And after a bit: "O.K. What do you want me to do?"

"I thought if you could invite him out to El Menar . . . Just for a few days . . ." she hastily added as he frowned. ". . . Just for two or three days. At least until I've had the opportunity of talking with her. You see, for some mad reason *she* seems quite taken with *him* as well. There's no explaining these things. But one must act. I shall be eternally grateful to you."

"Well," he said slowly, smoothing his hair, "I'm willing to extend the invitation, but how do I know he'll accept?"

"I think you can make it attractive to him if you really try," she said, smiling significantly. "Playing up the native life a bit . . . You know him, after all. You know what amuses him."

"Damn it!" he cried, suddenly annoyed. "I don't want him out three trailing me around all day while I work."

And seeing her face, he added resignedly: "But I'll ask him, I'll ask him."

"You *are* a darling," she said.

It was done. For some reason she felt no doubt that Monsieur Royer would accept. Fittingly, the sun was shining as she went through the garden to her cottage. It was almost an anticlimax when at tea-time Monsieur Royer came to announce his departure.

"We shall miss you," she smiled. "I expect you'll want to keep your cottage." And when he said that he did, she generously suggested: "We'll put you on demi-pension for those days. That way you'll only be paying a little more than the price of the room."

"No, no," he protested politely, but she saw that he was pleased.

A little while later she watched her two guests drive off in the open jeep into the twilight.

At dinner Mr. Callender looked around the room. "Where's everybody?" he said.

"Oh, Mr. Van Siclen's gone back to El Menar and taken Monsieur Royer along with him."

"*What?*" He was incredulous.

Charlotte said nothing. Several times during the meal Mrs. Callender glanced across at her, but if she was feeling any emotion she did not betray it.

"She's rather a little sneak," said Mrs. Callender to herself, disappointed; she had expected a little more reaction than this.

Charlotte was thinking: "He's gone, thank Heavens." But she meant Mr. Van Siclen. She went to bed immediately after dinner, slept soundly, and awoke early with a desire to see Gloria Gallegos, a friend from her *lycée* days. She breakfasted, dressed, and in the fresh of the morning set out on foot for town. It was not a great walk; she could make it in an hour. The moving air was a tonic. The sun had not yet begun to weight it down with its heat, nor the flowers with their noonday scent, nor the insects with their droning. When she arrived in the market she was startled to see Mr. Van Siclen's jeep parked by the Ciné Régis. She kept her face averted as she passed, lest he should be in it. But she came face to face with him at the corner.

"Hi there!" he said, grasping her arm, quite, she thought, as if nothing had ever occurred between them.

She was not effusive in her greeting. The crowd of Berbers passing pushed them this way and that.

"Where are you off to so early?" he demanded.

"Just up to the Boulevard," she said coldly.

"It's quite a walk. Let me take you up."

"I enjoy walking."

"Come on, be a good sport. Don't go on having hard feelings. You'll get old before your time."

He did not let go of her arm; the easiest way out was to accept. She let him lead her back to the jeep and help her in. As they went around the north end of the market they met the pension's station wagon which had just deposited Mr. Richmond at the bank. She waved to Pedro, who waved back.

"Am I forgiven?" asked Mr. Van Siclen.

"Only if you don't go on talking about it," she replied.

"That's the spirit," he said approvingly. "I had to come in for kerosene. There wasn't even enough for the lamps last night. Poor old Royer had to go to bed by moonlight, I guess. I didn't hear him come in."

He let her out at the Boulevard. At lunchtime she tried to telephone her mother to tell her that she was eating at the Gallegoses', but the line was having one of its frequent bad days, and she was unable to reach the pension.

"Bob, I *am* worried about Charlotte." Mrs. Callender was saying at lunch. (If the telephone had not been out of order it would have rung at that instant.) "She was already gone at eight when I went in to see her. It's not like her to go out so early. Where can she be?"

"Don't get so wrought up," said Mr. Callender gently.

"Quit thinking she's a kid. She's in town somewhere and she can't get through on the phone, that's all."

Mrs. Callender pouted. "She's been intolerable since the moment she arrived. Inconsiderate and perverse. I've done nothing all morning but worry about her."

"I know."

"And I've a fearful migraine as a result. It's that *beastly* Monsieur Royer," she added with vehemence.

At the next table Mr. Burton laid aside his book and feebly inquired: "I expect your daughter is pleased to be back home?"

Mrs. Callender turned to face him. "Oh, yes! She adores it here. Of course it's ideal for young people."

"Oh, quite! Yes, indeed."

After lunch she took more aspirin. Now she felt a slight nausea as well. She lay on her bed, the curtains drawn, reflecting with a dim satisfaction that at least Charlotte would know she had made her mother ill. The wind still blew, the trees still swayed and roared, and through their sound from time to time crept the shrill, tiny notes of the distant *rhaïta*. She dozed, woke, dozed. At tea-time Halima knocked to ask if she wanted tea in her room. She inquired if Señorita Charlotte had returned. Halima had not seen her.

Although she wanted Charlotte to find her ill in bed when she returned, she disliked having tea in her cottage alone and, deciding to run the risk of rising, went up to the salon in the main house for her tea. Only the nurses were there, but she sat down anyway. Soon she heard Pedro's voice in the hall and excused herself.

"*Oiga*, Pedro," she called, running out. "You haven't seen Señorita Charlotte this afternoon, have you?"

"*Esta tarde? Nó, señora.* Not since this morning in the market, riding with Señor Van Siclen in his car."

"*Cómo!*" she cried; the word was like an explosion. Her eyes had become very large. Pedro looked at her and thought that perhaps Señora Callender was about to faint.

"Get the *camioneta*," she said weakly. "*Vamos a El Menar.*"

"Now?" he asked, surprised.

"Immediately."

8

She sat in front with Pedro, her head pounding so hard that it was merely an enormous and imprecise pain she carried with her. The familiar landmarks as they passed made no sense. She could not have identified one. Nor did she know which of the three enraged her most: Charlotte, for her effrontery and disobedience, Mr. Van Siclen for his perfidy, or Monseiur Royer, for existing at all.

As long as she was sitting in the moving car her anger remained at fever pitch. But when Pedro stopped in the wilderness, pointing to a road strewn with large stones, and remarking that they would have to walk up to to get to the village, her annoyance at this unexpected obstacle somewhat calmed her. It was quite dark by this time, and the faint light from Pedro's torch wavered uncertainly. Out here the wind came directly off the Atlantic; it was violent and damp.

The road led upward, zigzagging among huge boulders. Each minute the sound of the sea became more audible. She had never been here before; the idea of this absurd village perched on the crags above the ocean filled her with terror. They met a Berber on his way down, and by the flashlight's feeble glimmer she saw him, stocky and dark-skinned, and carrying a shepherd's crook. "*Msalkheir,*" he said as he passed. He was in the darkness back of them before they could ask him how far the village was. Suddenly they came to a hut. There was a flickering light inside, and the sound of many goats and sheep. A little farther on Pedro spied the jeep. She caught herself thinking, "How does he ever drive up that trail?" and quickly remembered the seriousness of her errand.

"*Pregúnteles,*" she whispered to Pedro, indicating a group of dark figures at the right. The barnyard odors were overwhelming. As Pedro left her side to approach the men, she glanced up and saw the sky, uniformly black. Not a star showed through the huge curtain of cloud. Yes, far out over the invisible sea she thought she saw one shining, but it could have been a boat. She had neglected to bring a wrap, and she was shivering.

The house was up ahead, at the top of the village. She could see the lamp through the open door, the brightest light in the landscape. Several dogs went slinking away into the dark as they approached the house. Pedro called out, *"Señor!"* and Mr. Van Siclen appeared.

"Good God!" he cried when he saw them standing in the doorway. "What are you doing here?"

She pushed past him into the tiny room. There was a chair, a table littered with papers, and a mattress on the floor in the corner. And there were large native baskets everywhere, full of pieces of stone. The light hurt her eyes.

"Where's my daughter?" she said, going to the door of the adjoining room and peering in.

"What?"

She looked at him; for the first time since she had known him he seemed really perturbed—even frightened.

"Charlotte. Where is she?"

The expression on his face did not change. Her question seemed not to have reached it. "I have no idea. I let her off early this morning on the Boulevard by the French Consulate."

Mrs. Callender hesitated, not completely sure he was telling the truth. He took the initiative. "It'd be more to the point to ask where Monsieur Royer is. You haven't seen *him* by any chance? I don't mind telling you I'm worried."

"Monsieur Royer? Certainly not! Isn't he here with you?"

He shrugged his shoulders helplessly. "I'm afraid not. I don't know what's up. But it doesn't look good to me."

She sat down sideways on the straight-backed chair. For a second she heard the sea much closer that it should have been.

"He went out last night right after supper. There were some drums beating."

She had her hand to her head. And as so often happens in moments of great fatigue, she felt that the scene was one whose outcome she knew by heart, that although she was in it, it would go on and play itself through to the end without her participation. Mr. Van Siclen would reach into his hip-pocket, pull out a packet of cigarettes, extract one, light it, and hold the match a moment before blowing it out, just as he did do each of these things a fraction of a second after she had known he would. And he would go on speaking.

"—but I don't quite know what the hell to do. The worst thing about it is that the natives all claim not to have seen him, ever. They don't know there is such a person. I know damned well they're lying. It's too unanimous. I don't think he ever came back at all. The blankets on his mattress in there" —he indicated the next room—"haven't been touched. I didn't notice that until I got back from town this morning. I thought he was asleep."

She said nothing because she felt she was getting much too far ahead of him now. At the moment this bare room with the wind outside was the less strong of two realities. The other was a spoken sentence, a dreadful image, but she could recall neither the sentence nor the image it had evoked—only the brief horror she had felt at the time.

She was standing up, walking toward the door.

"I feel a bit ill." To say the words demanded a monstrous effort.

Outside, the sea-wind battered her face. She breathed deeply several times. Mr. Van Siclen's voice came from the door, solicitous. "Are you all right?"

"Yes," she said.

"Be careful out there. There's barbed wire strung along the edge where you are."

Now it was complete. Everything had been said. All she had to do was go on breathing deeply, facing the sea. Of course. A coil of wire around his neck. Behind a rock. A minute or two later she went back in.

"Better?"

"If I could have a drink," she said wanly. (She could not say to him: "It's not my fault. You yourself put the idea into my head," because to admit that much would establish her guilt firmly, for all time.)

"Whisky, you mean? Or water?"

"I think whisky."

As she drank it he said: "We'll have a searching party out looking for him the first thing in the morning. That is, if he doesn't turn up tonight. I'll drive you back now so you won't have to walk down the hill. And I think it might be a good idea to call the *comisaría* tonight, anyway."

She smiled ruefully. "The police won't be of much use, will they?"

"Never know," he said, slipping into his jacket. "He may be lying only a half mile from here with a broken leg."

Again she smiled: she was so sure it was not that. And so was he, she thought, but now that she was upset too he could afford to pretend.

"Well, shall we get going?" he asked her.

The wind blew, the great black cloud from the sea had covered everything. He put his arm about her waist as they stumbled downward. She thought of nothing, let herself bump against him as they avoided rocks.

They were in the jeep. At the foot of the hill Pedro got out. "Do you want to go in your own car?" said Mr. Van Siclen. "It'd be more comfortable, I guess."

"No. This air is just what I need."

Swiftly they left El Menar behind in the darkness.

9

From the spot where he lay, he could have heard the two motors grow fainter and be drowned by the vaster sound of the sea; he could have seen the two little red tail-lights moving away across the empty countryside. Could have, if all that had not been decided for him twenty-one hours earlier. In the bright moonlight he had sat with the child on his knee (for she was really no more than a child) letting her examine his watch. For some reason—probably the sight of this innocent animal holding the thin gold toy in her tattooed hands—he was put in mind of the phrase he had not been able to recall the evening of his arrival. He began to murmur it to himself, even at the moment her expression changed to one of terror as, looking up over his shoulder, she saw what was about to happen.

"Le temps qui coule ici n'a plus d'heures, mais, tant l'inoccupation de chacun est parfaite——"

This time he might have completed it.

A FRIEND
OF THE WORLD

SALAM rented two rooms and a kitchen on the second floor
of a Jewish house at the edge of the town. He had decided to
live with the Jews because he had already lived with Christians
and found them all right. He trusted them a little more than
he did other Moslems, who were like him and said: "No
Moslem can be trusted." Moslems are the only true people, the
only people you can understand. But because you do understand them, you do not trust them. Salam did not trust the
Jews completely, either, but he liked living with them because
they paid no attention to him. It had no importance if they
talked about him among themselves, and they never would talk
about him to Moslems. If he had a sister who lived here and
there, getting what money she could from whatever man she
found, because she had to eat, that was all right, and the Jews
did not point at her when she came to visit him. If he did
not get married, but lived instead with his brother and spent
his time smoking kif and laughing, if he got his money by
going to Tangier once a month and sleeping for a week with
old English and American ladies who drank too much whisky,
they did not care. He was a Moslem. Had he been rich he would
have lived in the Spanish end of the town in a villa with
concrete benches in the garden and a big round light in the
ceiling of the *sala*, with many pieces of glass hanging down
from it. He was poor and he lived with the Jews. To get to his
house he had to go to the end of the Medina, cross an open

83

space where the trees had all been cut down, go along the street where the warehouses had been abandoned by the Spanish when they left, and into a newer, dirtier street that led to the main highway. Halfway down was the entrance to the alley where he and his brother and fourteen Jewish families lived. There were the remains of narrow sidewalks along the edges of the wide gutter, full of mounds of rotten watermelon-rind and piles of broken bricks. The small children played here all day. When he was in a hurry he had to be careful not to step on them as they waded in the little puddles of dishwater and urine that were in front of all the doors. If they had been Moslem children he would have spoken to them, but since they were Jews he did not see them as children at all, but merely as nuisances in his way, like cactuses that had to be stepped over carefully because there was no way of going around them. Although he had lived here for almost two years, he did not know the names of any of the Jews. For him they had no names. When he came home and found his door locked, because his brother had gone out and taken both keys with him, he went into any house where the door was open and dropped his bundles on the floor, saying: "I'll be back in a little while." He knew they would not touch his property. The Jews were neither friendly nor unfriendly. They too, if they had had money, would have been living in the Spanish end of the town. It made the alley seem less like a Mellah, where only Jews live, to have the two Moslems staying among them.

Salam had the best house in the alley. It was at the end, and its windows gave onto a wilderness of fig trees and canebrake where squatters had built huts out of thatch and hammered pieces of tin. On the hot nights (for the town was in a plain and the heat stayed in the streets long after the sun had gone) his rooms had a breeze from the south that blew through and out onto the terrace. He was happy with his house and with the life that he and his brother had in it. "I'm a friend of the world," he would say. "A clean heart is better than everything."

One day he came home and found a small kitten sitting on the terrace. When it saw him it ran to him and purred. He unlocked the door into the kitchen and it went inside. After he had washed his hands and feet in the kitchen he went into his room. The kitten was lying on the mattress, still purring. "Mimí," he said to it. He gave it some bread. While it ate the bread it did not stop purring. Bou Ralem came home. He had been drinking beer with some friends in the Café Granada. At first he did not understand why Salam had let the kitten stay. "It's too young to be worth anything," he said. "If it saw a rat it would run and hide." But when the kitten lay in his lap and played with him he liked it. "Its name is Mimí," Salam told him. Nights it slept on the mattress with Salam near his feet. It learned to go down into the alley to relieve itself in the dirt there. The children sometimes tried to catch it, but it ran faster than they did and got to the steps before them, and they did not dare follow it upstairs.

During Ramadan, when they stayed up all night, they moved the mats and cushions and mattresses out on to the terrace and lived out there, talking and laughing until the daylight came. They smoked more kif than usual, and invited their friends home at two in the morning for dinner. Because they were living outside and the kitten could hear them from the alley, it grew bolder and began to visit the canebrake behind the house. It could run very fast, and even if a dog chased it, it could get to the stairs in time. When Salam missed it he would stand up and call to it over the railing, on one side down the alley and on the other over the trees and the roofs of the shacks. Sometimes when he was calling into the alley a Jewish woman would run out of one of the doors and look at him. He noticed that it was always the same woman. She would put one hand above her eyes and stare up at him, and then she would put both hands on her hips and frown. "A crazy woman," he thought, and he paid no attention to her. One day while he was calling the kitten, the woman shouted up to him in Spanish.

Her voice sounded very angry. *"Oyé!"* she cried, shaking her arm in the air, "why are you calling the name of my daughter?"

Salam kept calling: *"Mimí! Agi! Agiagi, Mimí!"*

The woman moved closer to the steps. She put both hands above her eyes, but the sun was behind Salam, so that she could not see him very well. "You want to insult people?" she screamed. "I understand your game. You make fun of me and my daughter."

Salam laughed. He put the end of his forefinger to the side of his head and made circles with it. "I'm calling my cat. Who's your daughter?"

"And your cat is called Mimí because you knew my little girl's name was Mimí. Why don't you behave like civilized people?"

Salam laughed again and went inside. He did not think of the woman again. Not many days after that the kitten disappeared, and no matter how much he called, it did not come back. He and Bou Ralem went out that night and searched for it in the canebrake. The moon was bright, and they found it lying dead, and carried it back to the house to look at it. Someone had given it a pellet of bread with a needle inside. Salam sat slowly on the mattress. "The *Yehoudía,*" he said.

"You don't know who did it," Bou Ralem told him.

"It was the *Yehoudía.* Throw me the *mottoui.*" And he began to smoke kif, one pipe after another. Bou Ralem understood that Salam was looking for an answer, and he did not talk. After a while he saw that the time had come to turn off the electricity and light the candle. When he had done this, Salam lay back quietly on the mattress and listened to the dogs barking outside. Now and then he sat up and filled his *sebsi.* Once he passed it to Bou Ralem, and lay back down on the cushions smiling. He had an idea of what he would do. When they went to bed he said to Bou Ralem: "She's one mother who's going to wet her pants."

The next day he got up early and went to the market. In

a little stall there he bought several things: a crow's wing, a hundred grams of *jduq jmel* seeds, powdered porcupine quills, some honey, a pressed lizard, and a quarter kilo of *fasoukh*. When he had finished paying for all this he turned away as if he were going to leave the stall, then he said: "*Khaï*, give me another fifty grams of *jduq jmel*." When the man had weighed the seeds out and put them into a paper and folded it up, he paid him and carried the paper in his left hand as he went on his way home. In the alley the children were throwing clots of mud at one another. They stopped while he went by. The women sat in the doorways with their shawls over their heads. As he passed before the house of the woman who had killed Mimí he let go of the package of *jduq jmel* seeds. Then he went upstairs on to his terrace, walked to the door, and pounded on it. No one answered. He stood in the middle of the terrace where everyone could see him, rubbing his hand over his chin. A minute later he climbed to the terrace next to his and knocked on that door. He handed his parcel to the woman who came to open. "I left my keys in the market," he told her. "I'll be right back." He ran downstairs, through the alley, and up the street.

Behind the Gailan Garage Bou Ralem was standing. When Salam passed him, he nodded his head once and went along without stopping. Bou Ralem began to walk in the other direction, back to the house. As he opened the gate on to the terrace, the woman from next door called to him. "Haven't you seen your brother? He left his keys in the market." "No," Bou Ralem said, and went in, leaving the door open. He sat down and smoked a cigarette while he waited. In a little while the talking in the alley below sounded louder. He stood up and went to the door to listen. A woman was crying: "It's *jduq jmel!* Mimí had it in her hand!" Soon there were many more voices, and the woman from the next terrace ran downstairs in her bathrobe, carrying a parcel. "That's it," Bou Ralem said to himself. When she arrived the shouting grew louder. He listened for a time, smiling. He went out and ran downstairs. They were all in the alley outside the woman's door, and the little girl was inside the house, screaming. Without looking toward them he ran by on the far side of the alley.

Salam was inside the café, drinking a glass of tea. "Sit down," he told Bou Ralem. "I'm not going to get Fatma Daifa before eleven." He ordered his brother a tea. "Were they making a lot of noise?" he asked him. Bou Ralem nodded his head. Salam smiled. "I'd like to hear them," he said. "You'll hear them," Bou Ralem told him. "They're not going to stop."

At eleven o'clock they left the café and went through the back passages of the Medina to Fatma Daifa's house. She was the sister of their mother's mother, and thus not of their family, so that they did not feel it was shameful to use her in the game. She was waiting for them at the door, and together they went back to Salam's house.

The old woman went into the alley ahead of Salam and Bou Ralem, and walked straight to the door where all the women were gathered. She held her *haïk* tightly around her head so that no part of her face showed, except one eye. She pushed against the Jewish women and held out one hand. "Give me my things," she told them. She did not bother to speak Spanish with them because she knew they understood Arabic. "You have my things." They did have them and they were still looking at them, but then they turned to look at her. She seized all the packages and put them into her *kouffa* quickly. "No shame!" she shouted at the women. "Go and look after your children." She pushed the other way and went back into the alley where Salam and Bou Ralem stood waiting. The three went upstairs and into Salam's house, and they shut the door. They had lunch there and stayed all day, talking and laughing. When everyone had gone to bed, Salam took Fatma Daifa home.

The next day the Jews all stared at them when they went out, but no one said anything to them. The woman Salam had wanted to frighten did not come to her door at all, and the little girl was not in the alley playing with the other children. It was clear that the Jews thought Fatma Daifa had put a spell on the child. They would not have believed Salam and Bou Ralem alone could do such a thing, but they knew a Moslem woman had the power. The two brothers were very much pleased with the joke. It is forbidden to practice magic, but the old woman was their witness that they had not done such a thing. She had taken home all the packages just as they had been when she had snatched them away from the Jewish women, and she had promised to keep them that way, so that in case of trouble she could prove that nothing had been used.

The Jewish woman went to the *comisaría* to complain. She found a young policeman sitting at his desk listening to a small radio he had in his hand, and she began to tell him that the Moslems in her *haouma* had bought charms to use against her daughter. The policeman did not like her, partly because she was Jewish and spoke Spanish instead of Arabic, and partly because he did not approve of people who believed in magic, but he listened politely until she said: "That Moslem is a *sinvergüenza*." She tried to go on to say that there were many very good Moslems, but he did not like her words. He frowned at the woman and said: "Why do you say all this? What makes you think they put a spell on your little girl?" She told him how the three had shut themselves in all day with the packages of bads things from the market. The policeman looked at her in surprise. "And for a dead lizard you came all the way here?" he laughed. He sent her away and went on listening to his radio.

The people in the alley still did not speak to Salam and Bou Ralem, and the little girl did not come out to play in the mud with the others. When the woman went to the market she took her with her. "Hold on to my skirt," she would tell her. But one day in front of the service station the child let go of the woman's skirt for a minute. When she ran to catch up with her mother, she fell and her knee hit a broken bottle. The woman saw the blood and began to scream. People stopped walking. In a few minutes a Jew came by and helped the woman carry the child to a pharmacy. They bandaged the little girl's knee and the woman took her home. Then she went back to the pharmacy to get her baskets, but on the way she stopped at the police station. She found the same policeman sitting at his desk.

"If you want to see the proof of what I told you, come and look at my little girl now," she told him. "Again?" said the policeman. He was not friendly with her, but he took her name and address, and later that day on his way home he called at her house. He looked at the little girl's knee and tickled her ribs so that she laughed. "All children fall down," he said. "But who is this Moslem? Where does he live?" The mother showed him the stairs at the end of the alley. He did not intend to speak with Salam, but he wanted to finish with the woman once and for all. He went out into the alley, and saw that the woman was watching him from the door, so he walked slowly to the foot of the stairs. When he had decided she was no longer looking, he started to go. At that moment he heard a voice behind him. He turned and saw Salam standing above him on the terrace. He did not much like his face, and he told himself that if he ever saw him in the street he would have a few words with him.

One morning Salam went early to the market to get fresh kif. When he found it he bought three hundred francs' worth. As he went out through the gates into the street the policeman, who was waiting for him, stopped him. "I want to speak with you," he told him. Salam stretched his fingers tightly around the kif in his pocket. "Is everything all right?" said the policeman. "Everything is fine," Salam replied. "No trouble?" the policeman insisted, looking at him as if he knew what Salam had just bought. Salam answered: "No trouble." The policeman said: "See that it stays like that." Salam was angry at being spoken to in this way for no reason, but the kif in his pocket he could only be thankful that he was not being searched. "I'm a friend of the world," he said, trying to smile. The policeman did not answer, and turned away.

"A very bad thing," thought Salam as he hurried home with the kif. No policeman had bothered him before this. When he reached his room he wondered if he should hide the package under a tile in the floor, but he decided that if he did that, he himself would be living like a Jew, who each time there is a knock at the door ducks his head and trembles. He spread the kif out on the table defiantly and left it there. During the afternoon he and Bou Ralem cut it. He did not mention the policeman, but he was thinking of him all the time they were working. When the sun had gone down behind the plain and the soft breeze began to come in through the windows he took off his shirt and lay back on the pillows to smoke. Bou Ralem filled his *mottoui* with the fresh kif and went out to a café. "I'm staying here," said Salam.

He smoked for an hour or more. It was a hot night. The dogs had begun to bark in the canebrake. A woman and a man in one of the huts below were cursing one another. Sometimes the woman stopped shouting and merely screamed. The sound bothered Salam. He could not be happy. He got up and dressed, took his *sebsi* and his *mottoui*, and went out. Instead of turning toward the town when he left the alley, he walked toward the highway. He wanted to sit in a quiet place in order to find out what to do. If the policeman had not suspected him, he would not have stopped him. Since he had stopped him once, he might do it again, and the next time he might search him. "That's not freedom," he said to himself. A few cars went by. Their headlights made the tree-trunks yellow as they passed. After each car had gone, there was only the blue light of the moon and the sky. When he got to the bridge over the river, he climbed down the bank under the girders, and went along a path to a rock that hung out high above the water. There he sat and looked over the edge at the deep muddy river that

91

was moving below in the moonlight. He felt the kif in his head, and he knew he was going to make it work for him. He put the plan together slowly. It was going to cost a thousand francs, but he had that, and he was willing to spend it. After six pipes, when he had everything arranged in his mind, he stuffed his *sebsi* into his pocket, jumped up, and climbed the path to the highway. He walked back to the town quickly, going into the Medina by a dirt road where the houses had gardens, and where behind the walls all along the way there were dogs barking at the moon. Not many people walked at night in this part of the town. He went to the house of his cousin Abdallah, who was married to a woman from Sidi Kacem. The house was never empty. Two or three of her brothers were always there with their families. Salam spoke privately with Abdallah in the street outside the door, asking for one of the brothers whose face was not known in the town. Abdallah went in and quickly came out again with someone. The man had a beard, wore a country *djellaba*, and carried his shoes in his hand. They spoke together for a few minutes. "Go with him," said Abdallah, when they had finished talking. Salam and the bearded man said goodnight and went away.

At Salam's house that night the man slept on a mat in the kitchen. When morning came, they washed and had coffee and pastries. While they were eating Salam took out his thousand-franc note and put it into an envelope. On the outside of it Bou Ralem had printed the word GRACIAS in pencil. Soon Salam and the man from the country got up and went out through the town until they came to a side street opposite the back entrance of the police station. There they stood against the fall and talked. "You don't know his name," said the man. "We don't have to," Salam told him. "When he comes out and gets into one of the cars and drives away, you run over to the office and give them the envelope, and say you tried to catch him before he left." He waved the envelope in his hand. "Ask them to give this to him when he comes back. They'll take it."

"He may walk," said the man. "Then what will I do?"

"The police never walk," Salam said. "You'll see. Then you run out again. This street is the best one. Keep going, that's all. I won't be here. I'll see you at Abdallah's."

They waited a long time. The sun grew hotter and they moved into the shade of a fig tree, always watching the door of the *comisaría* from where they stood. Several policemen came out, and for each one the man from the country was ready to run, but Salam held on to him and said: "No, no, no!" When the policeman they were waiting for finally did stand in the doorway, Salam drew in his breath and whispered: "There he is. Wait till he drives off, then run." He turned away and walked very fast down the street into the Medina.

When the man from the country had explained clearly who the envelope was for, he handed it to the policeman at the desk, said, "Thank you," and ran out quickly. The policeman looked at the envelope, then tried to call him back, but he had gone. Since all messages which came for any of the policemen had to be put on the captain's desk first, he sent the envelope in to his office. The captain held it up to the light. When the policeman came back he called him in and made him open it in front of him. "Who is it from?" said the captain. The policeman scratched his head. He could not answer. "I see," said the captain. The next week he had the man transferred. Word came from the capital that he was to be sent to Rissani. "See how many friends you can make in the desert," the captain told him. He would not listen to anything the policeman tried to say.

Salam went to Tangier. When he returned he heard that the policeman had been sent to the Sahara. This made him laugh a great deal. He went to the market and brought a half-grown goat. Then he invited Fatma Daifa and Abdallah and his wife and two of the brothers with their wives and children, and they killed the goat and ate it. It was nearly dawn by the time they all went home. Fatma Daifa did not want to go through the streets alone, and since Salam and Bou Ralem were too drunk to take her, she slept in the kitchen on the floor. When she woke up it was late, but Salam and Bou Ralem were still asleep. She got her things together, put on her *haïk* and went out. As she came to the house of the woman with the little girl, she stood still and looked in. The woman saw her and was frightened. "What do you want?" she cried. Fatma Daifa knew she was meddling, but she thought this was the right thing to do for Salam. She pretended not to see the woman's frightened face, and she shook her fist back at the terrace, crying into the air: "Now I see what sort of man you are! You think you can cheat me? Listen to me! None of it's going to work, do you hear?" She walked on down the alley shouting: "None of it!" The other Jewish women came and stood around the door and sat on the curb in front of it. They agreed that if the old woman had fought with the two men there was no more danger from the magic, because only the old woman had the power to make it work. The mother of the little girl was happy, and the next day the child was playing in the mud with the others.

Salam went in and out of the alley as always, not noticing the children or the people. It was half a month before he said one day to Bou Ralem: "I think the Jews are feeling better. I saw the wrong Mimí out loose this morning." He was free again now that the policeman was gone, and he could carry his kif in his pocket without worrying when he went out through the streets to the café. The next time he saw Fatma Daifa she asked him about the Jews in his alley. "It's finished. They've forgotten," he said. "Good," she replied. Then she went to her house and got out the porcupine quill powder and the crow's wing and the seeds and all the rest of the packages. She put them into her basket, carried them to the market, and sold them there, and with the money she bought bread, oil, and eggs. She went home and cooked her dinner.

HE OF
THE ASSEMBLY

He salutes all parts of the sky and the earth where it is bright. He thinks the color of the amethysts of Aguelmous will be dark if it has rained in the valley of Zerekten. The eye wants to sleep, he says, but the head is no mattress. When it rained for three days and water covered the flatlands outside the ramparts, he slept by the bamboo fence at the Café of the Two Bridges.

I T SEEMS there was a man named Ben Tajah who went to Fez to visit his cousin. The day he came back he was walking in the Djemaa el Fna, and he saw a letter lying on the pavement. He picked it up and found that his name was written on the envelope. He went to the Café of the Two Bridges with the letter in his hand, sat down on a mat and opened the envelope. Inside was a paper which read: "The sky trembles and the earth is afraid, and the two eyes are not brothers." Ben Tajah did not understand, and he was very unhappy because his name was on the envelope. It made him think that Satan was nearby. He of the Assembly was sitting in the same part of the café. He was listening to the wind in the telephone wires. The sky was almost empty of daytime light. "The eye wants to sleep," he thought, "but the head is no mattress. I know what that is, but I have forgotten it." Three days is a long time for rain to keep falling on flat bare ground. "If I got up and ran down the street," he thought, "a policeman would follow me and call to me to stop. I would run faster, and he would run after me. When he shot at me, I'd duck around the corners of houses." He felt the rough dried mud of the wall under his fingertips. "And I'd be running through the streets looking for a place to hide, but no door would be open, until finally I came to one door that was open, and I'd go in through the rooms and court-yards until finally I came to the kitchen. The old woman would be there." He stopped and wondered for a moment why an old woman should be there alone in the kitchen at that hour. She was stirring a big kettle of soup on the stove. "And I'd look for a place to hide there in the kitchen, and there'd be no place. And I'd be waiting to hear the policeman's footsteps, because he wouldn't miss the open door. And I'd look in the dark corner of the room where she kept the charcoal, but it wouldn't be dark enough. And the old woman would turn and look at me and say: 'If you're trying to get away, my boy, I can help you. Jump into the soup-kettle.'" The wind sighed in the tele-phone wires. Men came into the Café of the Two Bridges with their garments flapping. Ben Tajah sat on his mat. He had put the letter away, but first he had stared at it a long time. He of the Assembly leaned back and looked at the sky. "The old woman," he said to himself. "What is she trying to do? The soup is hot. It may be a trap. I may find there's no way out, once I get down there." He wanted a pipe of kif, but he was afraid the policeman would run into the kitchen before he was able to smoke it. He said to the old woman: "How can I get in? Tell me." And it seemed to him that he heard footsteps in the street, or perhaps even in one of the rooms of the house. He leaned over the stove and looked down into the kettle. It was dark and very hot down in there. Steam was coming up in clouds, and there was a thick smell in the air that made it hard to breathe. "Quick!" said the old woman, and she unrolled a rope ladder and hung it over the edge of the kettle. He began to climb down, and she leaned over and looked after him. "Until the other world!" he shouted. And he climbed all the way down. There was a rowboat below. When he was in it he tugged on the ladder and the old woman began to pull it up. And at that instant the policeman ran in, and two more were with him, and the old woman had just the time to throw the ladder down into the soup. "Now they are going to take her to the commissariat," he thought, "and the poor woman only did me a favor." He rowed around in the dark for a few minutes, and it was very hot. Soon he took off his clothes. For a while he could see the round top of the kettle up above, like a porthole in the side of a ship, with the heads of the police-men looking down in, but then it grew smaller as he rowed, until it was only a light. Sometimes he could find it and some-times he lost it, and finally it was gone. He was worried about the old woman, and he thought he must find a way to help her. No policeman can go into the Café of the Two Bridges because it belongs to the Sultan's sister. This is why there is so much kif smoke inside that a *berrada* can't fall over even if it is pushed, and why most customers like to sit outside, and even there keep one hand on their money. As long as the thieves stay inside and their friends bring them food and kif, they are all right. One day police headquarters will forget to send a man to watch the café, or one man will leave five minutes before the other gets there to take his place. Outside everyone smokes kif too, but only for an hour or two—not all day and night like the ones inside. He of the Assembly had forgotten to light his *sebsi*. He was in a café where no policeman could come, and he wanted to go away to a kif world where the police were chasing him. "This is the way we are now," he thought. "We work backwards." If we have something good, we look for something bad instead." He lighted the *sebsi* and smoked it. Then he blew the hard ash out of the *chqaf*. It landed in the brook beside the second bridge. "The world is too good. We can only work forward if we make it bad again first." This made him sad, so he stopped thinking, and filled his *sebsi*. While he was smoking it, Ben Tajah looked in his direction, and although they were facing each other, He of the Assembly did not notice Ben Tajah until he got up and paid for his tea. Then he looked at him because he took such a long time getting up off the floor. He saw his face and he thought: "That man has no one in the world." The idea made him feel cold. He filled his *sebsi* again and lighted it. He saw the man as he was going to go out of the café and walk alone down the long road outside the ramparts. In a little while he himself would have to go out to the *souks* to try and borrow money for dinner. When he smoked a lot of kif he did not like his aunt to see him, and he did not want to see her. "Soup and bread. No one can want more than that. Will thirty francs be enough the fourth time? The *qahouaji* wasn't satisfied last night. But he took it. And he went away and let me sleep. A Moslem, even in the city, can't refuse his brother shelter." He was not convinced, because he had been born in the mountains, and so he kept thinking back and forth in this way. He smoked many *chqofa*, and when he got up to go out into the street he found that the world had changed.

Ben Tajah was not a rich man. He lived alone in a room near Bab Doukkala, and he had a stall in the bazaars where he sold coathangers and chests. Often he did not open the shop because he was in bed with a liver attack. At such times he pounded on the floor from his bed, using a brass pestle, and the postman who lived downstairs brought him up some food. Sometimes he stayed in bed for a week at a time. Each morning and night the postman came in with a tray. The food was not very good because the postman's wife did not understand much about cooking. But he was glad to have it. Twice he had brought the postman a new chest to keep clothes and blankets in. One of the postman's wives a few years before had taken a chest with her when she had left him and gone back to her family in Kasba Tadla. Ben Tajah himself had tried having a wife for a while because he needed someone to get him regular meals and to wash his clothes, but the girl was from the mountains, and was wild. No matter how much he beat her she would not be tamed. Everything in the room got broken, and finally he had to put her out into the street. "No more women will get into my house," he told his friends in the bazaars, and they laughed. He took home many women, and one day he found that he had *en noua*. He knew that was a bad disease, because it stays in the blood and eats the nose from inside. "A man loses his nose only long after he has already lost his head." He asked a doctor for medicine. The doctor gave him a paper and told him to take it to the Pharmacie de l'Etoile. There he bought six vials of penicillin in a box. He took them home and tied each little bottle with a silk thread, stringing them so that they made a necklace. He wore this always around his neck, taking care that the glass vials touched his skin. He thought it likely that by now he was cured, but his cousin in Fez had just told him that he must go on wearing the medicine for another three months, or at least until the beginning of the moon of Chouwal. He had thought about this now and then on the way home, sitting in the bus for two days, and he had decided that his cousin was too cautious. He stood in the Djemaa el Fna a minute watching the trained monkeys, but the crowd pushed too much, so he walked on. When he got home he shut the door and put his hand in his pocket to pull out the envelope, because he wanted to look at it again inside his own room, and be sure that the name written on it was beyond a doubt his. But the letter was gone. He remembered the jostling in the Djemaa el Fna. Someone had reached into his pocket and imagined his hand was feeling money, and taken it. Yet Ben Tajah did not truly believe this. He was convinced that he would have known such a theft was happening. There had been a letter in his pocket. He was not even sure of that. He sat down on the cushions. "Two days in the bus," he thought. "Probably I'm tired. I found no letter." He searched in his pocket again, and it seemed to him he could still remember how the fold of the envelope had felt. "Why would it have my name on it? I never found any letter at all." Then he wondered if anyone had seen him in the café with the envelope in one hand and the sheet of paper in the other, looking at them both for such a long time. He stood up. He wanted to go back to the Café of the Two Bridges and ask the *qahouaji*: "Did you see me an hour ago? Was I looking at a letter?" If the *qahouaji* said, "Yes," then the letter was real. He repeated the words aloud: "The sky trembles and the earth is afraid, and the two eyes are not brothers." In the silence afterwards the memory of the sound of the words frightened him. "If there was no letter, where are these words from?" And he shivered because the answer to that was: "From Satan." He was about to open the door when a new fear stopped him. The *qahouaji* might say, "No," and this would be still worse, because it would mean that the words had been put directly into his head by Satan, that Satan had chosen him to reveal Himself to. In that case He might appear at any moment. "*Ach haddou laillaha ill'Allah. . . ,*" he prayed, holding his two forefingers up, one on each side of him. He sat down again and did not move. In the street the children were crying. He did not want to hear the *qahouaji* say: "No. You had no letter." If he knew that Satan was coming to tempt him, he would have that much less power to keep Him away with his prayers, because he would be more afraid.

He of the Assembly stood. Behind him was a wall. In his hand was the *sebsi*. Over his head was the sky, which he felt was about to burst into light. He was leaning back looking at it. It was dark on the earth, but there was still light up there behind the stars. Ahead of him was the pissoir of the Carpenters' Souk which the French had put there. People said only Jews used it. It was made of tin, and there was a puddle in front of it that reflected the sky and the top of the pissoir. It looked like a boat in the water. Or like a pier where boats land. Without moving from where he stood, He of the Assembly saw it approaching slowly. He was going toward it. And he re-

membered he was naked, and put his hand over his sex. In a
minute the rowboat would be bumping against the pier. He
steadied himself on his legs and waited. But at that moment a
large cat ran out of the shadow of the wall and stopped in the
middle of the street to turn and look at him with an evil face.
He saw its two eyes and for a while could not take his own eyes
away. Then the cat ran across the street and was gone. He was
not sure what had happened, and he stood very still looking at
the ground. He looked back at the pissoir reflected in the puddle
and thought: "It was a cat on the shore, nothing else." But the
cat's eyes had frightened him. Instead of being like cats' eyes,
they had looked like the eyes of a person who was interested in
him. He made himself forget he had had this thought. He was
still waiting for the rowboat to touch the landing pier, but
nothing had happened. It was going to stay where it was, that
near the shore but not near enough to touch. He stood still a
long time, waiting for something to happen. Then he began to
walk very fast down the street toward the bazaars. He had just
remembered that the old woman was in the police station. He
wanted to help her, but first he had to find out where they had
taken her. "I'll have to go to every police station in the Medina," he thought, and he was not hungry any more. It was one
thing to promise himself he would help her when he was far
from land, and another when he was a few doors from a commissariat. He walked by the entrance. Two policemen stood in
the doorway. He kept walking. The street curved and he was
alone. "This night is going to be a jewel in my crown," he said,
and he turned quickly to the left and went along a dark pas-
sageway. At the end he saw flames, and he knew that Mustapha
would be there tending the fire of the bakery. He crawled into
the mud hut where the oven was. "Ah, the jackal has come back
from the forest!" said Mustapha. He of the Assembly shook
his head. "This is a bad world," he told Mustapha. "I've got
no money," Mustapha said. He of the Assembly did not understand. "Everything goes backwards," he said. "It's bad now, and

101

we have to make it still worse if we want to go forwards."
Mustapha saw that He of the Assembly was *mkiyif ma rassou*
and was not interested in money. He looked at him in a more
friendly way and said: "Secrets are not between friends. Talk."
He of the Assembly told him that an old woman had done him
a great favor, and because of that three policemen had arrested
her and taken her to the police station. "You must go for me
to the commissariat and ask them if they have an old woman
there." He pulled out his *sebsi* and took a very long time filling
it. When he finished it he smoked it himself and did not offer
any to Mustapha, because Mustapha never offered him any of
his. "You see how full of kif my head is," he said laughing.
"I can't go." Mustapha laughed too and said it would not be a
good idea, and that he would go for him.

"I was there, and I heard him going away for a long time, so
long that he had to be gone, and yet he was still there, and his
footsteps were still going away. He went away and there was
nobody. There was the fire and I moved away from it. I wanted
to hear a sound like a muezzin crying *Allah akbar!* or a French
plane from the Pilot Base flying over the Medina, or news on
the radio. It wasn't there. And when the wind came in the door
it was made of dust high as a man. A night to be chased by dogs
in the Mellah. I looked in the fire and I saw an eye in there,
like the eye that's left when you burn *chibb* and you know
there was a *djinn* in the house. I got up and stood. The fire
was making a noise like a voice. I think it was talking. I went
out and walked along the street. I walked a long time and I
came to Bab el Khemiss. It was dark there and the wind was
cold. I went to the wall where the camels were lying and stood
there. Sometimes the men have fires and play songs on their
aouadas. But they were asleep. All snoring. I walked again and
went to the gate and looked out. The big trucks went by full of
vegetables and I thought I would like to be on a truck and ride
all night. Then in another city I would be a soldier and go to
Algeria. Everything would be good if we had a war. I thought

a long time. Then I was so cold I turned around and walked again. It was as cold as the belly of the oldest goat of Ijoukak. I thought I heard a muezzin and I stopped and listened. The only thing I heard was the water running in the *seguia* that carries the water out to the gardens. It was near the *mçid* of Moulay Boujemaa. I heard the water running by and I felt cold. Then I knew I was cold because I was afraid. In my head I was thinking: 'If something should happen that never happened before, what would I do?' You want to laugh? Hashish in your heart and wind in your head. You think it's like your grandmother's prayer-mat. This is the truth. This isn't a dream brought back from another world past the customs like a teapot from Mecca. I heard the water and I was afraid. There were some trees by the path ahead of me. You know at night sometimes it's good to pull out the *sebsi* and smoke. I smoked and I started to walk. And then I heard something. Not a muezzin. Something that sounded like my name. But it came up from below, from the *seguia*, *Allah istir!* And I walked with my head down. I heard it again saying my name, a voice like water, like the wind moving the leaves in the trees, a woman. It was a woman calling me. The wind was in the trees and the water was running, but there was a woman too. You think it's kif. No, she was calling my name. Now and then, not very loud. When I was under the trees it was louder, and I heard that the voice was my mother's. I heard that the way I can hear you. Then I knew the cat was not a cat, and I knew that Aïcha Qandicha wanted me. I thought of other nights when perhaps she had been watching me from the eyes of a cat or a donkey. I knew she was not going to catch me. Nothing in the seven skies could make me turn around. But I was cold and afraid and when I licked my lips my tongue had no spit on it. I was under the *safsaf* trees and I thought: 'She's going to reach down and try to touch me. But she can't touch me from the front and I won't turn around, not even if I hear a pistol.' I remembered how the policeman had fired at me and how I'd found only one

103

door open. I began to yell: 'You threw me the ladder and told me to climb down; You brought me here! The filthiest whore in the Mellah, with the pus coming out of her, is a thousand times cleaner than you, daughter of all the padronas and dogs in seven worlds.' I got past the trees and I began to run. I called up to the sky so she could hear my voice behind: 'I hope the police put a hose in your mouth and pump you full of salt water until you crack open!' I thought: 'Tomorrow I'm going to buy *fasoukh* and *tib* and *nidd* and *hasalouba* and *mska* and all the *bakhour* in the Djemaa, and put them in the *mijmah* and burn them, and walk back and forth over the *mijmah* ten times slowly, so the smoke can clean out all my clothes. Then I'll see if there's an eye in the ashes afterwards. If there is, I'll do it all over again right away. And every Thursday I'll buy the *bakhour* and every Friday I'll burn it. That will be strong enough to keep her away.' If I could find a window and look through and see what they're doing to the old woman! If only they could kill her! I kept running. There were a few people in the streets. I didn't look to see where I was going, but I went to the street near Mustapha's oven where the commissariat was. I stopped running before I got to the door. The one standing there saw me before that. He stepped out and raised him arm. He said to me: 'Come here.' "

He of the Assembly ran. He felt as though he were on horseback. He did not feel his legs moving. He saw the road coming toward him and the doors going by. The policeman had not shot at him yet, but it was worse than the other time because he was very close behind and he was blowing his whistle. "The policeman is old. At least thirty-five. I can run faster." But from any street others could come. It was dangerous and he did not want to think about danger. He of the Assembly let songs come into his head. When it rains in the valley of Zerekten the amethysts are darker in Aguelmous. The eye wants to sleep but the head is no mattress. It was a song. Ah, my brother, the ink on the paper is like smoke in the air. What words are there to tell how long a night can be? Drunk with love, I wander in the dark. He was running through the dye-souk, and he splashed into a puddle. The whistle blew again behind him, like a crazy bird screaming. The sound made him feel like laughing, but that did not mean he was not afraid. He thought: "If I'm seventeen I can run faster. That has to be true." It was very dark ahead. He had to slow his running. There was no time for his eyes to get used to the dark. He nearly ran into the wall of the shop at the end of the street. He turned to the right and saw the narrow alley ahead of him. The police had tied the old woman naked to a table with her thin legs wide apart and were sliding electrodes up inside her. He ran ahead. He could see the course of the alley now even in the dark. Then he stopped dead, moved to the wall, and stood still. He heard the footsteps slowing down. "He's going to turn to the left." And he whispered aloud: "It ends that way." The footsteps stopped and there was silence. The policeman was looking into the silence and listening into the dark to the left and to the right. He of the Assembly could not see him or hear him, but he knew that was what he was doing. He did not move. When its rains in the valley of Zerekten. A hand seized his shoulder. He opened his mouth and swiftly turned, but the man had moved and was pushing him from the side. He felt the wool of the man's *djellaba* against the back of his hand. He had gone through a door and the man had shut it without making any noise. Now they both stood still in the dark, listening to the policeman walking quickly by outside the door. Then the man struck a match. He was facing the other way, and there was a flight of stairs ahead. The man did not turn around, but he said, "Come up," and they both climbed the stairs. At the top the man took out a key and opened a door. He of the Assembly stood in the doorway while the man lit a candle. He liked the room because it had many mattresses and cushions and a white sheepskin under the tea-tray in the corner on the floor. The man turned around and said: "Sit down." His face looked serious and kind and unhappy. He of the Assembly had never seen it before, but he knew it was not the face of a policeman. He of the Assembly pulled out his *sebsi*.

Ben Tajah looked at the boy and asked him: "What did you mean when you said down there: 'It ends that way?' I heard you say it." The boy was embarrassed. He smiled and looked at the floor. Ben Tajah felt happy to have him there. He had been standing outside the door downstairs in the dark for a long time, trying to make himself go to the Café of the Two Bridges and talk to the *qahouaji*. In his mind it was almost as though he already had been there and spoken with him. He had heard the *qahouaji* telling him that he had seen no letter, and he had felt his own dismay. He had not wanted to believe that, but he would be willing to say yes, I made a mistake and there was no letter, if only he could find out where the words had come from. For the words were certainly in his head: ". . . and the two eyes are not brothers." That was like the footprint found in the garden the morning after a bad dream, the proof that there had been a reason for the dream, that something had been there after all. Ben Tajah had not been able to go or to stay. He had started and stopped so many times that now, although he did not know it, he was very tired. When a man is tired he mistakes the hopes of children for the knowledge of men. It seemed to him that He of the Assembly's words had a meaning all for him. Even though the boy might not know it, he could have been sent by Allah to help him at that minute. In a nearby street a police whistle blew. The boy looked at him. Ben Tajah did not care very much what the answer would be, but he said: "Why are they looking for you?" The boy held out his lighted *sebsi* and his *mottoui* fat with kif. He did not want to talk because he was listening. Ben Tajah smoked kif only when a friend offered it to him, but he understood that the police had begun once more to try to enforce their law against kif. Each year they arrested people for a few weeks, and then stopped arresting them. He looked

106

at the boy, and decided that probably he smoked too much. With the *sebsi* in his hand he was sitting very still listening to the voices of some passers-by in the street below. "I know who he is," one said. "I've got his name from Mustapha." "The baker?" "That's the one." They walked on. The boy's expression was so intense that Ben Tajah said to him: "It's nobody. Just people." He was feeling happy because he was certain that Satan would not appear before him as long as the boy was with him. He said quietly: "Still you haven't told me why you said: 'It ends that way.'" The boy filled his *sebsi* slowly and smoked all the kif in it. "I meant," he said, "thanks to Allah. Praise the sky and the earth where it is bright. What else can you mean when somethings ends?" Ben Tajah nodded his head. Pious thoughts can be of as much use for keeping Satan at a distance as camphor or *bakhour* dropped onto hot coals. Each holy word is worth a high column of smoke, and the eyelids do not smart afterward. "He has a good heart," thought Ben Tajah, "even though he is probably a guide for the Nazarenes." And he asked himself why it would not be possible for the boy to have been sent to protect him from Satan. "Probably not. But it could be." The boy offered him the *sebsi*. He took it and smoked it. After that Ben Tajah began to think that he would like to go to the Café of the Two Bridges and speak to the *qahouaji* about the letter. He felt that if the boy went with him the *qahouaji* might say there had been a letter, and that even if the man could not remember, he would not mind so much because he would be less afraid. He waited until he thought the boy was not nervous about going into the street, and then he said: "Let's go out and get some tea." "Good," said the boy. He was not afraid of the police if he was with Ben Tajah. They went through the empty streets, crossed the Djemaa el Fna and the garden beyond. When they were near the café, Ben Tajah said to the boy: "Do you know the Café of the Two Bridges?" The boy said he always sat there, and Ben Tajah was not surprised. It seemed to him that perhaps he had even seen him there. He seized the boy's arm. "Were you there today?" he asked him. The boy said, "Yes," and turned to look at him. He let go of the arm. "Nothing," he said. "Did you ever see me there?" They came to the gate of the café and Ben Tajah stopped walking. "No," the boy said. They went across the first bridge and then the second bridge, and sat down in a corner. Not many people were left outside. Those inside were making a great noise. The *qahouaji* brought the tea and went away again. Ben Tajah did not say anything to him about the letter. He wanted to drink the tea quietly and leave trouble until later.

When the muezzin called from the minaret of the Koutoubia, He of the Assembly thought of being in the Agdal. The great mountains were ahead of him and the olive trees stood in rows on each side of him. Then he heard the trickle of water and he remembered the *seguia* that is there in the Agdal, and he swiftly came back to the Café of the Two Bridges. Aïcha Qandicha can be only where there are trees by running water. "She comes only for single men by trees and fresh moving water. Her arms are gold and she calls in the voice of the most cherished one." Ben Tajah gave him the *sebsi*. He filled it and smoked it. "When a man sees her face he will never see another woman's face. He will make love with her all the night, and every night, and in the sunlight by the walls, before the eyes of children. Soon he will be an empty pod and he will leave this world for his home in Jehennem." The last carriage went by, taking the last tourists down the road beside the ramparts to their rooms in the Mamounia. He of the Assembly thought: "The eye wants to sleep. But this man is alone in the world. He wants to talk all night. He wants to tell me about his wife and how he beat her and how she broke everything. Why do I want to know all those things? He is a good man but he has no head." Ben Tajah was sad. He said: "What have I done? Why does Satan choose me?" Then at last he told the boy about the letter, about how he wondered if it had had his name on the envelope and how he was not even sure there had been a letter. When he finished he looked sadly at the boy. "And you didn't see me." He of the Assembly shut his eyes and kept them shut for a while. When he opened them again he said: "Are you alone in the world?" Ben Tajah stared at him and did not speak. The boy laughed. "I did see you," he said, "but you had no letter. I saw you when you were getting up and I thought you were old. Then I saw you were not old. That's all I saw." "No, it isn't," Ben Tajah said. "You saw I was alone." He of the Assembly shrugged. "Who knows?" He filled the *sebsi* and handed it to Ben Tajah. The kif was in Ben Tajah's head. His eyes were small. He of the Assembly listened to the wind in the telephone wires, took back the *sebsi* and filled it again. Then he said: "You think Satan is coming to make trouble for you because you're alone in the world. I see that. Get a wife or somebody to be with you always, and you won't think about it any more. That's true. Because Satan doesn't come to men like you." He of the Assembly did not believe this himself. He knew that Father Satan can come for anyone in the world, but he hoped to live with Ben Tajah, so he would not have to borrow money in the *souks* to buy food. Ben Tajah drank some tea. He did not want the boy to see that his face was happy. He felt that the boy was right, and that there never had been a letter. "Two days on a bus is a long time. A man can get very tired," he said. Then he called the *qahouaji* and told him to bring two more glasses of tea. He of the Assembly gave him the *sebsi*. He know that Ben Tajah wanted to stay as long as possible in the Café of the Two Bridges. He put his finger into the *mottoui*. The kif was almost gone. "We can talk," he said. "Not much kif is in the *mottoui*." The *qahouaji* brought the tea. They talked for an hour or more. The *qahouaji* slept and snored. They talked about Satan and the bad thing it is to live alone, to wake up in the dark and know that there is no one else nearby. Many times He of the Assembly told Ben Tajah that he must not worry.

The kif was all gone. He held his empty *mottoui* in his hand. He did not understand how he had got back to the town without climbing up out of the soup kettle. Once he said to Ben Tajah: "I never climbed back up." Ben Tajah looked at him and said he did not understand. He of the Assembly told him the story. Ben Tajah laughed. He said: "You smoke too much kif, brother." He of the Assembly put his *sebsi* into his pocket. "And you don't smoke and you're afraid of Satan," he told Ben Tajah. "No!" Ben Tajah shouted. "By Allah! No more! But one thing is in my head, and I can't put it out. The sky trembles and the the earth is afraid, and the two eyes are not brothers. Did you ever hear those words? Where did they come from?" Ben Tajah looked hard at the boy. He of the Assembly understood that these had been the words on the paper, and he felt cold in the middle of his back because he had never heard them before and they sounded evil. He knew, too, that he must not let Ben Tajah know this. He began to laugh. Ben Tajah took hold of his knee and shook it. His face was troubled. "Did you ever hear them?" He of the Assembly went on laughing. Ben Tajah shook his leg so hard that he stopped and said: "Yes!" When Ben Tajah waited and he said nothing more, he saw the man's face growing angry, and so he said: "Yes, I've heard them. But will you tell me what happened to me and how I got out of the soup-kettle if I tell you about those words?" Ben Tajah understood that the kif was going away from the boy's head. But he saw that it had not all gone, or he would not have been asking that question. And he said: "Wait a while for the answer to that question." He of the Assembly woke the *qahouaji* and Ben Tajah paid him, and they went out of the café. They did not talk while they walked. When they got to the Mouassine mosque, Ben Tajah held out his hand to say goodnight, but He of the Assembly said: "I'm looking in my head for the place I heard your words. I'll walk to your door with you. Maybe I'll remember." Ben Tajah said: "May Allah help you find it." And he took his arm and they walked to Ben Tajah's door while He of the Assembly said nothing. They stood outside the door in the dark. "Have you found it?" said Ben Tajah. "Almost," said He of the Assembly. Ben Tajah thought that perhaps when the kif had gone out of the boy's head he might be able to tell him about the words. He wanted to know how the boy's head was, and so he said: "Do you still want to know how you got out of the soup-kettle?" He of the Assembly laughed. "You said you would tell me later," he told Ben Tajah. "I will," said Ben Tajah. "Come upstairs. Since we have to wait, we can sit down." Ben Tajah opened the door and they went upstairs. This time He of the Assembly sat down on Ben Tajah's bed. He yawned and stretched. It was a good bed. He was glad it was not the mat by the bamboo fence at the Café of the Two Bridges. "And so, tell me how I got out of the soup-kettle," he said laughing. Ben Tajah said: "You're still asking me that? Have you thought of the words?" "I know the words," the boy said. "The sky trembles. . . ." Ben Tajah did not want him to say them again. "Where did you hear them? What are they? That's what I want to know." The boy shook his head. Then he sat up very straight and looked beyond Ben Tajah, beyond the wall of the room, beyond the streets of the Medina, beyond the gardens, toward the mountains where the people speak Tachelhait. He remembered being a little boy. "This night is a jewel in my crown," he thought. "It went this way." And he began to sing, making up a melody for the words Ben Tajah had told him. When he had finished ". . . and the two eyes are not brothers," he added a few more words of his own and stopped singing. "That's all I remember of the song," he said. Ben Tajah clapped his hands together hard. "A song!" he cried. "I must have heard it on the radio." He of the Assembly shrugged. "They play it sometimes," he said. "I've made him happy," he thought. "But I won't ever tell him another lie. That's the only one. What I'm going to do now is not the same as lying." He got up off the bed and went to the window. The meuzzins were calling the *fjer*. "It's almost morn-

111

ing," he said to Ben Tajah. "I still have kif in my head." "Sit down," said Ben Tajah. He was sure now there had been no letter. He of the Assembly took off his *djellaba* and got into bed. Ben Tajah looked at him in surprise. Then he undressed and got into bed beside him. He left the candle burning on the floor beside the bed. He meant to stay awake, but he want to sleep because he was not use to smoking kif and the kif was in his head. He of the Assembly did not believe he was asleep. He lay for a long time without moving. He listened to the voices of the muezzins, and he thought that the man beside him would speak or move. When he saw that Ben Tajah was surely asleep, he was angry. "This is how he treats a friend who has made him happy. He forgets his trouble and his friend too." He thought about it more and he was angrier. The muezzins were still calling the *fjer*. "Before they stop, or he will hear." Very slowly he got out of the bed. He put on his *djellaba* and opened the door. Then he went back and took all the money out of Ben Tajah's pockets. In with the banknotes was an envelope that was folded. It had Ben Tajah's name written across it. He pulled out the piece of paper inside and held it near the candle, and then he looked at it as he would have looked at a snake. The words were written there. Ben Tajah's face was turned toward the wall and he was snoring. He of the Assembly held the paper above the flame and burned it, and then he burned the envelope. He blew the black paper-ashes across the floor. Without making any noise he ran downstairs and let himself out into the street. He shut the door. The money was in his pocket and he walked fast to his aunt's house. His aunt awoke and was angry for a while. Finally he said: "It was raining. How could I come home? Let me sleep." He had a little kif hidden under his pillow. He smoked a pipe. Then he looked across his sleep to the morning and thought: "A pipe of kif before breakfast gives a man the strength of a hundred camels in the courtyard."

THE STORY OF
LAHCEN AND IDIR

T WO FRIENDS, Lahcen and Idir, were walking on the beach
at Merkala. By the rocks stood a girl, and her *djellaba* blew in
the wind. Lahcen and Idir stopped walking when they saw her.
They stood still, looking at her. Lahcen said: "Do you know
that one?" "No. I never saw her. "Let's go over," said Lahcen.
They looked up and down the beach for a man who might be
with the girl, but there was no one. "A whore," said Lahcen.
When they got closer to the girl, they saw that she was very
young. Lahcen laughed. "This is easy." "How much have you
got?" Idir asked him. "You think I'm going to pay her?" cried
Lahcen.

Idir understood that Lahcen meant to beat her. ("If you
don't pay a whore you have to beat her.") And he did not like
the idea, because they had done it before together, and it
nearly always meant trouble later. Her sister or someone in her
family went to the police and complained, and in the end
everybody was in jail. Being shut into prison made Idir
nervous. He tried to keep out of it, and he was usually able to.
The difference between Lahcen and Idir was that Lahcen liked
to drink and Idir smoked kif. Kif smokers want to stay quiet
in their heads, and drinkers are not like that. They want to
break things.

Lahcen rubbed his groin and spat onto the sand. Idir knew
he was going over the moves in the game he was going to play

with the girl, planning when and where he would knock her down. He was worried. The girl looked the other way. She held down the skirt of her *djellaba* so the wind would not blow it. Lahcen said: "Wait here." He went on to her and Idir saw her lips moving as she spoke to him, for she wore no veil. All her teeth were gold. Idir hated women with gold teeth because at fourteen he had been in love with a gold-toothed whore named Zohra, who never had paid him any attention. He said to himself: "He can have her." Besides, he did not want to be with them when the trouble began. He stood still until Lahcen whistled to him. Then he went over to where they stood. "Ready?" Lahcen asked. He took the girl's arm and started to walk along beside the rocks. "It's late. I've go to go," Idir told him. Lahcen looked surprised, but he said nothing. "Some other day," Idir told Lahcen, looking at him and trying to warn him. The girl laughed spitefully, as if she thought that might shame him into coming along.

He was glad he had decided to go home. When he went by the Mendoub's fig orchard a dog barked at him. He threw a rock at it and hit it.

The next morning Lahcen came to Idir's room. His eyes were red from the wine he had been drinking. He sat down on the floor and pulled out a handkerchief that had a knot tied in one corner. He untied the knot and let a gold ring fall out into his lap. Picking up the ring, he handed it to Idir. "For you. I got it cheap." Idir saw that Lahcen wanted him to take the ring, and he put it on his finger, saying: "May Allah give you health." Lahcen rubbed his hand across his chin and yawned. Then he said: "I saw you look at me, and afterward when we got to the quarry I thought that would be the best place. And then I remembered the night the police took us at Bou Khach Khach, and I remembered you looking at me. I turned around and left her there. Garbage!"

"So you're not in jail and you're drunk," said Idir, and he laughed.

"That's true," said Lahcen. "And that's why I give you the ring."

Idir knew the ring was worth at least fifty dirhams, and he could sell it if he needed money badly. That would end his friendship with Lahcen, but there would be no help for it.

Sometimes Lahcen came by in the evening with a bottle of wine. He would drink the whole bottle while Idir smoked his kif pipe, and they would listen to the radio until the end of the program at twelve o'clock. Afterward, very late, they would walk through the streets of Dradeb to a garage where a friend of Lahcen's was night watchman. When the moon was full, it was brighter than the street lights. With no moon, there was nobody in the streets, and in the few late cafés the men told one another about what thieves had done, and how there were more of them than ever before. This was because there was almost no work to be had anywhere, and the country people were selling their cows and sheep to be able to pay their taxes, and then coming to the city. Lahcen and Idir worked now and then, whenever they found something to do. They had a little money, they always ate, and Lahcen sometimes was able to afford his bottle of Spanish wine. Idir's kif was more of a problem, because each time the police decided to enforce the law they had made against it, it grew very scarce and the price went up. Then when there was plenty to be had, because the police were busy looking for guns and rebels instead, the price stayed high. He did not smoke any less, but he smoked by himself in his room. If you smoke in a café, there is always someone who has left his kif at home and wants to use yours. He told his friends at the Café Nadjah that he had given up kif, and he never accepted a pipe when it was offered to him.

Back in his room in the early evening, with the window open and the sleepy sounds of the town coming up, for it was summer and the voices of people filled the streets, Idir sat in the chair he had bought and put his feet on the windowsill. That way he could see the sky as he smoked. Lahcen would come in and talk. Now and then they went together to Emsallah to a *barraca* there near the slaughter house where two sisters lived with their feeble-minded mother. They would get the mother drunk and put her to bed in the inner room. Then they would get the girls drunk and spend the night with them, without paying. The cognac was expensive, but it did not cost as much as whores would have.

In midsummer, at the time of Sidi Kacem, it suddenly grew very hot. People set up tents made of sheets on the roofs of their houses and cooked and slept there. At night in the moonlight Idir could see all the roofs, each one with its box of sheets flapping in the wind, and inside the sheets the red light made by the fire in the pot. Daytimes, the sun shining on the sea of white sheets hurt his eyes, and he remembered not to look out when he passed the window as he moved about his room. He would have liked to live in a more expensive room, one with a blind to keep out the light. There was no way of being protected from the bright summer day that filled the sky outside, and he waited with longing for dusk. His custom was not to smoke kif before the sun went down. He did not like it in the daytime, above all in summer when the air is hot and the light is powerful. When each day came up hotter than the one before it, he decided to buy enough food and kif to last several days, and to shut himself into his room until it got cooler. He had worked two days at the port that week and had some money. He put the food on the table and locked the door. Then he took the key out of the lock and threw it into the drawer of the table. Lying with the packages and cans in his market basket was a large bundle of kif wrapped in a newspaper. He unfolded it, took out a sheaf and sniffed of it. For the next two hours he sat on the floor picking off the leaves and cutting them on a breadboard, sifting, and cutting, again and again. Once, as the sun reached him, he had to move to get out of its heat. By the time the sun went down he had enough ready for three or four days. He got up off the floor and sat in his chair with his pouch and his pipe in his lap, and smoked, while the radio played the Chleuh music that was always broadcast at this hour for the Soussi shopkeepers. In cafés men often got up and turned it off. Idir enjoyed it. Kif smokers usually like it, because of the *naqous* that always pounds the same design.

The music played a long time, and Idir thought of the market at Tiznit and the mosque with the tree trunks sticking out of its mud walls. He looked down the floor. The room still had daylight in it. He opened his eyes wide. A small bird was walking slowly along the floor. He jumped up. The kif pipe fell, but its bowl did not break. Before the bird had time to move, he had put his hand over it. Even when he held it between his two hands it did not struggle. He looked at it, and thought it was the smallest bird he had ever seen. Its head was gray, and its wings were black and white. It looked at him, and it did not seem afraid. He sat down in the chair with the bird in his lap. When he lifted his hand it stayed still. "It's a young bird and can't fly," he thought. He smoked several pipes of kif. The bird did not move. The sun had gone down and the houses were growing blue in the evening light. He stroked the bird's head with his thumb. Then he took the ring from his little finger and slipped it over the smooth feathers of its head. The bird paid no attention. "A gold collar for the sultan of birds," he said. He smoked some more kif and looked at the sky. Then he began to be hungry, and he thought the bird might like some breadcrumbs. He put his pipe down on the table and tried to take the ring from the bird's head. It would not come off over the feathers. He pulled at it, and the bird fluttered its wings and struggled. For a second he let go of it, and in that instant it flew straight from his lap into the sky. Idir jumped up and stood watching it. When it was gone, he began to smile. "The son of a whore!" he whispered.

He prepared his food and ate it. After that he sat in the chair smoking and thinking about the bird. When Lahcen came he told him the story. "He was waiting all the time for a chance to steal something," he said. Lahcen was a little drunk, and he was angry. "So he stole my ring!" he cried. "Ah," said Idir. "Yours? I thought you gave it to me."

"I'm not crazy yet," Lahcen told him. He went away still angry, and did not return for more than a week. The morning he came into the room Idir was certain that he was going to begin to talk again about the ring, and he quickly handed him a pair of shoes he had bought from a friend the day before. "Do these fit you?" he asked him. Lahcen sat down in the chair, put them on, and found they did fit. "They need new bottoms, but the tops are like new," Idir told him. "The tops are good," said Lahcen. He felt of the leather and squeezed it between his thumb and fingers. "Take them," said Idir. Lahcen was pleased, and he said nothing about the ring that day. When he got the shoes to his room he looked carefully at them and decided to spend the money that it would cost to have new soles made.

The next day he went to a Spanish cobbler, who agreed to repair the shoes for fifteen dirhams. "Ten," said Lahcen. After a long discussion the cobbler lowered his price to thirteen, and he left the shoes there, saying that he would call for them in a week. The same afternoon he was walking through Sidi Bouknadel, and he saw a girl. They talked together for two hours or more, standing not very near to each other beside the wall, and looking down at the ground so that no one could see they were talking. The girl was from Meknes, and that was why he had never seen her before. She was visiting her aunt, who lived there in the quarter, and soon her sister was coming from Meknes. She looked to him the best thing he had seen that year, but of course he could not be sure of her nose and mouth because her veil hid them. He got her to agree to meet him at the same place the next day. This time they took a walk along the Hafa, and he could see that she would be willing. But she would not tell him where her aunt's house was.

Only two days later he got her to his room. As he had expected, she was beautiful. That night he was very happy, but in the morning when she had gone, he understood that he wanted to be with her all the time. He wanted to know what her aunt's house was like and how she was going to pass her day. In this way a bad time began for Lahcen. He was happy only when she was with him and he could get into bed and see her lying on one side of him and a bottle of cognac on the other, upright on the floor beside his pillow, where he could reach it easily. Each day when she had gone he lay thinking about all the men she might be going to see before she came back to him. When he talked about it to her she laughed and said she spent all her time with her aunt and sister, who now had arrived from Meknes. But he could not stop worrying about it.

Two weeks went by before he remembered to go and get his shoes. On his way to the cobbler's he thought about how he would solve his problem. He had an idea that Idir could help him. If he brought Idir and the girl together and left them alone, Idir would tell him afterward everything that had happened. If she let Idir take her to bed, then she was a whore and could be treated like a whore. He would give her a good beating and then make it up with her, because she was too good to throw away. But he had to know whether she was really his, or whether she would go with others.

When the cobbler handed him his shoes, he saw that they looked almost like new, and he was pleased. He paid the thirteen dirhams and took the shoes home. That night when he was going to put them on to wear to the café, he found that his feet would not go into them. They were much too small. The cobbler had cut down the last in order to stitch on the new soles. He put his old shoes back on, went out, and slammed the door. That night he had a quarrel with the girl. It took him until almost dawn to stop her crying. When the sun came up and she was asleep, he lay with his arms folded behind his head looking at the ceiling, thinking that the shoes had cost him thirteen dirhams and new he was going to have to spend the day trying to sell them. He got rid of the girl early and went in to Bou Araqia with the shoes. No one would give him more than eight dirhams for them. In the afternoon he went to the Joteya and sat in the shade of a grapevine, waiting for the buyers and sellers to arrive. A man from the mountains finally offered him ten dirhams, and he sold the shoes. "Three dirhams gone for nothing," he thought when he put the money into his pocket. He was angry, but instead of blaming the cobbler, he felt that the fault was Idir's.

That afternoon he saw Idir, and he told him he would bring a friend with him to Idir's room after the evening meal. Then he went home and drank cognac. When the girl arrived he had finished the bottle, and he was drunk and more unhappy than ever. "Don't take it off," he told her when she began to unfasten her veil. "We're going out." She said nothing. They took the back streets to Idir's room.

Idir sat in his chair listening to the radio. He had not expected a girl, and when he saw her take off her veil the beating of his heart made his head ache. He told her to sit in the chair, and then he paid no more attention to her and sat on the bed talking only with Lahcen, who did not look at her either. Soon Lahcen got up. "I'm going out to get some cigarettes," he said. "I'll be right back." He shut the door after him, and Idir quickly went and locked it. He smiled at the girl and sat on the table beside her, looking down at her. Now and then he smoked a pipe of kif. He wondered why Lahcen was taking so long. Finally he said: "He's not coming back, you know." The girl laughed and shrugged. He jumped up, took her hand, and led her to the bed.

In the morning when they were getting dressed, she told him she lived at the Hotel Sevilla. It was a small Moslem hotel in the center of the Medina. He took her there and left her. "Will you come tonight?" she asked him. Idir frowned. He was thinking of Lahcen. "Don't wait for me after midnight," he said. On his way home he stopped at the Café Nadjah. Lahcen was there. His eyes were red and he looked as though he had not slept at all. Idir had the feeling that he had been waiting for him to appear, for when he came into the café Lahcen quickly got up and paid the *qahouaji*. They walked down the main street of Dradeb without saying anything, and when they got to the road that leads to the Merkala beach, they turned down it, still without speaking.

It was low tide. They walked on the wet sand while the small waves broke at their feet. Lahcen smoked a cigarette and threw stones into the water. Finally he spoke. "How was it?"

Idir shrugged, tried to keep his voice flat. "All right for one night," he said. Lahcen was ready to say carelessly: "Or even two." But then he realized that Idir did not want to talk about the night, which meant that it had been a great event for him. And when he looked at his face he was certain that Idir wanted the girl for himself. He was sure he had already lost her to him, but he did not know why he had not thought of that in the beginning. Now he forgot the true reason why he had wanted to take her to Idir.

"You thought I brought her just to be good to you!" he cried. "No, sidi! I left her there to see if you were a friend. And I see what kind of friend you are! A scorpion!" He seized the front of Idir's garments and struck him in the face. Idir moved backward a few steps, and got ready to fight. He understood that Lahcen had seen the truth, and that now there was nothing at all to say, and nothing to do but fight. When they were both bloody and panting, he looked for a flash at Lahcen's face, and saw that he was dizzy and could not see very well. He drew back, put his head down, and with all his force ran into Lahcen, who lost his balance and fell onto the sand. Then quickly he kicked him in the head with the heel of his shoe. He left him lying there and went home.

In a little while Lahcen began to hear the waves breaking on the sand near him. "I must kill him," he thought. "He sold my ring. Now I must go and kill him." Instead, he took off his clothes and bathed in the sea, and when he had finished, he lay in the sun on the sand all day and slept. In the evening he went and got very drunk.

At eleven o'clock Idir went to the Hotel Sevilla. The girl was sitting in a wicker chair by the front door, waiting for him. She looked carefully at the cuts on his face. Under her veil he saw her smile.

"You fought?" Idir nodded his head. "How is he?" He shrugged. This made her laugh. "He was always drunk, anyway," she said. Idir took her arm, and they went out into the street.

THE WIND
AT BENI MIDAR

At BENI MIDAR there is a barracks. It has many rows of small buildings, whitewashed, and everything is in the middle of big rocks, on the side of the mountain behind the town. A quiet place when the wind is not blowing. A few Spanish still live in the houses along the road. They run the shops. But now the people in the street are Moslems, mountain men with goats and sheep, or soldiers from the *cuartel* looking for wine. The Spanish sell wine to men they know. One Jew sells it to almost anybody. But there never is enough wine in the town for everybody who wants it. Beni Midar has only one street, that comes down out of the mountains, curves back and forth like a snake between the houses for a while, and goes on, back into the mountains. Sunday is a bad day, the one free time the soldiers have, when they can walk back and forth all day between the shops and houses. A few Spaniards in black clothes go into the church at the hour when the Rhmara ride their donkeys out of the *souk*. Later the Spaniards come out of the church and go home. Nothing else happens because all the shops are shut. There is nothing the soldiers can buy.

Driss had been stationed for eight months in Beni Midar. Because the cabran in charge of his unit had been a neighbor of his in Tetuan, he was not unhappy. The cabran had a friend with a motorcycle. Together they went each month to Tetuan. There the cabran always saw Driss's sister, who made a big bundle of food to send back to the barracks for him. She sent him chickens and cakes, cigarettes and figs, and always many hard-boiled eggs. He shared the eggs with two or three friends, and did not complain about being in Beni Midar.

Not even the brothels were open on Sunday. It was the day when everyone walked from one end of the town to the other, back and forth, many times. Sometimes Driss walked like this with his friends. Usually he took his gun and went down into the valley to hunt for hares. When he came back at twilight he stopped in a small café at the edge of the town and had a glass of tea and a few pipes of kif. If it had not been the only café he would never have gone into it. Shameful things happened there. Several times he had seen men from the mountains get up from the mat and do dances that left blood on the floor. These men were Djilala, and no one thought of stopping them, not even Driss. They did not dance because they wanted to dance, and it was this that made him angry and ashamed. It seemed to him that the world should be made in such a way that a man is free to dance or not as he feels. A Djilali can do only what the music tells him to do. When the musicians, who are Djilala too, play the music that has the power, his eyes shut and he falls on the floor. And until the man has shown the proof and drunk his own blood, the musicians do not begin the music that will bring him back to the world. They should do something about it, Driss said to the other soldiers who went with him to the café, and they agreed.

He had talked about it with his cabran in the public garden. The cabran said that when all the children in the land were going to school every day there would be no more *djenoun*. Women would no longer be able to put spells on their husbands. And the Djilala and the Hamatcha and all the others would stop cutting their legs and arms and chests. Driss thought about this for a long time. He was glad to hear that the government knew about these bad things. "But if they know," he thought, "why don't they do something now? The

124

day they get every one of the children in school I'll be lying beside Sidi Ali el Mandri." He was thinking of the cemetery at Bab Sebta in Tetuan. When he saw the cabran again he said: "If they can do something about it, they ought to do it now." The cabran did not seem interested. "Yes," he said.

When Driss got his permission and went home he told his father what the cabran had said. "You mean the government thinks it can kill all evil spirits?" he father cried.

"That's right. It can," said Driss. "It's going to."

His father was old and had no confidence in the young men who now ran the government. "It's impossible," he said. "They should let them alone. Leave them under their stones. Children have gone to school before, and how many were hurt by *djenoun*? But if the government begins to make trouble for them, you'll see what will happen. They'll go after the children first."

Driss had expected his father to speak this way, but when he heard the words he was ashamed. He did not answer. Some of his friends were without respect for God. They ate during Ramadan and argued with their fathers. He was glad not to be like them. But he felt his father was wrong.

One hot summer Sunday when the sky was very blue Driss lay in bed late. The men who slept in his room at the barracks had gone out. He listened to the radio. "It would be good down in the valley on a day like this," he thought. He saw himself swimming in one of the big pools, and he thought of the hot sun on his back afterward. He got up and unlocked the cupboard to look at his gun. Even before he took it out he said, "*Yah latif!*" because he remembered that he had only one cartridge left, and it was Sunday. He slammed the cupboard door shut and got back into bed. The radio began to give the news. He sat up, spat as far out as he could from the bed, and turned it off. In the silence he heard many birds singing in the *safsaf* tree outside the window. He scratched his head. Then he got up and dressed. In the courtyard he saw Mehdi going toward

125

the stairs. Mehdi was on his way to do sentry duty in the box outside the main gate.

"*Khái!* Does four rials sound good to you?"

Mehdi looked at him. "Is this number sixty, three, fifty-one?" This was the name of an Egyptian song that came over the radio nearly every day. The song ended with the word nothing. Nothing, nothing, sung over and over again.

Why not? As they walked along together, Driss moved closer, so that his thigh rubbed against Mehdi's.

"The price is ten, *khoya*."

"With all its cartridges?"

"You want me to open it up and show you here?" Mehdi's voice was angry. The words came out of the side of his mouth.

Driss said nothing. They came to the top of the stairs. Mehdi was walking fast. "You'll have to have it back here by seven," he said. "Do you want it?"

In his head Driss saw the long day in the empty town. "Yes," he said. "Stay there." He hurried back to the room, unlocked his cupboard, and took out his gun. From the shelf he pulled down his pipe, his kif, and a loaf of bread. He put his head outside the door. There was no one in the courtyard but Mehdi sitting on the wall at the other end. Then with the old gun in his hands he ran all the way to Mehdi. Mehdi took it and went down the stairs, leaving his own gun lying on the wall. Driss took up the gun, waited a moment, and followed him. When he went past the sentry box he heard Mehdi's voice say softly: "I need the ten at seven, *khoya*."

Driss grunted. He knew how dark it was in there. No officer ever stuck his head inside the door on Sundays. Ten rials, he thought, and he's running no risk. He looked around at the goats among the rocks. The sun was hot, but the air smelled sweet, and he was happy to be walking down the side of the mountain. He pulled the visor of his cap further down over his eyes and began to whistle. Soon he came out in front of the town, below it on the other side of the valley. He could see the

people on the benches in the park at the top of the cliff, small
but clear and black. They were Spaniards and they were waiting
for the bell of their church to begin to ring.

He got to the highest pool about the time the sun was overhead. When he lay on the rocks afterward eating his bread,
the sun burned him. No animals will move before three, he
thought. He put his trousers on and crawled into the shade of
the oleander bushes to sleep. When he awoke the air was
cooler. He smoked all the kif he had, and went walking
through the valley. Sometimes he sang. He found no hares,
and so he put small stones on the tops of the rocks and fired at
them. Then he climbed back up the other side of the valley
and followed the highway into the town.

He came to the café and went in. The musicians were playing
an *aaita* and singing. The tea drinkers clapped their hands with
the music. A soldier cried: "Driss! Sit down!" He sat with his
friends and smoked some of their kif. Then he bought four
rials' worth from the cutter who sat on the platform with the
musicians, and went on smoking. "Nothing was moving in the
valley today," he told them. "It was dead down there."

A man with a yellow turban on his head who sat nearby
closed his eyes and fell against the man next to him. The
others around him moved to a further part of the mat. The
man toppled over and lay on the floor.

"Another one?" cried Driss. "They should stay in Djebel
Habib. I can't look at him."

The man took a long time to get to his feet. His arms and
legs had been captured by the drums, but his body was fighting,
and he groaned. Driss tried to pay no attention to him. He
smoked his pipe and looked at his friends, pretending that no
Djilali was in front of him. When the man pulled out his
knife he could not pretend any longer. He watched the blood
running into the man's eyes. It made a blank red curtain over
each hole. The man opened his eyes wider, as if he wanted to
see through the blood. The drums were loud.

Driss got up and paid the *qahouaji* for his tea. He said good-by to the others and went out. The sun would soon go below the top of the mountain. Its light made him want to shut his eyes, because he had a lot of kif in his head. He walked through the town to the higher end and turned into a lane that led up into another valley. In this place there was no one. Cactuses grew high on each side of the lane, and the spiders had built a world of webs between their thorns. Because he walked fast, the kif began to boil in his head. Soon he was very hungry, but all the fruit had been picked from the cactuses along the lane. He came to a small farmhouse with a thatched roof. Behind it on the empty mountainside there were more cactuses still pink with hundreds of *hindiyats*. A dog in a shed beside the house began to bark. There was no sign of people. He stood still for a while and listened to the dog. Then he walked toward the cactus patch. He was sure no one was in the house. Many years ago his sister had shown him how to pick *hindiyats* without letting the needles get into the flesh of his hands. He laid his gun on the ground behind a low stone wall and began to gather the fruit. As he picked he saw in his head the two blind red holes of the Djilali's eyes, and under his breath he cursed all Djilala. When he had a great pile of fruit on the ground he sat down and began to eat, throwing the peels over his shoulder. As he ate he grew hungrier, and so he picked more. The picture he had in his head of the man's face shiny with blood slowly faded. He thought only of the *hindiyats* he was eating. It was almost dark there on the mountainside. He looked at his watch and jumped up, because he remembered that Mehdi had to have his gun at seven o'clock. In the dim light he could not see the gun anywhere. He searched behind the wall, where he thought he had laid it, but he saw only stones and bushes.

"It's gone, *Allah istir*," he said. His heart pounded. He ran back to the lane and stood there a while. The dog barked without stopping.

It was dark before he reached the gate of the barracks. Another man was in the sentry box. The cabran was waiting for him in the room. The old gun Driss's father had given him lay on his bed.

"Do you know where Mehdi is?" the cabran asked him.

"No," said Driss.

"He's in the dark house, the son of a whore. And do you know why?"

Driss sat down on the bed. The cabran is my friend, he was thinking. "It's gone," he said, and told him how he had laid the gun on the ground, and a dog had been barking, and no one had come by, and still it had disappeared. "Maybe the dog was a *djinn*," he said when he had finished. He did not really believe the dog had anything to do with it, but he could not think of anything else to say then.

The cabran looked at him a long time and said nothing. He shook his head. "I thought you had some brains," he said at last. Then his face grew very angry, and he pulled Driss out into the courtyard and told a soldier to lock him up.

At ten o'clock that night he went to see Driss. He found him smoking his *sebsi* in the dark. The cell was full of kif smoke. "Garbage!" cried the cabran, and he took the pipe and the kif away from him. "Tell the truth," he said to Driss. "You sold the gun, didn't you?"

"On my mother's head, it's just as I told you! There was only the dog."

The cabran could not make him say anything different. He slammed the door and went to the café in the town to have a glass of tea. He sat listening to the music, and he began to smoke the kif he had taken from Driss. If Driss was telling the truth, then it was only the kif in Driss's head that had made him lose the gun, and in that case there was a chance that it could be found.

The cabran had not smoked in a long time. As the kif filled his head he began to be hungry, and he remembered the times when he had been a boy smoking kif with his friends. Always

129

they had gone to look for *hindiyats* afterward, because they tasted better than anything else and cost nothing. They always knew where there were some growing. "A *kouffa* full of good *hindiyats*," he thought. He shut his eyes and went on thinking.

The next morning early the cabran went out and stood on a high rock behind the barracks, looking carefully all around the valley and the bare mountainside. Not far away he saw a lane with cactuses along it, and further up there was a whole forest of cactus. "There," he said to himself.

He walked among the rocks until he came to the lane, and he followed the lane to the farmhouse. The dog began to bark. A woman came to the doorway and looked at him. He paid no attention to her, but went straight to the high cactuses on the hillside behind the house. There were many *hindiyats* still to be eaten, but the cabran did not eat any of them. He had no kif in his head and he was thinking only of the gun. Beside a stone wall there was a big pile of *hindiya* peelings. Someone had eaten a great many. Then he saw the sun shining on part of the gun's barrel under the peelings. "Hah!" he shouted, and he seized the gun and wiped it all over with his handkerchief. On his way back to the barracks he felt so happy that he decided to play a joke on Driss.

He hid the gun under his bed. With a glass of tea and a piece of bread in his hand he went to see Driss. He found him asleep on the floor in the dark.

"Daylight is here!" he shouted. He laughed and kicked Driss's foot to wake him up. Driss sat on the floor drinking the tea and the cabran stood in the doorway scratching his chin. He looked down at the floor, but not at Driss. After a time he said: "Last night you told me a dog was barking?"

Driss was certain the cabran was going to make fun of him. He was sorry he had mentioned the dog. "Yes," he said, not sounding sure.

"If it was the dog," the cabran went on, I know how to get it back. You have to help me."

Driss looked up at him. He could not believe the cabran was being serious. Finally he said in a low voice: "I was joking when I said that. I had kif in my head."

The cabran was angry. "You think it's a joke to lose a gun that belongs to the Sultan? You did sell it! You haven't got kif in your head now. Maybe you can tell the truth. He stepped toward Driss, and Driss thought he was going to hit him. He stood up quickly. "I told you the truth," he said. "It was gone."

The cabran rubbed his chin and looked down at the floor again for a minute. "The next time a Djilali begins to dance in the café, we'll do it," he told him. He shut the door and left Driss alone.

Two days later the cabran came again to the dark house. He had another soldier with him. "Quick!" he told Driss. "There's one dancing now."

They went out into the courtyard and Driss blinked his eyes. "Listen," said the cabran. "When the Djilali is drinking his own blood he has power. What you have to do is ask him to make the *djinn* bring me the gun. I'm going to sit in my room and burn *djaoui*. That may help."

"I'll do it," said Driss. "But it won't do any good."

The other soldier took Driss to the café. The Djilali was a tall man from the mountains. He had already taken out his knife, and he was waving it in the air. The soldier made Driss sit down near the musicians, and then he waited until the man began to lick the blood from his arms. Then, because he thought he might be sick if he watched any longer, Driss raised his right arm toward the Djilali and said in a low voice: "In the name of Allah, *khoya*, make the *djinn* that stole Mehdi's gun take it now to Aziz the cabran." The Djilali seemed to be staring at him, but Driss could not be sure whether he had heard his words or not.

The soldier took him back to the barracks. The cabran was sitting under a plum tree beside the kitchen door. He told the soldier to go away and jumped up. "Come," he said, and he led Driss to the room. The air was blue with the smoke of the *djaoui* he had been burning. He pointed to the middle of the floor. "Look!" he cried. A gun was lying there. Driss ran and picked it up. After he had looked at it carefully, he said: "It's the gun." And his voice was full of fear. The cabran could see that Driss had not been sure the thing was possible, but that now he no longer had any doubt.

The cabran was happy to have fooled him so easily. He laughed. "You see, it worked," he said. "It's lucky for you Mehdi's going to be in the dark house for another week."

Driss did not answer. He felt even worse than when he had been watching the Djilali slicing the flesh of his arms.

That night he lay in bed worrying. It was the first time he had had anything to do with a *djinn* or an *affrit*. Now he had entered into their world. It was a dangerous world and he did not trust the cabran any longer. "What am I going to do?" he thought. The men all around him were sleeping, but he could not close his eyes. Soon he got up and stepped outside. The leaves of the *safsaf* tree were hissing in the wind. On the other side of the courtyard there was light in one of the windows. Some of the officers were talking there. He walked slowly around the garden in the middle and looked up at the sky, thinking of how different his life was going to be now. As he came near the lighted window he heard a great burst of laughter. The cabran was telling a story. Driss stopped walking and listened.

"And he said to the Djilali: 'Please, sidi, would you ask the dog that stole my gun—' "

The men laughed again, and the sound covered the cabran's voice.

He went quickly back and got into bed. If they knew he had heard the cabran's story they would laugh even more. He lay in the bed thinking, and he felt poison come into his heart. It was the cabran's fault that the *djinn* had been called, and now in front of his superior officers he was pretending that he had

had nothing to do with it. Later the cabran came in and went to bed, and it was quiet in the courtyard, but Driss lay thinking for a long time before he went to sleep.

In the days that came after that, the cabran was friendly again, but Driss did not want to see him smile. He thought with hatred: "In his head I'm afraid of him now because he knows how to call a *djinn*. He jokes with me now because he has power."

He could not laugh or be happy when the cabran was nearby. Each night he lay awake for a long time after the others had gone to sleep. He listened to the wind moving the hard leaves of the *safsaf* tree, and he thought only of how he could break the cabran's power.

When Mehdi came out of the dark house he spoke against the cabran. Driss paid him his ten rials. "A lot of money for ten days in the dark house," Mehdi grumbled, and he looked at the bill in his hand. Driss pretended not to understand. "He's a son of a whore," he said.

Mehdi snorted. "And you have the head of a needle," he said. "It all came from you. The wind blows the kif out your ears!"

"You think I wasn't in the dark house too?" cried Driss. But he could not tell Mehdi about the Djilali and the dog. "He's a son of a whore," he said again.

Mehdi's eyes grew narrow and stiff. "I'll do his work for him. He'll think he's in the dark house himself when I finish."

Mehdi went on his way. Driss stood watching him go.

The next Sunday Driss got up early and walked into Beni Midar. The *souk* was full of rows of mountain people in white clothes. He walked in among the donkeys and climbed the steps to the stalls. There he went to see an old man who sold incense and herbs. People called him El Fqih. He sat down in front of El Fqih and said: "I want something for a son of a whore."

El Fqih looked at him angrily. "A sin!" He raised his forefinger and shook it back and forth. "Sins are not my work."

133

Driss did not say anything. El Fqih spoke more quietly now. "To balance that, it is said that each trouble in the world has its remedy. There are cheap remedies and remedies that cost a lot of money." He stopped.

Driss waited. "How much is this one?" he asked him. The old man was not pleased because he wanted to talk longer. But he said: "I'll give you a name for five rials." He looked sternly at Driss, leaned forward and whispered a name in his ear. "In the alley behind the sawmill," he said aloud. "The blue tin shack with the canebrake in back of it." Driss paid him and ran down the steps.

He found the house. The old woman stood in the doorway with a checked tablecloth over her head. Her eyes had turned white like milk. They looked to Driss like the eyes of an old dog. He said: "You're Anisa?"

"Come into the house," she told him. It was almost dark inside. He told her he wanted something to break the power of a son of a whore. "Give me ten rials now," she said. "Come back at sunset with another ten. It will be ready."

After the midday meal he went out into the courtyard. He met Mehdi and asked him to go with him to the café in Beni Midar. They walked through the town in the hot afternoon sun. It was still early when they got to the café, and there was plenty of space on the mats. They sat in a dark corner. Driss took out his kif and his *sebsi* and they smoked. When the musicians began to play, Mehdi said: "The circus is back!" But Driss did not want to talk about the Djilala. He talked about the cabran. He gave the pipe many times to Mehdi, and he watched Mehdi growing more angry with the cabran as he smoked. He was not surprised when Mehdi cried: "I'll finish it tonight!"

"No, *khoya*," said Driss. "You don't know. He's gone way up. He's a friend of all the officers now. They bring him bottles of wine."

"He'll come down," Mehdi said. "Before dinner tonight. In the courtyard. You be there and watch it."

Driss handed him the pipe and paid for the tea. He left Mehdi there and went into the street to walk up and down because he did not want to sit still any longer. When the sky was red behind the mountain he went to the alley by the sawmill. The old woman was in the doorway.

"Come in," she said as before. When they were inside the room she handed him a paper packet. "He has to take all of it," she said. She took the money and pulled at his sleeve. "I never saw you," she said. "Good-by."

Driss went to his room and listened to the radio. When dinner time came he stood inside the doorway looking out into the courtyard. In the shadows at the other end he thought he could see Mehdi, but he was not sure. There were many soldiers walking around in the courtyard, waiting for dinner. Soon there was shouting near the top of the steps. The soldiers began to run toward the other end of the courtyard. Driss looked from the doorway and saw only the running soldiers. He called to the men in the room. "Something's happening!" They all ran out. Then with the paper of powder in his hand he went back into the room to the cabran's bed and lifted up the bottle of wine one of the officers had given the cabran the day before. It was almost full. He pulled out the cork and let the powder slide into the bottle. He shook the bottle and put the cork back. There was still shouting in the courtyard. He ran out. When he got near the crowd, he saw Mehdi being dragged along the ground by three soldiers. He was kicking. The cabran sat on the wall with his head down, holding his arm. There was blood all over his face and shirt.

It was almost a half hour before the cabran came to eat his dinner. His face was covered with bruises and his arm was bandaged and hung in a sling. Mehdi had cut it with his knife at the last minute when the soldiers had begun to pull them apart. The cabran did not speak much, and the men did not try to talk with him. He sat on his bed and ate. While he was eating he drank all the wine in the bottle.

That night the cabran moaned in his sleep. A dry wind blew between the mountains. It made a great noise in the *safsaf* tree outside the window. The air roared and the leaves rattled, but Driss still heard the cabran's voice crying. In the morning the doctor came to look at him. The cabran's eyes were open but he could not see. And his mouth was open but he could not speak. They carried him out of the room where the soldiers lived and put him somewhere else. "Maybe the power is broken now," thought Driss.

A few days later a truck came to the barracks, and he saw two men carrying the cabran on a stretcher to the truck. Then he was sure that the cabran's soul had been torn out of his body and that the power was truly broken. In his head he made a prayer of thanks to Allah. He stood with some other soldiers on a rock above the barracks watching the truck grow smaller as it moved down the mountain.

"It's bad for me," he told a man who stood nearby. "He always brought me food from home." The soldier shook his head.

THE HYENA

A STORK was passing over desert country on his way north. He was thirsty, and he began to look for water. When he came to the mountains of Khang el Ghar, he saw a pool at the bottom of a ravine. He flew down between the rocks and lighted at the edge of the water. Then he walked in and drank.

At that moment a hyena limped up and, seeing the stork standing in the water, said: "Have you come a long way?" The stork had never seen a hyena before. "So this is what a hyena is like," he thought. And he stood looking at the hyena because he had been told that if the hyena can put a little of his urine on someone, that one will have to walk after the hyena to whatever place the hyena wants him to go.

"It will be summer soon," said the stork. "I am on my way north." At the same time, he walked further out into the pool, so as not to be so near the hyena. The water here was deeper, and he almost lost his balance and had to flap his wings to keep upright. The hyena walked to the other side of the pool and looked at him from there.

"I know what is in your head," said the hyena. "You believe the story about me. You think I have that power? Perhaps long ago hyenas were like that. But now they are the same as everyone else. I could wet you from here with my urine if I wanted to. But what for? If you want to be unfriendly, go to the middle of the pool and stay there."

The stork looked around at the pool and saw that there was no spot in it where he could stand and be out of reach of the hyena.

"I have finished drinking," said the stork. He spread his wings and flapped out of the pool. At the edge he ran quickly ahead and rose into the air. He circled above the pool, looking down at the hyena.

"So you are the one they call the ogre," he said. "The world is full of strange things."

The hyena looked up. His eyes were narrow and crooked. "Allah brought us all here," he said. "You know that. You are the one who knows about Allah."

The stork flew a little lower. "That is true," he said. "But I am surprised to hear you say it. You have a very bad name, as you yourself just said. Magic is against the will of Allah."

The hyena tilted his head. "So you still believe the lies!" he cried.

"I have not seen the inside of your bladder," said the stork. "But why does everyone say you can make magic with it?"

"Why did Allah give you a head, I wonder? You have not learned how to use it." But the hyena spoke in so low a voice that the stork could not hear him.

"Your words got lost," said the stork, and he let himself drop lower.

The hyena looked up again. "I said: 'Don't come too near me. I might lift my leg and cover you with magic!' " He laughed, and the stock was near enough to see that his teeth were brown.

"Still, there must be some reason," the stork began. Then he looked for a rock high above the hyena, and settled himself on it. The hyena sat and stared up at him. "Why does everyone hate you?" the stork went on. "Why do they call you an ogre? What have you done?"

The hyena squinted. "You are very lucky," he told the stork. "Men never try to kill you, because they think you are holy.

They call you a saint and a sage. And yet you seem like neither a saint nor a sage."

"What do you mean?" said the stork quickly.

"If you really understood, you would know that magic is a grain of dust in the wind, and that Allah has power over everything. You would not be afraid."

The stork stood for a long time, thinking. He lifted one leg and held it bent in front of him. The ravine grew red as the sun went lower. And the hyena sat quietly looking up at the stork, waiting for him to speak.

Finally the stork put his leg down, opened his bill, and said: "You mean that if there is no magic, the one who sins is the one who believes there is."

The hyena laughed. "I said nothing about sin. But you did, and you are the sage. I am not in the world to tell anyone what is right or wrong. Living from night to night is enough. Everyone hopes to see me dead."

The stork lifted his leg again and stood thinking. The last daylight rose into the sky and was gone. The cliffs at the sides of the ravine were lost in the darkness.

At length the stork said: "You have given me something to think about. That is good. But now night has come. I must go on my way." He raised his wings and started to fly straight out from the boulder where he had stood. The hyena listened. He heard the stork's wings beating the air slowly, and then he heard the sound of the stork's body as it hit the cliff on the other side of the ravine. He climbed up over the rocks and found the stork. "Your wing is broken," he said. "It would have been better for you to go while there was still daylight."

"Yes," said the stork. He was unhappy and afraid.

"Come home with me," the hyena told him. "Can you walk?"

"Yes," said the stork. Together they made their way down the valley. Soon they came to a cave in the side of the mountain. The hyena went in first and called out: "Bend your head."

When they were well inside, he said: "Now you can put your head up. The cave is high here."

There was only darkness inside. The stork stood still. "Where are you?" he said.

"I am here," the hyena answered, and he laughed.

"Why are you laughing?" asked the stork.

"I was thinking that the world is strange," the hyena told him. "The saint has come into my cave because he believed in magic."

"I don't understand," said the stork.

"You are confused. But at least now you can believe that I have no magic. I am like anyone else in the world."

The stork did not answer right away. He smelled the stench of the hyena very near him. Then he said, with a sigh: "You are right, of course. There is no power beyond the power of Allah."

"I am happy," said the hyena, breathing into his face. "At last you understand." Quickly he seized the stork's neck and tore it open. The stork flapped and fell on his side.

"Allah gave me something better than magic," the hyena said under his breath. "He gave me a brain."

The stork lay still. He tried to say once more: "There is no power beyond the power of Allah." But his bill merely opened very wide in the dark.

The hyena turned away. "You will be dead in a minute," he said over his shoulder. "In ten days I shall come back. By then you will be ready."

Ten days later the hyena went to the cave and found the stork where he had left him. The ants had not been there. "Good," he said. He devoured what he wanted and went outside to a large flat rock above the entrance to the cave. There in the moonlight he stood a while, vomiting.

He ate some of his vomit and rolled for a long time in the rest of it, rubbing it deep into his coat. Then he thanked Allah for eyes that could see the valley in the moonlight, and for a nose that could smell the carrion on the wind. He rolled some more and licked the rock under him. For a while he lay there panting. Soon he got up and limped on his way.

THE GARDEN

A MAN who lived in a distant town of the southern country was working in his garden. Because he was poor his land was at the edge of the oasis. All the afternoon he dug channels, and when the day was finished he went to the upper end of the garden and opened the gate that held back the water. And now the water ran in the channels to the beds of barley and the young pomegranate trees. The sky was red, and when the man saw the floor of his garden shining like jewels, he sat down on a stone to look at it. As he watched, it grew brighter, and he thought: "There is no finer garden in the oasis."

A great happiness filled him, and he sat there a long time, and did not get home until very late. When he went into the house, his wife looked at him and saw the joy still in his eyes.

"He has found a treasure," she thought; but she said nothing.

When they sat face to face at the evening meal, the man was still remembering his garden, and it seemed to him that now that he had known this happiness, never again would he be without it. He was silent as he ate.

His wife too was silent. "He is thinking of the treasure," she said to herself. And she was angry, believing that he did not want to share his secret with her. The next morning she went to the house of an old woman and bought many herbs and powders from her. She took them home and passed several days mixing and cooking them, until she had made the medi-

cine she wanted. Then at each meal she began to put a little
of the *tseuheur* into her husband's food.

It was not long before the man fell ill. For a time he went
each day to his garden to work, but often when he got there
he was so weak that he could merely sit leaning against a palm
tree. He had a sharp sound in his ears, and he could not follow his thoughts as they came to him. In spite of this, each
day when the sun went down and he saw his garden shining
red in its light, he was happy. And when he got home at night
his wife could see that there was joy in his eyes.

"He has been counting the treasure," she thought, and she
began to go secretly to the garden to watch him from behind
the trees. When she saw that he merely sat looking at the
ground, she went back to the old woman and told her about it.

"You must hurry and make him talk, before he forgets where
he has hidden the treasure," said the old woman.

That night the wife put a great amount of *tseuheur* into his
food, and when they were drinking tea afterward she began to
say many sweet words to him. The man only smiled. She tried
for a long time to make him speak, but he merely shrugged
his shoulders and made motions with his hands.

The next morning while he was still asleep, she went back
to the old woman and told her that the man could no longer
speak.

"You have given him too much," the old woman said. "He
will never tell you his secret now. The only thing for you to do
is go away quickly, before he dies."

The woman ran home. Her husband lay on the mat with his
mouth open. She packed her clothing and left the town that
morning.

For three days the man lay in a deep sleep. The fourth day
when he awoke, it was as if he had made a voyage to the other
side of the world. He was very hungry, but all he could find in
the house was a piece of dry bread. When he had eaten that,
he walked to his garden at the edge of the oasis and picked

many figs. Then he sat down and ate them. In his mind there was no thought of his wife, because he had forgotten her. When a neighbor came by and called to him, he answered politely, as if speaking to a stranger, and the neighbor went away perplexed.

Little by little the man grew healthy once more. He worked each day in the garden. When dusk came, after watching the sunset and the red water, he would go home and cook his dinner and sleep. He had no friends, because although men spoke to him, he did not know who they were, and he only smiled and nodded to them. Then the people in the town began to notice that he no longer went to the mosque to pray. They spoke about this among themselves, and one evening the imam went to the man's house to talk with him.

As they sat there, the imam listened for sounds of the man's wife in the house. Out of courtesy he could not mention her, but he was thinking about her and asking himself where she might be. He went away from the house full of doubts.

The man went on living his life. But the people of the town now talked of little else. They whispered that he had killed his wife, and many of them wanted to go together and search the house for her remains. The imam spoke against this idea, saying that he would go and talk again with the man. And this time he went all the way to the garden at the edge of the oasis, and found him there working happily with the plants and the trees. He watched him for a while, and then he walked closer and spoke a few words with him.

It was late in the afternoon. The sun was sinking in the west, and the water on the ground began to be red. Presently the man said to the imam: "The garden is beautiful."

"Beautiful or not beautiful," said the imam, "you should be giving thanks to Allah for allowing you to have it."

"Allah?" said the man. "Who is that? I never heard of him. I made this garden myself. I dug every channel and planted every tree, and no one helped me. I have no debts to anyone."

The imam had turned pale. He flung out his arm and struck the man very hard in the face. Then he went quickly out of the garden.

The man stood with his hand to his cheek. "He has gone mad," he thought, as the imam walked away.

That night the people spoke together in the mosque. They decided that the man could no longer live in their town. Early the next morning a great crowd of men, with the imam going at the head of it, went out into the oasis, on its way to the man's garden.

The small boys ran ahead of the men, and got there long before them. They hid in the bushes, and as the man worked they began to throw stones and shout insults at him. He paid no attention to them. Then a stone hit the back of his head. He jumped up quickly. As they ran away, one of them fell, and the man caught him. He tried to hold him still so he could ask him: "Why were you throwing stones at me?" But the boy only screamed and struggled.

And the townspeople, who were on their way, heard the screaming, and they came running to the garden. They pulled the boy away from him and began to strike at the man with hoes and sickles. When they had destroyed him, they left him there with his head lying in one of the channels, and went back to the town, giving thanks to Allah that the boy was safe.

Little by little the sand covered everything. The trees died, and very soon the garden was gone. Only the desert was there.

DOÑA
FAUSTINA

1

No ONE could understand why Doña Faustina had bought the inn. It stood on one of the hairpin curves in the old highway leading up from the river valley to the town, but the route had been made useless by the building of the new paved road. Now it was impossible to reach the inn except by climbing up a stony path over the embankment and walking several hundred feet down the old road which, no longer kept in repair, already was being washed away by the rains and strangled by the shiny vegetation of that lowland region.

On Sundays the people used to walk out from the town, the women carrying parasols and the men guitars (for this was before the days of the radio, when almost everyone knew how to make a little music); they would get as far as the great breadfruit tree and look up the road at the faded façade of the building, more than half hidden by young bamboo and banana plants, stare a few seconds, and turn around to go back. "Why does she leave the sign up?" they would say. "Does she think anyone would ever spend the night there now?" And they were quiet right: no one went near the inn any more. Only the people of the town knew that it existed, and they had no need of it.

There remained the mystery of why she had bought it. As usual when there is something townspeople cannot understand, they invented a whole series of unpleasant explanations for

Doña Faustina's behavior. The earliest and most common one, which was that she had decided to transform the place into a house of ill-repute, soon fell to pieces, for there was absolutely nothing to substantiate such a theory. No one had been seen to go near the inn for weeks, except Doña Faustina's younger sister Carlota who arrived from Jalapa, and the old servants José and Elena, who went to market each morning and minded their business strictly enough to satisfy even the most vicious gossips. As for Carlota, she appeared occasionally at Mass, dressed in black. It was said that she had taken their father's death very much to heart, and would probably not remove the mourning, ever.

The other suppositions evolved by the people of the town in their effort to bring light to the mystery proved as unlikely as the first. It was rumored that Doña Faustina was giving asylum to Chato Morales, a bandit whom the police of the region had been trying for months to capture, but he was caught soon afterward in a distant part of the province. Then it was said that the inn was a depository for a drug ring; this also proved to be false. The leaders of the ring, having been arrested, divulged their secrets, and the cache proved to be in a room above the Farmácia Ideal. There were darker hints to the effect that Carlota might be luring lone voyagers to the inn, where they met the fate that traditionally befalls such solitary visitors to lonely inns. But people did not take such suggestions seriously. The opinion grew that Doña Faustina had merely gone a little mad, and that her madness, having taken an anti-social turn, had induced her to retire to the outskirts of town where she could live without ever seeing anyone. To be sure, this theory was contested by certain younger members of the community who claimed that she was no more crazy than they, that on the contrary she was extremely crafty. They said that having a great deal of money she had bought the inn because of the ample lands which surrounded it, and that there in the privacy of the plant-smothered gardens and orchards she had devised all kinds of clever ways of hiding her riches. The older citizens of the town took no stock in this, however, since they clearly remembered both her husband and her father, neither of whom had evinced any unusual prowess in collecting money. And she had bought the inn for practically nothing. "Where would she have got the pesos?" they said sceptically. "Out of the trees, perhaps?"

2

Once when a child disappeared from the town (small children were often stolen in those days and taken off to distant places where they were made to work), the parents insisted that the police search the inn. Doña Faustina, who was a large woman in the prime of life, met the little policeman at the door and refused to let him in. Indeed, she was so brusque with him and glared at him with such malignity that he felt obliged to go back to the *comisaría* and get reinforcements. when he and the three extra men returned to the inn, they made a complete but unrewarding search of the place, followed at every step by Doña Faustina, who did not cease to shower them with insults until they had left the premises. But they returned to town with a story. The rooms were a shambles, they said, the furniture was broken, there was rubbish and garbage everywhere in the corridors, the railing of the second-story balcony had given way and been replaced by a single strand of barbed wire, and the place looked generally as though innumerable picnic parties had been held there over a period of years. This report helped to fortify people in their belief that Doña Faustina had more or less lost her mind, and for a time the town ceased thinking about her.

Some time afterward it was noted that she and her sister had taken to making trips to neighboring towns; they had been

seen in such widely separated places as Tlacotalpam and Zem-
poala. But even these peregrinations failed to elicit true interest. Heads were shaken, sympathetically or otherwise, and
it was remarked that Doña Faustina was growing less and less
sane, but that was all.

When the mistresses of the house were absent they did not
return for three or four days, and José and Elena remained
alone to guard the property, not even venturing forth to the
town for marketing until the two reappeared. On their return
the sisters would take an old covered carriage that went each
day to the station to await the train. They would pile their
numerous bundles and baskets in and drive as far as the curve,
where they would get down, the driver helping them up the
embankment with their effects and then leaving them to get
to the house in whatever way they could. Carlota would go
and bring up José to help carry the things, but Doña Faustina always insisted on carrying the heaviest baskets herself. A
few trips would be made back and forth through the undergrowth, and then the abandoned road would be quiet again
until the old servants went to market the next morning.

In another fortnight or so they would set out once more,
always to a new place; necessarily this led them farther and
farther afield. Someone even claimed to have seen them once
in Vera Cruz, although, given the number of false stories which
were circulated about the two women, there was no particular
reason to believe this.

Before the house had been made into an inn it had been a
prosperous *finca*, with terraced lands planted with fruit trees,
leading downward rather steeply for a mile or so to a high bluff
above the river. For fifty years or more the land had been totally
neglected, so that now it was hard to find the avocado and
mango trees in the tangle of new, eager parasites which had
sprung up on every side and often reached above even the tallest
of the older trees. Lianas looped down from the branches,

149

climbing plants stretched up to clutch at them, and a person could not stray more than fifty feet down one of the orchard paths from the house without coming face to face with an impenetrable curtain of leaves. And now no one really knew how far it was from the house to the river, because the borders of the property gave on even thicker jungle.

3

Not even José would have known the tank existed, if he had not strayed a bit farther down than usual one afternoon, to see if he could find some *zapotes*. In the deep silence of the undergrowth there, far beneath the regions where the sun could reach, he had heard a heavy splash not far distant, as though a boulder had been flung into deep water. He had listened intently, but there had been no other sound. The next afternoon during siesta time he went back to the same spot carrying a machete, and laboriously hacked his way through the stubborn vegetation. It was nearly twilight when he caught sight of the water ahead. Finally he stood near the edge of the tank. The stagnant water gave off a heavy odor, and insects hovered in swarms in the still air above it. And as he watched, it seemed to him that there was a faint movement down in the brown depths; for some reason the water was not competely motionless. For a while he stood there staring downward, lost in contemplation; then, as the light was fading, he turned and started back, resolving without knowing why he did so, to say nothing about the tank to Elena when he returned to the house.

Several times in the course of the following months José returned there, always with the hope of discovering what had made the splash. Even a man diving into the tank could scarcely have caused such a noise. There was a stone-paved ramp at the far end (the tank doubtless had been built to bathe cattle) and on two occasions he found the ramp partially wet, which merely added to his perplexity. The second time he noticed this, he began to cut his way through the vines along the edge, in order to examine the ramp closely. And half-way along he found the path. Someone had cleared a narrow but practicable passage to the tank from some point back near the house. Abandoning his project, he followed the path and came out in a corner of what had once been a rose garden, on a lower terrace between the door to the laundry and the ruined stables. As he stood blinking in the sunlight, Doña Faustina appeared coming down the short flight of steps outside the laundry door. By its handle she carried a basket with a newspaper tucked over the top. Automatically old José walked toward her to take the basket from her. Evidently she had not been expecting to see him, for when she looked up and realized he was near her, her face took on an extraordinary expression. But all she said was: "What are you doing down here? Go to the kitchen." Then she stepped to a stone bench under an arbor near her and sat down, putting the basket on the bench beside her.

As he went on up towards the house José thought he had never seen his *patrona* look quite so fierce. She was always severe, and often forbidding, but not to the point of being able to frighten him as she had today. It was as if a demon had peered out at him for a moment from beneath her heavy lids.

"It must be true," he thought. "Doña Faustina is going mad. What will become of Elena and me?"

This time when he got to the kitchen he took Elena into a corner and whispered to her, telling her his fears, and of how strange the señora had looked in the garden. Elena crossed herself. "Oh, God," she murmured. But he did not mention the tank to her, either now or later. He did not even want to think about it, because he suspected that in some way it was connected with Doña Faustina's madness, and being the only one who knew about it gave him a certain feeling of security which he would have lost had he shared the knowledge with Elena.

4

One cold evening of *llovizna*, as the mealy fog slowly turned to water and drenched the countryside, there was a knock at the entrance door. Doña Faustina, who spent much of her time pottering about in the basement where the baths and laundry were, heard it from there, and straightway mounted the stairs, her face dark with fury. Carlota stood in the *comedor*, undecided as to whether she should answer. The knocking was repeated as Doña Faustina reached her.

"Again the police?" said Carlota a bit fearfully.

"*Ya veremos*," muttered Doña Faustina. And she went out and stood behind the door, calling out in a loud voice: "Who?"

There was no answer.

"Don't open it," whispered Carlota, who stood behind her.

Doña Faustina made an impatient gesture to silence her sister. They waited several minutes, but the knock did not come again. There was only the irregular dripping of the water from the balcony above on to the ground.

"Stay here," said Doña Faustina, and she went through the *comedor*, down the stairs and into the laundry again. Here she gathered up all the refuse that strewed the floor and the wash-tubs, and packing it into two large baskets, continued out the side door which gave on the grape arbor. From here, descending the steps slowly, she disappeared into the darkness of the rose garden.

Within a half-hour she was back in the entrance hall where Carlota still stood listening by the door.

"Nothing," said Carlota in answer to Doña Faustina's questioning gesture. Doña Faustina's beckoned to her. They went into the *comedor* and whispered together. One candle flame cowered behind a pitcher on the newspaper-covered sideboard.

"It's not the police," said Doña Faustina. "Your room has a key. Go immediately. Lock the door and go to bed."

"But you. . .?"

"I'm not afraid."

Left alone in the *comedor*, Doña Faustina poured herself a glass of water and drank it. Then she took the candle and went up the long staircase to her room. She closed the door and set the candle down. By her sagging bed, around which Elena had draped the patched mosquito-net, stood a man. Swiftly he stepped over to her, and putting one arm around her neck tightly, stuffed a crumpled cloth into her mouth. She swung her arms about wildly, and managed to hit him once in the face, but almost immediately he had tied her wrists together. There was no further struggle. He propelled her roughly to the bed, yanked aside the netting and pushed her down. She looked at him: he was a tall young man, a *mestizo* probably, and badly dressed. As he moved about the room looking into the crates and boxes that lay in wild disorder about the floor, he snorted with distaste. Finally he overturned a chair in anger and with a scornful gesture swept all the empty bottles and piles of newspapers off the bureau onto the floor. He approached the bed again and looked at Doña Faustina in the wavering light. Then, to her surprise (although it cannot be said to her annoyance) he lay down and had his way with her quietly, impersonally. A few minutes later he sat up and pulled the cloth out of her mouth. She lay perfectly still and looked up at him. Finally she said: "What do you want here? I have no money."

"Who knows if you have or not?"

"I tell you there is none."

"We'll see."

He got up. Again he spent a quarter of an hour or so searching the room, scuffing piles of refuse under the tables, kicking the furniture over to examine the under part, emptying drawers of their dust and litter. He lit a small cigar and returned to the bed. His oblique eyes looked almost closed in the light of the candle.

"Where is it?" he said.

"There is none. But I have something more precious."

"What?" He looked at her with scornful disbelief. What could be more precious than money?

"Untie my hands."

He gave her the use of one hand, holding the other arm firmly while she fumbled in her clothing. In a moment she drew forth a small parcel done up in newspaper, and handed it to him. He placed it on the bed and bound her hands together. Then in a gingerly fashion he lifted the parcel and smelled of it. It was soft, and slightly wet.

"What is it?"

"Open it, *hombre*. Eat it. You know what it is."

Suspiciously he removed the outer layer of paper and held the contents close to the candle.

"What is this?" he cried.

"*Ya sabes, hombre*," she said calmly. "*Cómelo*."

"What is it?" he said again, trying to sound stern; but there was fear in his voice.

"Eat it, son. You don't have the chance every day."

"Where did you get it?"

"Ah!" Doña Faustina looked mysterious and wise, and gave no further answer.

"What do I want of it?" said the young man presently, looking down at the little object in his hand.

"Eat it! Eat it and have the power of two," she said cajolingly.

"*Brujerías!*" he exclaimed, still without putting the thing down.

A moment later he added, speaking slowly: "I don't like witchcraft. I don't like it."

"Bah!" Doña Faustina snorted. "Don't be stupid, son. Don't ask questions. Eat it, and go on your way with the force of two. Who will ever know? Tell me that! Who?"

This argument appeared to weigh with the young man. Suddenly he lifted the thing to his mouth and bit into it as if it had been a plum. While he ate he looked once at Doña Faustina darkly. When he had finished, he walked around the room tentatively for a moment, his head slightly on one side. Doña Faustina watched him closely.

"How do you feel?" she inquired.

"*Bien*," he said.

"Two," she reminded him. "Now you have the power of two."

As if inspired by the fortifying suggestion, he walked to the bed, threw himself down on it and lay with her again briefly. This time she kissed his forehead. When it was over he rose, and without undoing the rope that bound her hands, without saying a word, he went out of the door and down the stairs. A minute or so later she heard the front door close. At the same time the candle, which had burned down to its base, began to flicker wildly, and soon the room was in darkness.

5

All night Doña Faustina lay perfectly still on her bed, sleeping now and then, and during the periods of wakefulness listening to the slow dripping of the mist outside her windows. In the morning Carlota, still fearful, opened her door a crack, and apparently finding everything in the corridors in a normal state went to Doña Faustina's room.

"*Ay, Dios!*" she cried when she saw Doña Faustina lying with her clothing partially ripped away and her hands lashed together. "Oh, God! Oh, God!"

But Doña Faustina was calm. As Carlota undid the rope, she said: "He did no harm. But I had to give him the heart."

Carlota looked at her sister with horror.

"You're mad!" she cried. "The police will be here any minute."

"No, no," Doña Faustina reassured her, and she was right: no police arrived to search the house again. Nothing happened.

At the end of two weeks they made another trip, and a little while later still another. Two days after they had returned from this one, Doña Faustina called Carlota into her room and said to her: "There will be a child."

Carlota sat down slowly on the bed.

"How terrible!"

Doña Faustina smiled. "No, no. It's perfect. Think. It will have the power of thirty-seven."

But Carlota did not seem convinced. "We don't know about those things," she said. "It may be a vengeance."

"No, no, no," said Doña Faustina, shaking her head. "But now we must be more careful than ever."

"No more trips?" said Carlota hopefully.

"I shall think about it."

A few days later they were both in the rose garden sitting on a bench.

"I have thought," said Doña Faustina. "And there will be no more trips."

"Good," replied Carlota.

Toward the end of the year Doña Faustina was confined to bed, awaiting the birth of the child. She lay back comfortably in the crooked old bed, and had Elena come and sweep out the room for the first time in many months. Even when the floor was clean, the room still reeked of the garbage that had lain there for so long. Carlota had bought a tiny crib in the town; the purchase had awakened interest in their activities on the part of the townspeople.

When the time arrived, Elena and Carlota were both in the room to assist at the birth. Doña Faustina did not scream once. The baby was washed and laid beside her in the bed.

"A boy," said Elena, smiling down at her.

"Of course," said Doña Faustina, beginning to nurse him.

Elena went down to the kitchen to tell José the good news. He shook his head gloomily.

"Something bad in all this," he muttered.

"In all what?" said Elena sharply.

"Who is the father?" said José, looking up.

"That is Doña Faustina's secret," Elena replied smugly, rather as if it had been her own.

"Yes. I think so too," said José meaningfully. "I think there is no father, if you want to know. I think she got the child from the Devil."

Elena was scandalized. "Shameless!" she cried. "How can you say such a thing?"

"I have reasons," said José darkly. And he would say no more.

Things went smoothly at the inn. Several months passed. The baby had been named Jesus Maria and was in perfect health— "*un torito*," said Elena, "a real little bull."

"Of course," Doña Faustina had replied on that occasion. "He has the power of thirty-seven. . ." Exactly then Carlota had been taken with a violent fit of coughing which managed to cover the rest of the sentence. But Elena had noticed nothing.

The rainy season had finished again, and the bright days of sunlight and green leaves had come. José went in search of fruit once more, wandering down through the garden, crouching over most of the time to creep beneath the hanging walls of vines and tendrils. Again one day he cut his way to the tank, and stood on the edge of it looking toward the ramp. And this time he saw the monster just as it slid forward and disappeared beneath the surface of the water. His mouth dropped open. Only one word came out: "*Caimán!*"

He stood still for several minutes looking down at the dark water. Then he edged along the side of the tank to the place where the path had been the year before. It had completely disappeared. No one had been to the tank in many months; there was no indication that such a corridor had ever existed there in the mass of vegetation. He returned the way he had come.

It was a scandal, thought José, that such a beast should be living on Doña Faustina's property, and he determined to speak to her about it immediately. He found her in the kitchen talking with Elena. From his face she saw that something was wrong, and fearful perhaps that he was going to say just what he did say a moment later, she tried to get him out of the room.

"Come upstairs. I want you to do something for me," she said, walking over to him and pulling him by the arm.

But José's excitement was too great. He did not even notice that she was touching him. "Señora!" he cried. "There is a crocodile in the garden!"

Doña Faustina looked at him with black hatred. "What are you saying?" she said softly and with a certain concern in her voice, as if the old man needed to be treated with gentleness.

"An enormous *caimán!* I saw it!"

Elena looked at him apprehensively. "He's ill," she whispered to Doña Faustina. José heard her. "Ill!" he laughed scornfully. "Come with me and wait a little. I'll show you who's ill! Just come!"

"You say in the garden?" repeated Doña Faustina incredulously. "But where?"

"In the great tank, señora."

"Tank? What tank?"

"The señora doesn't know about the tank? There's a tank down below in the orchard. *Sí, sí, sí,*" he insisted, seeing Elena's face. "I've been there many times. It's not far. Come."

Inasmuch as Elena seemed to be on the point of removing her apron and, accepting his invitation, Doña Faustina changed her tactics. "Stop this nonsense!" she shouted. "If you're ill, José, go to bed. Or are you drunk?" She stepped close to him and sniffed suspiciously. "No? *Bueno.* Elena, give him some hot coffee and let me know in an hour how he is."

But in her room Doña Faustina began to worry.

6

They got out just in time. Carlota was not sure they ought to leave. "Where shall we go?" she said plaintively.

"Don't think about that," said Doña Faustina. "Think about the police. We must go. I know. What good does it do me to have the power of thirty-seven if I pay no attention to what they tell me? They say we must leave. Today."

As they sat in the train, ready to pull out of the station, surrounded by baskets, Doña Faustina held Jesus Maria up to the window and made his tiny arm wave good-by to the town. "The capital is a better place for him in any case," she whispered.

They went to a small *fonda* in the capital, where the second day Doña Faustina conceived the idea of applying at the nearest *comisaría* for employment as police matron. Her physical build, plus the fact that, as she told the lieutenant, she was afraid of no human being, impressed those who interviewed her, and after various examinations, she was accepted into the force.

"You'll see," she said to Carlota when she returned that evening in high spirits. "From now on we have nothing to worry about. Nothing can harm us. We have new names. We are new people. Nothing matters but Jesus Maria."

At that very moment the inn was swarming with police. The news of the *caimán*, which José in his obstinacy insisted was really there, first to Elena and then to others in the market, had reached them and awakened their curiosity once again. When it was found that there was not one, but a pair of the beasts, in the hidden tank, the police began to look more closely. No one really believed even now that it was Doña Faustina and her sister who were responsible for the disappearance of the dozens of infants who had vanished during the past two or three years, but it was felt that it would do no harm to investigate.

In a dark corner of the laundry, under one of the washtubs, they found a bundle of bloodstained rags which on closer inspection proved beyond a doubt to be the garments of an infant.

Then they discovered other such rags stuffed in the windows to fill the spaces left by broken panes. "They must be Jesus Maria's," said the loyal Elena. "The señora will be back in a day or so, and she will tell you." The police leered.

The *jefe* came and looked around the laundry. "She was not stupid," he said admiringly. "She did the work here, and *they*" —he pointed out toward the orchard—"took care of the rest."

Little by little all the stories from roundabout concurred to make one unified mass of evidence; there was no longer much doubt as to Doña Faustina's guilt, but finding her was another matter. For a while the papers were full of the affair. Indignant articles were spread across the pages, and always there was the demand that the readers be on the lookout for the two monstrous women. But it turned out that no picture was available of either of them.

Doña Faustina saw the newspapers, read the articles, and shrugged her shoulders. "All that happened long ago," she said. "It has no importance now. And even if it had, they could not catch me. I have too much power for them." Soon the papers spoke of other things.

Fifteen years passed quietly. Jesus Maria, who was unusually bright and strong for his age, was offered a position as servant in the home of the Chief of Police. He had seen the boy about with his mother for several years, and liked him. This was a great triumph for Doña Faustina.

"I know you will be a great man," she told Jesus Maria, "and will never bring dishonor upon us."

But eventually he did, and Doña Faustina was inconsolable.

After three years he grew bored with his menial work, and went into the army, carrying with him a recommendation from his employer to a close friend, a certain colonel who saw to it that Jesus Maria was pleasantly treated in the barracks. Everything went well for him; he was constantly promoted, so that by the time he was twenty-five he had become a colonel himself. It may be observed that to be a colonel in the Mexican army is not so great an attainment, nor is it necessarily a sign of exceptional merit. However, there is little doubt that Jesus Maria's military career would have continued its upward course, had he not happened to be in Zacatecas at the time of the raids on the villages thereabout by Fermín Figueroa and his band. As one more privilege in the endless chain of favors granted him by his superiors he was put in charge of the punitive expedition that was sent out in pursuit of Figueroa. Jesus Maria could not have been completely without ability, nonetheless, since on the third day out he succeeded in taking the leader prisoner along with thirty-six of his men.

No one ever really knew what happened in the small mountain village where the capture took place, save that Figueroa and the bandits had all been tied up in a sheep corral, ready to be shot, and when a few hours later a corporal had arrived with six soldiers to carry out the execution, the corral was empty. And it was even said, after Jesus Maria had been stripped of his rank, that a sheepherder had seen him enter the corral in the bright afternoon sunlight when everyone else was asleep, loosen the ropes that bound Figueroa, and then hand him his knife, whereupon he turned his back and walked away. Few believed the sheepherder's story: colonels do not do such things. Still, it was agreed that he had been inexcusably careless, and that it was entirely his fault that the thirty-seven bandits had escaped and thus lived to continue their depredations.

The evening Jesus Maria arrived back at his barracks in the capital, he stood alone in the latrine looking at himself in the fly-specked mirror. Slowly he began to smile, watching the movements of of his facial muscles. "No," he said, and tried again. He opened his eyes wider and smiled with all his might. The man's face had looked something like that; he would never be able to get it exactly, but he would go on trying because it made him happy to recall that moment—the only time he had ever known how it feels to have power.

TAPIAMA

J UST behind the hotel was the river. If it had come from very far inland it would have been wide and silent, but because it was really only a creek swollen by the rains, and its bed was full of boulders, it made a roaring noise which the photographer briefly mistook for more rain. The heat and the trip had tired him out; he had eaten the cold fried fish and the leathery omelet that oozed grease, the brown bean paste with rice and burned bananas, and had been overtaken suddenly by a sleepiness powerful as the effect of a drug. Staggering to his bed, he had ripped off his shirt and trousers, lifted the stiff mosquito-net that reeked of dust, and dropped like a stone onto the mattress, only distantly noticing its hardness before he lost himself in sleep.

But in the night when he awoke he realized he had been in the false sleep of indigestion; staring into the blackness over his head he told himself that it was going to be hard to find the way back into oblivion. It was then that he had become aware of the night's changeless backdrop of sound, and had taken it for rain. Now and then, far above his head (how could the ceiling be that high?) a firefly's nervous little light flashed its indecipherable code for an instant or two. He was lying on his back; something small was crawling down his chest. He put his hand there: it was a slowly moving drop of sweat. The rough sheet under him was wet. He wanted to move, but if he did

162

there would be no end to the shifting, and each new position would be more uncomfortable than the last. In the anonymous darkness of a nearby room someone coughed from time to time; he could not tell whether it was a man or a woman. The meal he had eaten lay like ten meals in his stomach. Slowly the memory of it was being suffused with a nebulous horror—particularly the heavy cold omelet shining with grease.

Lying there smelling the dust from the netting was like being tied up inside a burlap bag. To get out into the street and walk —that was what he wanted, but there were difficulties. The electricity went off at midnight; the old man who ran the hotel had told him that. Instead of putting the matches under his pillow he had left them in his trouser-pocket, and the idea of stepping out on to the floor barefoot without a light did not appeal to him. Besides, he reminded himself, listening again to the wide, strangely distant clamor out there, it was raining. But to move along the dead streets even under the invisible rain would be a pleasure. . . . If he lay quite still, sleep might return. Finally, in desperation he yanked the net aside and sprang out of bed, across the room in the direction of the chair over which he had thrown his clothes.

He managed to get into his shirt and trousers in the space of three matches; his shoes he pounded on the concrete floor in the dark, to tumble out a possible centipede or scorpion. Then he struck a fourth match and opened the door into the *patio*. Here it was no longer pitch-black. The huge potted plants were visible in the night's lead-colored light, but the sky, stifled by a cloud that no starlight could pierce, seemed not to be there at all. It was not raining. "The river must be very close," he thought.

He walked along the covered *corredor*, grazing the tentacles of orchids that hung in baskets and jars from the eaves, bumping into the pieces of wicker furniture, and found the entrance door, closed and doubly bolted. Carefully he slid back the metal bars and opened the door, pulling it shut after him. The gloom of the street was as profound as that of the *patio*, and the air as still as it had been under the mosquito-net. But it had an indefinite vegetable scent—a sweet odor of both fulfilment and exhaustion.

He turned to the left: the long empty main street, lined with one-story buildings, led straight down to the *paseo* along the sea. As he walked, the unmoving hot-house air became veined with the fresher smell of seaweed on the beach. At each intersecting street he had to go down six steps to the road level, cross, and climb up again to the sidewalk. In the rainy season, the *propietario* of the hotel had told him, there was a rowboat at each corner to ferry the pedestrians across. Like the intermingling of the land and sea odors that he breathed, two opposing but entwined sensations took possession of him: a relief amounting almost to delight, and a faint feeling of nausea which he decided to combat because he felt that not to have been able to leave all suggestion of illness behind showed a lack of strength. He tried to put more springiness into his walk, but discovered almost immediately that it was too hot to make any more than a minimum of effort. He was sweating even more now than he had been in his bed. He lighted an Ovalado. The taste of the sweet tobacco was a part of the night.

The *paseo* bordering the sea-front was about half a mile long. He had imagined there would be some slight stirring of the air here, but he could detect no difference. Still, now and then there was the soft intimate sound of a small wave breaking gently on the sand just below. He sat down on the balustrade and rested, in the hope of cooling off a little. The sea was invisible. He could have been sitting on the peak of a cloud-covered mountain—the gloom in front of him would have been that formless and all-embracing. Yet the sea's casual noises had no element of distance in them, as sea sounds have. It was as though they were taking place in a vast, closed courtyard. The concrete slabs on which he sat were damp, and a little cooler than his flesh. He smoked two cigarettes and strained his ears to hear some sound, made even indirectly, by human agency. But there was nothing more than the desultory slipping and sucking of the lazy water on the beach below. He glanced up and down the empty *paseo*. Far out along the shore to the west there was a light. It was orange, it flickered: a bonfire? He resumed walking, more slowly than before, ahead of him the distant blaze, the one point of light in the landscape.

A wide flight of steps led down on to the beach. Just beyond, he could see the flimsy structure of a pier that had been built out over the water. He stood still and listened. The fitful licking of small waves around the piles sounded as though it were happening in an echo-chamber.

He ran lightly down the steps and passed underneath the pier. It was definitely cooler walking along on the sand than it had been up on the *paseo*. He felt wide-awake now, and decided to see how much nearer to the light down the shore fifteen minutes would put him. Night-colored crabs hurried along the sand just ahead of his moving feet, completely soundless and almost invisible. A little beyond the end of the *paseo* the sand gave place to a hard coral surface which was easier to walk on. Out of prudence he kept as near to the water's edge as possible.

There was a difference between this walk and innumerable other midnight jaunts he had made, and he was inclined to wonder what made it so pleasant. Perhaps he was enjoying it simply because the fabric here was of pure freedom. He was not looking for anything; all the cameras were back in the hotel room.

Occasionally he lifted his eyes from the dim brainlike configurations of coral beneath his feet and looked inland, to see whether he could make out any signs of habitation. It seemed to him that there might be sand dunes a few hundred feet back, but in the absence of light it was impossible to be certain of even that much. The sweat trickled down his spine and over his coccyx, sliding in between his buttocks. Maybe the best idea would be to undress completely. But then there would be the bother of carrying his clothing, and he wanted his hands free, even at the risk of chafing.

The question of freedom was governed by the law of diminishing returns, he said to himself, walking faster. If you went beyond a certain point of intensity in your consciousness of desiring it, you furnished yourself with a guarantee of not achieving it. In any case, he thought, what is freedom in the last analysis, other than the state of being totally, instead of only partially, subject to the tyranny of chance?

There was no doubt that this walk was dispelling the miasma of indigestion that had lain within him. Three minutes to go, said the bright minute-hand of his watch; the orange light ahead seemed smaller than it had from the town. Why an arbitrary fifteen minutes? He smiled at the precise urban pattern in which his mind had automatically moved. If he lifted his arm he could touch the sky, and it would be moist, tepid and voluptuously soft.

And now in the distance ahead, on the landward side, he heard sounds which he quickly identified as the voices of hundreds of young frogs. The light, now that he studied it, was moving in a strange fashion: slightly up and down, and sideways as well, but without appearing to alter its position. All at once it became a huge flame belching upward, an instant later scattering cascades of red sparks, and he understood that he had arrived. The bonfire burned on the floor of a gently swaying craft not a hundred feet ahead of him. A naked man stood above it, tossing it palm branches. The photographer stopped walking and listened for the sound of human voices, but the happy chorus of frogs filled the air.

He stepped ahead several paces and decided to call out. "*Hola!*" The man wheeled about, jumped over the nearer side of the boat (the water was extremely shallow) and came running up to him.

Without greeting him, taking him perhaps for someone else,

the man said: *"Tapiama? Vas a Tapiama?"* The photographer, never having heard of Tapiama, stuttered a bit and finally said, *"Sí,"* whereupon the other seized his arm and pulled him along to the edge of the water. "The tide's all the way out. We'll start in a minute."

He could see two other people in the craft, lying flat on the floor, one on each side of the fire, as far from its heat as possible. The photographer squatted down and removed his shoes and socks, then waded to the boat. When he stood in the center of it (the fire was still crackling brightly) he turned and watched the naked man loosening the rope that held the craft in place.

"The whole thing is absurd." He could only distrust the very naturalness with which all this was coming about—the indifference to his unexpected arrival on the part of the two passengers, and perhaps even more, the highly suspect readiness of the boatmen to take off the moment he had appeared. He told himself, "Things don't happen this way," but since beyond a doubt they were doing so, any questioning of the process could lead only in the direction of paranoia. He dropped to the floor of the boat and pulled out his packet of Ovalados. The naked boatman, the coil of dripping rope around his black forearm like a bracelet, sprang aboard, and with his big toe nudged one of the supine passengers who stirred, rose to his knees, and glanced about with annoyance. "Where is it?" he demanded. Without replying, the boatman handed him the shorter of two poles that had lain along the gunwale. Together they began to propel the punt along the invisible surface of the water. The frogs' canticle and the fire's flare filled the night.

Having answered *"Sí"* to the Tapiama question, the photographer felt he could scarcely take the retrogressive step of asking "What is Tapiama?" or "Where is Tapiama?" And so, much as he would have liked to know, he decided to wait. This shallow body of water beneath them—estuary, lagoon? River more likely, since the boatman had said the tide was out. But

167

not the stream whose troubled passage among the boulders he had heard from his bed.

They pushed on, now and then passing beneath clumps of high vegetation where the frogs' song was briefly covered by another sound, inexplicable and brutal, like the sudden tearing of a vast sheet of strong linen. From time to time something solid and heavy splashed nearby, as if a man had fallen into the water. And occasionally the other passenger raised himself on one elbow and without too much effort managed to revive the dying fire with another dry palm-leaf.

Probably it was less than an hour before they came to a landing in the mud. The two passengers leapt out and hurried away into the darkness. The boatman, after carefully donning a pair of short underpants, tapped the photographer on the arm and asked him for sixty centavos. He gave him seventy-five and clambered out into the soft mud, his shoes in his hand.

"Wait a minute," said the man. "I'll go with you." The photographer was pleased. When the boatman, looking blacker now in his white shorts, had secured the punt to an upright log driven into the mud, he led the way upward through a tangle of undergrowth, saying casually at one point: "Are you going across tomorrow?"

"Across? No."

"Aren't you here for the company?" The voice implied that to be here otherwise than for the company laid one open to unnameable suspicion.

The time had come to be truthful, he feared, although he did not relish the position he knew it would put him in. "I never heard of the company," he said. "I just arrived in Rio Martillo tonight. What sort of company?"

"Sugar," said the other. Then he stood still in the dark and spoke slowly: "*Entonces*—why have you come to Tapiama? They don't like *millonarios* here, you know." Understanding that this was the contemptuous coastal term for Americans, the photographer quickly lied. "I'm Danish," he said, but feeling that his voice lacked conviction he immediately added: "Do we go through any more mud, or can I put my shoes on?"

The man had started up again. "Wash your feet at the *cantina*, if you like," he told him over his shoulder. In another minute they were there: all in the dimness an open space, a dozen or so palm-leaf huts at one end of it, at the other a platform which must be a loading dock, the empty night and openness of water behind it; and half-way between the dock and the cluster of dwellings, the *cantina*, itself only a very large hut without a front wall.

A faint light came from within; there was no sound but the frogs on all sides, and the occasional tearing rasp in the branches high overhead. "Why is the place open at this hour?" demanded the photographer. The boatman stopped in the middle of the clearing and adjusted his shorts briefly. "Don Octavio runs it from six in the morning until six at night. His brother runs it from six at night until six in the morning. The company lets the men off from work at different hours. They come here with their *pago* and spend it. They like it better here than at home. Not so many mosquitoes." It could have been the photographer's imagination that made the man's voice sound bitter as he spoke the last words. They continued across the clearing and stepped into the *cantina*.

There was no floor; the ground was covered with white sand. A counter of boards had been built diagonally across a far corner. Here an oil lamp smoldered and two men stood drinking. Wooden packing-cases were scattered here and there, some standing on end with empty beer bottles on them, and others on their sides, to be used as seats. "*Muy triste*," commented the boatman, glancing around. Then he went behind the bar and disappeared through a small door in the wall there. Apart from the two at the bar, who had ceased their conversation and now stood staring at the photographer, there was no one else in the place. "When in doubt, speak," he told himself, advancing toward them, although it occurred to him that he might just as

169

well have made it, "When in doubt, keep quiet," even as he opened his mouth to say, *"Buenas noches,"* for their expressions did not alter in any manner that he could detect. For a full three seconds they continued to gaze at him before they replied, which they then did more or less simultaneously. These two had nothing in common, he noted: one was a soldier in uniform, an Indian boy of perhaps eighteen, the other a tired-looking mulatto civilian of indeterminate age. Or perhaps—the idea came to him as he put his elbow on the bar with a show of casualness—they did have at least a common antagonism, now that he had entered the *cantina*. "Oh, well, I'm barefoot and my shoes are covered with mud," he thought.

"Hay alguien?" he said aloud to the palm-leaf wall behind the bar. The two neither resumed their conversation nor spoke further with him, and he did not turn his head again toward them. Presently the small door opened and a fat man pushed through. He stood with his hands outspread on the bar, his eyebrows raised in anticipation. "I'll have a *cumbiamba*," said the photographer, remembering the name of the coastal region's favorite drink, a herbal concoction famous for its treacherous effects.

It was foul-tasting but strong. The second one seemed less objectionable. He walked across to the open side of the *cantina* and sat down on a packing-case, looking out at the formless night. The two at the bar were talking again now in low tones. It was not long before five men appeared from the platform end of the clearing; they straggled in and stood at the bar, laughing as they waited for their drinks. All of them were black, and wore only underpants, like the boatman. Now a mulatto girl with gold teeth came through the little door behind the bar and joined them. Almost immediately, however, she became aware of the photographer sitting by himself, and with her hands on her hips, half dancing, she made her way across the open space toward him. When she arrived, she squatted down beside him grinning and with one thin yellow hand reached out to unfasten his fly. His reaction was instantaneous and automatic: he drew back his leg and kicked her full in the breast, so that she toppled over backward in silence on to the sand. The noise of the resulting laughter at the bar was not sufficient to cover her thin voice, made sharp by rage: "*Qué bruto, tú! Pendejo!*" Hands on hips again, she retreated to the bar and was given a beer by one of the workmen. Although the photographer had not meant to kick her, he felt no regret at the turn the incident had taken. The *cumbiambas* seemed to be having their effect; he was beginning to feel very well. He sat still a while, tapping rhythms on the side of his empty glass. Soon more Negro workmen came in and joined the others at the bar. One carried a guitar on which he set to work strumming a syncopated chordal accompaniment for a melody which failed to appear. However, it was music of a sort, and everyone was pleased with it. Perhaps awakened by the sound, the dogs of the village had now started an angry chrous of barking; this was particularly audible to the photographer who sat at the entrance, and it bothered him. He rose and moved over to an empty crate alongside the opposite wall, resting his head against a rough-hewn pole that was one of the supports of the roof. A foot or so above his head there was a strange object dangling from a nail. Now and then he rolled his eyes upward and studied it.

All at once he jumped up and began violently to brush the back of his neck and head. The pole behind him was swarming with tiny ants, thousands upon thousands of them: someone had hung a small crushed coral snake over the nail, and they had come to eat the flesh. It took him a good while not to feel any more of the insects running over his back; during that time two other individuals had come into the *cantina* (whether from the outside or through the door behind the counter, he had not noticed), and now sat between him and the bar in such a fashion that both of them faced him. The old man looked Nordic, the innocent-looking one-legged boy with him could be Spanish; the old man was telling the boy a humorous story, leaning toward him with great interest, occasionally poking his arm with a forefinger to drive home a point, but the boy was distraughtly making designs in the sand with the tip of his crutch.

The photographer stood up; he had never before had such an effect from two drinks. "A very peculiar sensation," he said to himself. "Very peculiar," he repeated aloud under his breath as he started toward the bar to order another. It was not that he felt drunk so much as that he had become someone who was not he, someone for whom the act of living was a thing so different from what he had imagined it could be, that he was left stranded in a region of sensation far from any he had heretofore known. It was not unpleasant: it was merely indefinable. *"Dispénseme,"* he said to a tall Negro in pink and white striped BVD's, and he handed his empty glass to the fat man. He wanted to see what went into a *cumbiamba,* but the barman did everything quickly beneath the counter and handed him back the glass, brimming with the slightly frothy mixture. He took a good swallow of it and set it down, turning a little to his right as he did so. Standing beside him was the Indian soldier, his cap at an angle atop a pre-Colombian face. "Why does the army put such big visors on them?" he wondered.

He saw that the soldier was about to speak. "Whatever he says is going to turn out to be an insult," he warned himself, in the hope that this would help him to avoid possible anger later.

"Do you like this place?" the soldier said; his voice was silken.

"Es simpático. Yes, I like it."

"Why?" The dogs outside had come nearer; he could hear their yapping now above the laughter.

"Can you tell me why they hung that dead snake on the wall there?" he found himself asking, and supposed it was to

172

change the subject. But the soldier was going to be even more boring than he had feared. "I asked you why you like this *cantina*," he insisted.

"And I told you it was *simpático*. Isn't that enough?"

The soldier tilted his head back and looked down his nose.

"Far from being enough," he replied, his manner pedantic, his expression infuriating.

The photographer returned to his drink, picked it up, slowly finished it off. Then he pulled out his cigarettes and offered one to the other. With exaggerated deliberateness the soldier reached for the cigarette, took it, and began to tap it on the counter. The man playing the guitar at last had started to sing in a small falsetto voice along with it, but most of the words were in a dialect the photographer could not understand. When the cigarettes were lighted, he found himself wondering who had lighted them—he or the soldier.

"Just where did you come from?" asked the soldier.

He was not bothering to answer, but the soldier misunderstood even this. "I can see you're inventing something," he said, "and I don't want to hear it."

The photographer, disgusted, exclaimed, "Aaah!" and ordered another *cumbiamba*. This most recent one had done something extraordinary to him: he felt that he had become very precise, thin and hard, an object made of enamel or some similar material, something other than a living being, but intensely conscious all the same. "Four ought to do the trick," he thought.

The empty glass was in his hand, the fat barman was staring at him, and at that point he had not the slightest idea whether he had already drunk the fourth one or whether it was still the moment just after he had ordered it. He felt himself laughing, but he could not hear whether any sound was coming out or not. The mangled snake, seething with ants, had upset him a little; recognizing it, he had then been made aware of its smell, which he was not sure he had escaped even now. Here at the bar the kerosene lamp smoked heavily; its strong fumes choked him. "*Gracias a Dios,*" he confided to the barman, handing him the glass.

The old man who had been sitting on the crate behind them rose and came vaguely toward the bar. "Where did this come from?" said the photographer, laughing apologetically, looking at the full glass in his hand. The frenzied dogs out in the clearing yapped and howled, an exasperating sound. "*Qué tienen esos perros?*" he demanded of the soldier.

The old man had stopped beside them. "Say, Jack, I don't mean to butt in or anything," he began. He was bald, sunburned; he wore a fishnet shirt. The furrows between his ribs showed as parallel shadows, and irregular tufts of gray hair waved out from his chest between the meshes of the shirt. He stretched his lips in a smile, showing naked white gums. The soldier's stance became over-nonchalant; he stared at the newcomer, open hatred suddenly in his eyes, and gently blew the smoke from his cigarette into the old man's face.

"You from Milwaukee? Siddown."

"In a little while, thanks," said the photographer.

"A little while?" the old man echoed incredulously, running his hand over the top of his head. Then he called out in Spanish to the one-legged boy. The photographer was thinking: "This is not going to work out right, at all. It's just not going to work out." He wished the Negro would stop singing and the dogs would stop barking. He looked at the glass in his hand, full of what looked like soapsuds. Someone tapped him on the shoulder. "Say, bud, lemme give you a little advice." The old man again. "There's money in this country if you know where to look. But the guy that finds it is the guy that sticks to his own kind, if you know what I mean." He put his face nearer. and lowered his voice. Three skeletal fingers touched the photographer's arm. "You take it from me, from one white man to another. I'm tellin' you!" The three fingers, dark with tobacco stain, lifted themselves, trembled, and dropped back. "These guys all mean trouble from the word go."

The boy having both gathered up his crutch and managed to rise from where he had beeh sitting, had now arrived at the bar. "Take a look at this, Jack," the old man said. "Show him," he told the boy in Spanish, and the boy, leaning on his crutch, bent over and rolled up the right leg of his ragged khaki shorts until he had exposed the stump of his amputated leg. It was not far below the groin; the scar tissue had puckered and wrinkled curiously in countless tiny convolutions. "See?" cried the old man. "Two hundred and sixty tons of bananas went over that. Feel it."

"You feel it," said the photographer, wondering how it was possible for him to go on standing and talking exactly as if he were a person like the rest of them. (Could it be that what had happened to him did not show?) He turned his head and looked towards the entrance. The mulatto girl was vomiting just outside. With a cry the barman rushed across and furiously pushed her farther away, out into the clearing. When he came back in he was theatrically holding his nose. "That prostitute ape!" he yelled. "In another minute we'd have had the dogs inside here."

The boy was still looking expectantly at the old man, to see if it was time to lower his trouser leg. "You think he got a centavo from them?" said the old man sadly. "Hah!"

The photographer had begun to suspect that something had gone very wrong inside him. He felt sick, but since he was no longer a living creature he could not conceive it in those terms. He had shut his eyes and put his hand over his face. "It's going around backward," he said. The undrunk *cumbiamba* was in his other hand.

Saying the sentence had made it more true. It was definitely going around backward. The important thing was to remember that he was alone here and that this was a real place with real people in it. He could feel how dangerously easy it would be to go along with the messages given him by his senses, and dismiss the whole thing as a nightmare in the secret belief that when the breaking-point came he could somehow manage to escape by waking himself up. A little unsteadily he set his drink down on the counter. An argument which had arisen a while ago between the Indian soldier and his sad companion had now reached its noisy stage, with the companion attempting to drag the soldier away from the bar against his will, and the soldier, his two booted legs firmly apart, breathing rapidly, noisily in his resistance. Suddenly there was a small, shining knife in his right hand, and his face assumed the look of a little boy about to burst into tears. The old man quickly moved around to the photographer's other side. "That guy's bad news in any language," he muttered, gesturing nervously to the boy with the crutch as he bade him move out of the way.

The photographer was saying to himself: "If I can hold out. If I can only hold out." The whole place was slipping away from him, downward and outward; the guitar strummed and the dogs barked, the soldier flashed his knife and pouted, the old American talked about caves with buried emeralds only six days up the Tupurú, the lamp grew redder and more smoke came out of it. He understood nothing except that he must stay there and suffer; to try to escape would be fatal. The soldier's face was very near his own now, breathing black tobacco smoke at him. Languorously, with an insane natural coquetry, he made his long lashes tremble as he asked: "Why have you not offered me a *copita*? All night I have been waiting for you to invite me." The hand holding the knife hung listlessly at his side; the photographer thought of a sleeping baby still clutching its rattle.

"*Sí quieres. . . . Qué tomas?*" he murmured, reflecting that his shoes should be in his hand and were not; then where were they? Someone had brought a large spider monkey into the *cantina* and was forcing it to dance to the guitar's syncopations, making it stand upright by holding its two front paws. With an air of distraught gravity it stepped about, peering this way and that, grimacing nervously at the loud peals of laughter that came from those at the bar watching its antics. The dogs, having noticed its arrival, had rushed to the very entrance of the *cantina*, where they braced themselves to shriek and snap with determined fury.

The soldier's drink had been bought and paid for, but he was not drinking it. He was leaning far back against the bar, reclining on his elbow almost as though he were in bed, his eyes simple black slits, whispering: "You don't like it here. You want to go, *verdad?* But you are afraid to go."

In spite of the constant sliding away, everything had remained just as it was. It would have been better if he could have sat down. "Oh, God," he asked himself. "Am I going to be able to stand this?"

"Why are you afraid to go?" pursued the other tenderly, smiling so that the photographer could admire his small, perfect teeth. The photographer laughed silently, did not reply.

The face of the soldier, ovoid, honey-colored, so near to his, moved now with consummate smoothness into another face, that of a general. ("*Sí, mi general,*" with stiff *bigotes* sprouting from beneath the nostrils, almond eyes, black, deadly with a delicate lust, the uniform svelte, plaited steel riding crop in hand, sharpened spurs shining by the anklebone. "*Bien, mi general.*" Lying on the hot barrack mattress, *tarde tras tarde,* the soldier had dreamed of being the general. Which mountain village had he said he was from? How long had he been talking?)

". . .and that day alone they killed forty-one pigs before my eyes. There in the corral. *Me hizo algo; no sé. . . .*" His smile was apologetic, intimate; he lowered his eyes imperceptibly, made the effort and raised them again to look at the photographer in such a way that, since they were wider than before, they glistened. "I never forgot it; I don't know why."

Between them the gold-toothed girl came sliding, her hands wriggling over her head, her hips circling, her thin voice shouting: "*Ahii! Ahii! El fandango de la Guajira*" The soldier must have pushed her, for all at once she slapped him. But it was

177

happening very slowly. How could it take the soldier so long to bring up his knife, and as he raised his hand, how could the stupid girl wait that way before screaming and ducking aside? Even so, the blade caught her only on the arm; she was in the middle of the floor, kneeling on the sand, moaning: "He cut me! Oh, God! He cut me!" And because the man who had been dancing with the spider monkey let go of it to get as quickly as all the others to the bar, the beast toddled over to the girl and distractedly wrapped one long hairy arm around her neck. But then the photographer was being roughly jostled, his bare feet were being stepped on as everyone tried to get at the soldier and disarm him. (A demon mask shiny with venom, a voice of barbed wire that rasped: "Os mato a todos! A todos!"

It was exactly nineteen steps from the place where he had stood to the trunk of a small papaya tree in front of the entrance. The tree was not very strong; it swayed slightly as he leaned against it. The dogs were yelping now from inside the cantina. Here the air was sweet and almost cool; the faintest glimmer of morning was in the sky and water behind the landing. "I must start to walk," he told himself; it seemed important to believe it. The shouts and screams inside the cantina were growing in volume, and people were beginning to call to one another from the doors of their huts. The landing platform was empty—just boards and no railing. Shuffling along with great care because he was not used to going barefoot, he followed what he thought was the path he had taken earlier, through the undergrowth back down to the river's edge, and there was the punt, mud-beached in the mangroves.

It was easy to get in, easy to untie the rope, and easy (for the level of the water had risen considerably since the craft had been left) to pry it loose from the shelf of mud where it rested. But once he was floating among the now nearly visible trunks and branches, bumping against them and being spun to face first the dark chaotic riverbank and then the wide whitening emptiness of open sky and water, he understood dimly that it

178

was not going to be possible to pole his way back to the beach whence he had come, since the tide was still coming in. It was a comforting thought, he decided, because it meant that everything was going ahead instead of backward. A minute later he was floating quietly by the base of the landing: people were running around the clearing. Quickly he lay down flat on the bottom of the punt, and there he stayed, looking straight up at the gray sky, hoping in this way to remain invisible until he had been carried out of sight, beyond Tapiama.

It was going to be one of those stillborn tropical days, when there would be no sun, no wind, no clouds—because the entire sky was enfolded in one vast suffocating blanket of cloud—when nothing at all would happen save that hourly it would grow hotter until an approximate dusk came along. Already the eastern side of the sky was the hot side, arching above the flatness of the swampland. The punt scarcely moved now, the channel having broadened into this wide marshy lake. The photographer lay still and groaned. Little by little the fear that someone might see him gave way to the hope that what current there was would propel the craft in the direction of the shore rather than out toward the wilderness of water and tiny islands; sometimes, even though suffering be implicit in it, contact with others is preferable to the terror of solitude and the unknown. He laid an arm over his eyes to shield them from the corrosive gray light that beat down upon him from the spaces above. The other hand lay in the ashes of last night's fire. And he floated in utter silence on the calm bosom of the lagoon, not stirring as the morning hours moved along, but growing increasingly conscious of the infernal seething of the *cumbiambas* in his brain, a seething which expressed itself as a senseless nightmare imposed from without, in the face of which he could only be totally passive. It was an invisible spectacle whose painful logic he followed with the entire fiber of his being, without, however, once being given a clear vision of what agonizing destinies were at stake.

Some time towards mid-morning the punt grazed a submerged root and was swung into an eddyless pool in the shelter of the vegetation near the shore. Here fierce flies stung him, and from among the leaves high above, a talking bird remarked casually, over and over again: "*Idigaraga. Idigaraga. Idigaraga.*"

It was no particular consolation to him, so intent was he on the obscure drama being enacted within him, to hear human voices presently, or to feel the craft seized by the hands of someone splashing in the water alongside. Only when several people had climbed in and crouched chattering around him did he move his arm and squint up at them. Five young men, all of whom looked remarkably alike, surrounded him. Water dripped down upon him from their naked bodies. He shut his eyes again: it was too unlikely a scene. During this time one of them dived overboard, was gone a short while, and returned with a green coconut whose top he had sliced off. He began to let the water dribble into the photographer's face, whereupon the photographer partially sat up and drank the rest of it. In a minute he looked around at them again, and said: "Are you brothers?"

"*Sí, sí,*" they chorused. This was for some reason a consolation. "*Hermanos,*" he sighed, sliding down into the ashes again. Then he added desperately, hoping they could still hear him: "Please take me to Rio Martillo."

It had been a brief interlude of clarity. Now they poled the punt back out under the hot sky, letting him lie there and moan as he liked. At one point he felt he must try to explain that he would give them each seventy-five centavos for their trouble, but they giggled and pushed him back down.

"My shoes!" he cried. "There are no shoes," they told him. "Lie still."

"And when we get to the beach," he panted, seizing a brown ankle beside his face, "how will you get me to Rio Martillo?" "We are not going to any beach," they replied. "We go through the swamp and the canal."

He lay still a while, trying to disassociate himself from the irrational ideas boiling up in his head. "Is this the way to Rio Martillo?" he demanded, thrusting himself up a little and gasping, trying to see beyond the enclosing thicket of brown legs and arms, and feeling a deep unreasoned shame at have once again accepted defeat. They laughed, pushed him gently down to the floor, and went on rhythmically poling the craft eastward. "The factory chimney," they said to one another, pointing into the distance. His mind took him back to the quiet region by the riverbank where the small bird had spoken, high up in the trees, and he heard again the ridiculous conversational tone. "*Idigaraga*," he said aloud, imitating perfectly its voice and intonation. There was an explosion of mirth around him. One of the youths took his arm, shook it lightly. "You know that bird?" he said. "It is a very comic bird. It goes to the nests of other birds and wants to sit there, and when the other birds fight with it and drive it away, it sits down in the same tree there and says: '*Idigaraga*.' That means:'*Iri garagua, nadie me quiere*, nobody likes me.' And it says it over and over, until they make it go farther away so they can't hear it any more. You said it just right. Say it again." "*Sí, sí*," the others agreed, "*otra vez!*"

The photographer had no intention of saying it again. His shame at having accepted defeat already troubled him less. It was hard in his present condition to fit the bird correctly into the pattern, but he knew it had to be done.

When the Compañía Azucarera Riomartillense blew a long blast on its whistle to announce the advent of noon, the sound hovered for an instant over the empty swampland like an invisible trail of smoke. "*Las doce*," said one of the brothers. A great black and gold dragonfly came skimming across the water and lighted on the photographer's bare foot. After raising and lowering its wings twice, it was away again on its crooked course, curving and swooping over the lagoon toward Tapiama. "Say it again," the brothers begged him.

IF I SHOULD
OPEN MY MOUTH

Monday 26th——

AT LAST succeeded in finding the correct mixture of gum-arabic, sugar and essence of peppermint. Had the most complicated time getting Mrs. Crawford out of the house and keeping her out for a sufficiently long time so that I could clean up the kitchen properly before she returned. I find this plan most exhilarating, however, and I intend to carry it through to its conclusion in the face of all obstacles. The subway station details are clear in my mind, and I have worked out the entire plan of action. In fact, the project is so extremely simple that it seems at times almost suspect. It is as if I were constantly being reassured by an invisible person whose face, if only I could see it, might easily prove to be wearing a falsely benign expression. However, it is only in the evenings that I begin to think of such things. A seconal or two ought to arrange matters, at least for tonight, so that I can knit up some of that raveled sleeve of care. Curious how disturbing the sound of a motorcycle can be out here in the still night air. There has been one idling somewhere up the road for the past ten minutes, popping and sputtering in a way calculated to drive a listener crazy. When it finally purred off into the distance it was like a relief from a constant pain. Why were machines ever invented? And what is this strange calm confidence that mankind has placed in these senseless toys it has managed to put together? That question I don't

182

expect ever to be able to answer. I can only say that I know it
is wrong.

Wednesday 28th——

More complications, getting rid of Mrs. C. while I dipped the
tablets. The rest, gluing the ends of the boxes and so on, can
be done up here in my room. A ridiculous facet of my feeling
about all this is that while I am quite aware of the reprehensible
aspects of my silly little project, for some unfathomable reason
I feel hugely righteous about it all—more satisfyingly virtuous
than I have in years. A quirk of human nature, I suppose.

Saturday 1st——

I don't know why it is that ideas never occur to me except
when I lack the time to put them down or when it is literally
impossible to do so, as for instance when I am seated in a
dentist's chair or surrounded by talking people at a dinner
party, or even sound asleep, when often the best things come
to light and are recognized as such by a critical part of my
mind which is there watching, quite capable of judging but
utterly unable to command an awakening and a recording.
Sick-bed and fever often bring up astonishing things, but again,
to what avail? A less ingenuous man than I might ask just why
it should be of any importance to me that what goes on inside
my mind should be put down. I am not a literary person and I
never expect to be one, nor have I any intention of showing my
notebooks to my friends. But that is a point not even to be
discussed; long ago I determined to extract from my mind whatever by-products it could furnish. I have done it, I am still doing it, and I expect to continue to do it. The only difficulty is
that whatever I am able to catch hold of is captured only after
engaging in the most elaborate intrigues with my mind, playing
hide-and-seek with various parts of it, exhausting myself in inventing disguises with which to surprise it, and in general having a most unpleasant time. Such as this very moment, this very
page. A typical example of an occasion when there is not a

single idea in view on the vast inner horizon. I am using up pages of my notebook, minutes when I might be strolling on the beach smelling the sea, in scribbling these absurd excuses, inventing alibis for not living, trying to find one more reason why I should feel justified in keeping these nonsensical journals year after year. Year after year, and life does not last for ever, not even an unsatisfactory one like mine. Perhaps this is the very thing which is keeping my life so unsatisfactory. If I could argue myself into stopping it all, even into destroying the notebooks, would it be better? Yes. Each minute would be complete in itself, like a room with four walls in which one can stand, sit, move about. Each day would be like a complete city shining in the sun, with its streets, parks and crowds. And the years would be whole countries to roam in. That much is certain. But the whole? That is to say, the interstices in time, the tiny chinks in consciousness when the total is there, enveloping one, and one knows that life is not made of time any more than the world is made of space. They would still occur, and they would be illicit because there would have been no arrangements made for them. What a man can distil and excrete will necessarily have some value for him (if only for him, as in my case) because its essence is of the interstices in time. One more justification, as idiotic as all the others, of the need for living an unsatisfactory life.

It seems to me that if one could accept existence as it is, partake of it fully, the world could be magical. The cricket on my balcony at the moment piercing the night repeatedly with its hurried needle of sound, would be welcome merely because it is there, rather than an annoyance because it distracts me from what I am trying to do. Here I am, a man of fifty-five, who enjoys a certain respect on the part of his friends, cursing a small black insect outside the window. But I dare say all this is merely procrastination. I am probably trying to put off writing down what is really on my mind. It must go down, of course, because everything must go down, and truthfully. (I thought the cricket had stopped just then, but it has started again, quite the same as before.) I delivered the first twenty boxes today.

Sunday 2nd——

The cricket got to be too much for me last night. It seemed to keep increasing its tempo, although I don't know how it could have managed to chirp any faster than it had been doing at the beginning. In any case, when I put down the great fact, I waited a while trying to decide how to go about describing the distribution. Nothing untoward happened, it is quite true, while I was making the deliveries, but still, it seemed to me last night in my overwrought condition that a special effort was required for me to be able to go into the details. And while I waited, the cricket went on and on and on; faster and faster, or so it seemed to me, until it would have been impossible to set down another word. This morning, however, I am in fine shape.

It was raining a little when I started out, a warm, fine summer drizzle. One of the things I have noticed about myself since Anna and I split up is the fact that I have a sneaking fondness for walking in the rain without rubbers or a hat. Doubtless this is a predilection I have always had without realizing it, since first it was Mother and then Anna who always seemed somehow to prevent me from indulging in it. Quite rightly, too; I should probably have caught pneumonia and died long before this if it had not been for them. But since Anna left me and I have been here in Manor Heights alone, I occasionally slip out bareheaded and without rubbers, if the rain is not too heavy. Mrs. Crawford, like a good housekeeper, has sometimes caught me at it, and brought it to my attention, hurrying to supply the needed accessories and thus obliging me to wear them. Yesterday morning, however, I managed to get out of the front door while she was in the kitchen talking to the delivery man from Macy's. I knew he would be coming, and I had everything ready, the twenty little boxes in the left-hand pocket of my jacket, the pennies in the right-hand trouser-pocket. The only way to do anything is to have it so well rehearsed in one's imagination that when the moment comes one does it automatically, as though for the hundredth time. Then it is all natural, and there is little likelihood of a slip-up. And there was no slip-up anywhere along the way. It was a heavy day, but not too hot because of the rain, which fell quietly as I walked down the road to the station. On the train I was not in the slightest degree perturbed: I knew there was no chance of any trouble. I kept marveling at the peculiar pleasure afforded by the knowledge that one has planned a thing so perfectly there can be no room for the possibility of failure, all the while being conscious that both the pleasure and the idea itself were completely childish, and that my conviction of success was, at the very least, ill-founded. But certain situations call forth certain emotions, and the mind is a thing entirely apart. I have cakes of soap that I bought twenty-five years ago, still in their wrappers, and I am saving them in the perfect confidence that the right day will come to unwrap each one and use it. And there are probably a hundred books downstairs in the library that I am eager to read, have been eager to read for years, yet refuse to read until the days comes, the day that says to me: This is the morning to start Villiers de l'Ile Adam, or George Borrow, or Psichari, or someone else. Now, in my logical mind, I know quite well that these promised days are not likely ever to arrive: I shall never use those old cakes of soap that are stored in the linen closet, and I am reasonably sure of never reading *Romany Rye*, because it doesn't interest *me*. But there is that other person, the ideal one that I ought to be, and whom it does interest, and it comforts me to think that those things are there waiting for him. Certainly, the mind is a thing absolutely apart.

From Grand Central I took the shuttle across to Times Square, then walked underground to the Eighth Avenue Subway. I chose the Independent as my territory, because of the great length of the stations. The air in that tunnel was almost steamy, and smelled of wet cement, hot metal and sewage. I took an express all the way up to Fort Tryon, worked slowly down through Harlem and then all the way to Canal Street. There was no hitch, no real difficulty, anywhere. The only place where there was even a meeting of any sort was at Twenty-third Street, where a colored woman who was standing near the machine came up behind me as I was reaching in to take out the real package, which of course made it impossible for me to put in the one I held in my left hand. I did not hesitate for a fraction of a second. It was my determination that everything be carried off perfectly. I turned aside, put my left hand back into my coat pocket, and proceeded to open the little box, shake out its two while candy-coated pellets into my hand and pop them into my mouth. If I were to suggest to anyone that this was an excellent piece of strategy, it would sound laughable, and yet it required quick thinking and a certain courage. In the first place, I have never chewed gum, and the idea of it disgusts me. (It occurs to me now that this distaste may easily have had some bearing on my choice of method for carrying out my project.) But much more than that secondary consideration was the fact that my co-ordination is not always of the best. On occasion it takes terrific concentration for me to distinguish right from left. And a second before, I had held in my left hand the *other* box, one of *my* boxes. What if, I said to myself, through some dark perversity of the subconscious, I should somehow have opened the wrong box? And as I crunched through the enamal walls of mint-sugar I found myself wondering if what I was tasting was the normal flavor, or whether it might be my flavor, my special mixture. I did not wait to get at that machine again, but continued downtown, skipping the West Fourth Street station because of the central platforms and the undesirable placing of the machines.

At Canal Street I had the pleasure of actually seeing the bait snapped up. I had no sooner put the penny in, retrieved the untouched box, and placed one of mine at the back of the shelf, when a young girl (Italian, I think) pushed past me and worked the machine. There was an expression of amusement on her face as she rejoined her friends at the edge of the platform. "Gee, I'm gettin' good," she said. "I got two."

I delivered the three final boxes in Brooklyn, returned to Manhattan, had a light meal at a Longchamps on Madison Avenue, and came home, feeling that the day had certainly not been wasted. I venture to say that I am embarked on the biggest comedy to be played in the subways of New York until the day Russia's super-bombs lay them all bare to the sun. This is an infantile pastime I have devised, but at the same time it carries its own weight, and thus must have a meaning. However, I paid for my jaunt with a feeling of considerable fatigue, mostly of nervous origin, I suppose. Naturally, it was something of a strain. On an ordinary evening a cricket would not have been able to disturb me. Mrs. Crawford was indignant about the rubbers and the hat and the fact that my clothes were quite damp, of course. She is a good old soul. Today I have done nothing but sit in the garden reading the Sunday *Times*. The sun was out and in, all day, but it was not too hot.

This morning the Stewarts very kindly invited me on a picnic to Rye Beach. I could not entertain the thought of going, certainly. It's bad enough to have them living next door, to have to hear their abominable radio at all hours of the day and night, and put up with the depredations wrought in the garden by that untrained brat of theirs, without going out of my way to accompany them on an outing. It was a kind thought, however, and I have decided to go downtown the first thing tomorrow morning and buy a toy of some sort for little Dorothy. Maybe a tricycle, or something that will keep her on the sidewalk. Anywhere, anywhere, out of my garden!

Monday 3rd——

I scarcely dared open the paper this morning, for fear of what I should find. Still, reading of the consequences is most assuredly a part of the procedure, and so I went ahead. But for some reason the police are keeping it quiet. There was nothing, anywhere. This silence managed to make me feel uncomfortable; in a way I feel as though I were being watched.

The Stewarts were most pleased with the velocipede, or whatever the chromium-plated contraption is called. Little Dorothy seemed quite overwhelmed by its splendor. As yet I have not seen her use it. I dare say she is too small to pull it by herself, up and down the two flights of steps between the front door and the sidewalk. I imagine for a while her parents will have to take it up and down for her.

Thursday 6th——

The newspapers continue to maintain a stubborn silence, being filled instead with asinine stories about the electoral campaign. As if it could possibly change the course of history which of the two scarecrows gets into the seat of power. It was already too late to do that a hundred and seventy-five years ago. Too late to avert the sheer, obscene horror that has been on its way ever since, and is nearly here now. Voltaire, Marx, Roosevelt, Stalin, what were they but buds along the branch, like sores that have a way of bursting through the skin where it is thinnest? Who planted the tree of poison, who infected the blood? I am not qualified to say; the complexities of the question are endless. But I believe that one of the culprits was our friend Rousseau. That unpardonable mechanism, the intellect, has several detestable aspects. Perhaps the worst is the interpenetration of minds; the influence, unconscious, even, that one mind can have over millions, is unforeseeable, immeasurable. You never know what form it will take, when it will make itself manifest.

Saturday 8th——

The police assuredly are playing some sort of game. There must have been at least fifteen deaths, and not a word about one of them has appeared. That of course is their business,

189

but I am amused and a little mystified to see how they are conducting it. Mrs. C. has a heavy summer cold. I tried hard to make her stay in bed, but she is the soul of conscientiousness, and insists on continuing with her regular work.

Sunday 9th——

It is an odd thing, that part of the mind which invents dreams and retains them, sometimes making of a certain dream a colored lens, as it were, which comes between one's consciousness and one's vision of what passes for reality. That is, the feeling of the dream can remain when every detail has been lost. For several days now a particular atmosphere, taste, sensation, or whatever it may be called, has been haunting me. It can only be a dream-vestige, yet in spite of the fact that I have forgotten the dream it is very strong. And since it is gone it is unlocatable in time. It may have been this week or many years ago that the dream itself took place. The feeling, if it can be put into words at all, is one connected with languor, forgetfulness, lostness, emptiness, endlessness—one thing which would be all those things. Living my life and thinking my thoughts through that lens makes for a certain melancholy. I have tried desperately to find a door into the dream; perhaps if I could recall it, get back there, I could destroy its power. It is often a way. But it is almost as if it were an entity in itself, aware of my efforts to find it, and determined to remain hidden. As I feel I am approaching it I seem to sense a springing away, a definite recoil into some airless, unreachable region within. I don't like it; it worries me.

Monday 10th——

When things become wholly unbelievable, all one can do is laugh. There is nothing to fall back upon but the bare fact of one's existence; one must forsake logic for magic. Because it was raining this morning (a morning rather like the day of my excursion to the city) and I wanted to take a short stroll, I went to the clothes closet and took out my gray flannel suit. I was entirely dressed when I suddenly recalled that there was a large hole in the right trouser-pocket. A strange feeling of confusion came over me, even before I started to think. But then the mental process commenced. How had the pennies stayed in my pocket that day? It was quite simple. I had changed my suit; now I remembered clearly taking off the gray flannel and putting on the herring-bone tweed. Perhaps if I had been able to live completely in the mind at that moment, I should have given it no further thought, and the unacceptable discovery would not have been made—at least, not then. But evidently I could not be satisfied with anything so simple. Another reflex sent my left hand to the pocket of the jacket, and that was the instant of my undoing. Later I took them all out and counted them sitting on the bed, but then I merely stood still, my hand inside the pocket feeling the jumble of small cardboard boxes, my mouth hanging open like an idiot's. It was inescapable—they were there. A second later I said aloud: "Oh." And I rushed over to the bureau drawer and opened it, because I wanted to be sure that these were not the untouched boxes I had collected. But they too were there, scattered among the piles of clean handkerchiefs. Then the others——? There is nothing to think. I *know* I delivered them.

At least, I believe I know. If I am to doubt my own eyes and ears, then it is time I gave up entirely. But in connection with that idea a ghastly little thought occurs to me: am I doubting my eyes and ears? Obviously not; only my memory. Memory is a cleverer trickster by far. In that case, however, I am stark, raving mad, because I remember every detail of those hours spent in the subway. But here are the boxes piled in front of me on the desk, all twenty. I know them intimately. I glued down each little flap with the maximum of care. There is no mistaking them. It is a shattering experience, and I feel ill, ill in every part of my being. A voice in me says: "Accept the impossible. Leave off trying to make this fit in with your preconceived ideas of logic and probability. Life would be a sad affair if it reserved no surprises at all." "But not this sort!" I reply. "Nothing quite so basically destructive of my understanding of the world!" I am going to bed. Everything is all wrong.

The dream has emerged from its wrappings of fog. Not all of it, but that does not matter. I recognized it immediately when only a piece of it appeared, as I was lying here in the dark, half asleep. I relaxed and let more of it come. A senseless dream, it would seem, and yet powerful enough to have colored all these past few days with its sadness. It is almost impossible to put down, since nothing *happens* in it: I am left only with vague impressions of being solitary in the park of some vast city. Solitary in the sense that although life is going on all around me, the cords that could connect me in any way with that life have been severed, so that I am as alone as if I were a spirit returned from the dead. Traffic moves past at some distance from where I am reclining on the ground under the trees. The time—timeless. I know there are streets full of people behind the trees, but I will never be able to touch them. If I should open my mouth to cry out, no sound would come forth. Or if I should stretch my arms toward one of the figures that occasionally wanders along the path nearby, that would have no effect, because I am invisible. It is the terrible contradiction that is unbearable: being there and yet knowing that I am not there, for in order to *be*, one must not only be to one's self: it is absolutely imperative that one be for others. One must have a way of basing one's being on the certainly that others know one is there. I am telling myself that somewhere in this city Mrs. Crawford is thinking of me. If I could find her, she would be able to see me, and could give me a sign that would mean everything was all right. But she will never come by this place. I am hidden. I cannot move, I was born here, have always been here under these trees on this wet grass. And if I was born,

192

perhaps I can die, and the city making its roar out beyond this park will stop being. That is my only hope. But it will take almost for ever. That is about all there is to the dream. Just that static picture of sadness and lostness.

The boxes are still there on my desk. They at least are no dream!

That little Dorothy is a horror. This evening at dusk I was returning from a short walk. It was nearly dark, and for some reason the street lights had not yet been put on. I turned into the front walk, climbed up the steps, and had almost reached the house, when I banged full-force into her damned tricycle. I am afraid my anger ran away with me, for I deliberately gave it such a push that it bumped all the way down both flights of steps and ran out into the middle of the street. A truck coming down the hill finished it off in a somewhat spectacular fashion. When I got inside I found the child in the kitchen talking with Mrs. C. I did not mention the incident, but came directly upstairs.

It is a lovely evening. After dinner I am going to take all forty boxes to the woods behind the school and throw them on to the rubbish heap there. It's too childish a game to go on playing at my age. Let the kids have them.

THE
FROZEN FIELDS

THE train was late because the hot-box under one of the coaches had caught fire in the middle of a great flat field covered with snow. They had stayed there about an hour. After the noise and rushing of the train, the sudden silence and the embarrassed stirring of people in their seats induced a general restlessness. At one point another train had shot by on the next track with a roar worse than thunder; in the wake of that, the nervousness of the passengers increased, and they began to talk fretfully in low voices.

Donald had started to scratch pictures with his fingernail in the ice that covered the lower part of the windowpane by his seat. His father had said: "Stop that." He knew better than to ask "Why?" but he thought it; he could not see what harm it would do, and he felt a little resentful toward his mother for not intervening. He could have arranged for her to object to the senseless prohibition, but experience had taught him that she could be counted on to come to his defense only a limited number of times during any given day, and it was imprudent to squander her reserve of good will.

The snow had been cleared from the station platform when they got out. It was bitter cold; a fat plume of steam trailed downward from the locomotive, partially enveloping the first coach. Donald's feet ached with the cold.

"There's Uncle Greg and Uncle Willis!" he cried, and he jumped up and down several times.

"You don't have to shout," said his father. "We see them. And stand still. Pick up your bag."

Uncle Willis wore a black bearskin coat that almost touched the ground. He put his hands under Donald's arms and lifted him up so that his head was at a level with his own, and kissed him hard on the mouth. Then he swung him over into Uncle Greg's arms, and Uncle Greg did the same thing. "How's the man, hey?" cried Uncle Greg, as he set him down.

"Fine," said Donald, conscious of a feeling of triumph, because his father did not like to see boys being kissed. "Men shake hands," he had told him. "They don't kiss each other."

The sky was crystal clear, and although it was already turning lavender with the passing of afternoon, it still shone with an intense light, like the sky in one scene at the Russian Ballet. His mother had taken him a few weeks earlier because she wanted to see Pavlova; it was not the dancing that had excited him, but the sudden direct contact with the world of magic. This was a magic sky above him now, nothing like the one he was used to seeing above the streets of New York. Everything connected with the farm was imbued with magic. The house was the nucleus of an enchanted world more real than the world that other people knew about. During the long green summers he had spent there with his mother and the members of her family he had discovered that world and explored it, and none of them had ever noticed that he was living in it. But his father's presence here would constitute a grave danger, because it was next to impossible to conceal anything from him, and once aware of the existence of the other world he would spare no pains to destroy it. Donald was not yet sure whether all the entrances were safely guarded or effectively camouflaged.

They sat in the back of the sleigh with a brown buffalo robe tucked around them. The two big gray horses were breathing out steam through their wide nostrils. Silently the white countryside moved past, its frozen trees pink in the late light. Uncle Greg held the reins, and Uncle Willis, sitting beside him, was turned sideways in his seat, talking to Donald's mother.

"My feet hurt," said Donald.

"Well, God Almighty, boy!" cried Uncle Willis. "Haven't you got 'em on the bricks? There are five hot bricks down there. That's what they're there for." He bent over and lifted up part of the heavy lap-robe. The bricks were wrapped in newspaper.

"My feet are like blocks of ice, too," said Donald's mother. "Here, take your shoes off and put your feet on these." She pushed two of the bricks toward Donald.

"He just wants attention," said Donald's father. But he did not forbid him to have the bricks.

"Is that better?" Uncle Willis asked a moment later.

"It feels good. How many miles is it to the farm?"

"Seven miles to The Corner, and a mile and a half from there."

"Oh, I know it's a mile and a half from The Corner," said Donald. He had walked it many times in the summer, and he knew the names of the farms along the road. "First you come to the Elders, then the Landons, then the Madisons——"

His father pushed him hard in the ribs with his elbow. "Just keep quiet for a while."

Uncle Willis pretended not to have heard this. "Well, well. You certainly have a good memory. How old are you now?"

Donald's throat had constricted; it was a familiar occurrence which did not at all mean that he was going to cry—merely that he felt like crying. He coughed and said in a stifled voice: "Six." Then he coughed again; ashamed, and fearful that Uncle Willis might have noticed something amiss, he added: "But I'll be seven the day after New Year's."

They were all silent after that; there were only the muffled rhythm of the horses' trot and the soft, sliding sound of the runners on the packed snow. The sky was now a little darker

196

than the white meadows, and the woods on the hill-side beyond, with their millions of bare branches, began to look frightening. Donald was glad to be sitting in the middle. He knew there were no wolves out there, and yet, could anybody be really certain? There had been wolves at one time—and bears as well —and simply because nobody had seen one in many years, they now said there weren't any. But that was no proof.

They came to The Corner, where the road to the farm turned off from the main road. Seven rusty mail-boxes stood there in a crooked row, one for each house on the road.

"R. F. D. Number One," said Uncle Willis facetiously. This had always been a kind of joke among them, ever since they had bought the farm, because they were townspeople and thought the real farmers were very funny.

Now Donald felt he was on home ground, and it gave him the confidence to say: "Rural Free Delivery." He said the words carefully, since the first one sometimes gave him difficulty. But he pronounced it all right, and Uncle Greg, without turning round, shouted: "That's right! You go to school now?"

"Yes." He did not feel like saying more, because he was following the curves in the road, which he knew by heart. But everything looked so different from the way he remembered it that he found it hard to believe it was the same place. The land had lost its intimacy, become bare and unprotected. Even in the oncoming night he could see right through the leafless bushes that should have hidden the empty fields beyond. His feet were all right now, but his hands in their woolen mittens under the buffalo skin were numb with cold.

The farm came into view; in each downstairs window there was a lighted candle and a holly wreath. He bent over and put his shoes on. It was hard because his fingers ached. When he sat up again the sleigh had stopped. The kitchen door had opened; someone was coming out. Everyone was shouting "Hello!" and "Merry Christmas!" Between the sleigh and the kitchen he was aware only of being kissed and patted, lifted up and set down, and told that he had grown. His grandfather helped him take off his shoes again and removed a lid from the top of the stove so he could warm his hands over the flames. The kitchen smelled, as in summer, of woodsmoke, sour milk and kerosene.

It was always very exciting to be in the midst of many people. Each one was an added protection against the constant watchfulness of his mother and father. At home there were only he and they, so that mealtimes were periods of torture. Tonight there were eight at the supper table. They put an enormous old leather-bound dictionary in a chair so he would be high enough, and he sat between his grandmother and Aunt Emilie. She had dark brown eyes and was very pretty. Uncle Greg had married her a year ago, and Donald knew from many overheard conversations that none of the others really liked her.

Gramma was saying: "Louisa and Ivor couldn't get down till tomorrow. Mr. Gordon's driving them down as far as Portersville in his car. They'll all stay in the hotel tonight, and we've got to go in first thing in the morning and bring them out."

"Mr. Gordon, too, I suppose," said his mother.

"Oh, probably," Uncle Greg said. "He won't want to stay alone Christmas Day."

His mother looked annoyed. "It seems sort of unnecessary," she said. "Christmas is a *family* day, after all."

"Well, he's part of the family now," said Uncle Willis with a crooked smile.

His mother replied with great feeling: "I think it's terrible."

"He's pretty bad these days," put in Grampa, shaking his head.

"Still on the old fire-water?" asked his father.

Uncle Greg raised his eyebrows. "That and worse. You know. . . . And Ivor too."

Donald knew they were being mysterious because of him. He pretended not to be listening, and busied himself making marks on the tablecloth with his napkin ring.

His father's mouth had fallen open with astonishment. "Where do they get it?" he demanded.

"Prescription," said Uncle Willis lightly. "Some crooked Polack doctor up there."

"Oh, honestly," cried his mother. "I don't see how Louisa *stands* it."

Aunt Emilie, who had been quiet until now, suddenly spoke. "Oh, I don't know," she said speculatively. "They're both very good to her. I think Mr. Gordon's very generous. *He* pays the rent on her apartment, you know, and gives her the use of the car and chauffeur most afternoons."

"You don't know anything about it," said Uncle Greg in a gruff, unpleasant voice which was meant to stop her from talking. But she went on, a bit shrilly, and even Donald could hear that they were in the habit of arguing.

"I *do* happen to know that Ivor's perfectly willing to give her a divorce any time she wants it, because she told me so herself."

There was silence at the table; Donald was certain that if he had not been there they would all have begun to talk at that point. Aunt Emilie had said something he was not supposed to hear.

"Well," said Uncle Willis heartily, "how about another piece of cake, Donald, old man?"

"How about bed, you mean," said his father. "It's time he went to bed."

His mother said nothing, helped him from his chair and took him upstairs.

The little panes of his bedroom window were completely covered with ice. Opening his mouth, he breathed on one pane until a round hole had been melted through and he could see blackness outside. "Don't do that, dear," said his mother. "Gramma'll have to clean the window. Now come on; into bed with you. There's a nice hot brick under the covers so your feet won't get cold." She tucked the blankets around him, kissed

199

him, and took the lamp from the table. His father's voice, annoyed, came up from the foot of the stairs. "Hey, Laura! What's going on up there? Come on."

"Won't there be any light in my room at all?" Donald asked her.

"I'm coming," she called. She looked down at Donald. "You never have a light at home."

"I know, but home I can turn it on if I need it."

"Well, you're not going to need it tonight. Your father would have a fit if I left the lamp. You know that. Now just go to sleep."

"But I won't be able to sleep," he said miserably.

"Laura!" shouted his father.

"Just a *minute!*" she cried, vexed.

"Please, Mother. . .?"

Her voice was adamant. "This cold air will put you to sleep in two shakes of a lamb's tail. Now go to sleep." She went to the doorway, the lamp in her hand, and disappeared through it, closing the door behind her.

There was a little china clock on the table that ticked very loud and fast. At infrequent intervals from below came a muffled burst of laughter which immediately subsided. His mother had said: "I'll open this window about an inch; that'll be enough." The room was growing colder by the minute. He pushed the sole of one foot against the heated brick in the middle of the bed, and heard the crackle of the newspaper that enfolded it. There was nothing left to do but go to sleep. On his way through the borderlands of consciousness he had a fantasy. From the mountain behind the farm, running silently over the icy crust of the snow, leaping over the rocks and bushes, came a wolf. He was running toward the farm. When he got there he would look through the windows until he found the dining-room where the grownups were sitting around the big table. Donald shuddered when he saw his eyes in the dark through the glass. And now, calculating every movement perfectly, the wolf sprang, smashing the panes, and seized Donald's father by the throat. In an instant, before anyone could move or cry out, he was gone again with his prey still between his jaws, his head turned sideways as he dragged the limp form swiftly over the surface of the snow.

The white light of dawn was in the room when he opened his eyes. Already there were bumpings in the bowels of the house: people were stirring. He heard a window slammed shut, and then the regular sound of someone splitting wood with a hatchet. Presently there were nearer noises, and he knew that his parents in the next room had gotten up. Then his door was flung open and his mother came in, wearing a thick brown flannel bathrobe, and with her hair falling loose down her back. "Merry Christmas!" she cried, holding up a gigantic red mesh stocking crammed with fruit and small packages. "Look what I found hanging by the fireplace!" He was disappointed because he had hoped to go and get his stocking himself. "I brought it up to you because the house is as cold as a barn," she told him. "You stay put right here in bed till it's warmed up a little."

"When'll we have the tree?" The important ritual was the tree: the most interesting presents were piled under it.

"You just hold your horses," she told him. "You've got your stocking. We can't have the tree till Aunt Louisa gets here. You wouldn't want her to miss it, would you?"

"Where's my present for Aunt Louisa and Uncle Ivor? Uncle Ivor's coming, too, isn't he?"

"Of course he's coming," she replied, with that faintly different way of speaking she used when she mentioned Uncle Ivor. "I've already put it under the tree with the other things. Now you just stay where you are, all covered up, and look at your stocking. I'm going to get dressed." She shivered and hurried back into her room.

The only person he had to thank at breakfast was his grandfather, for a box of colored pencils which had been jammed into the foot of the stocking. The other gifts had been tagged:

"For Donald from Santa." Uncle Willis and Uncle Greg had eaten an early breakfast and gone in the sleigh to the hotel in Portersville to fetch Aunt Louisa and Uncle Ivor. When they go back, Donald ran to the window and saw that Mr. Gordon had come. Everyone had talked so mysteriously about Mr. Gordon that he was very eager to see him. But at that moment his mother called him upstairs to help her make the beds. "We all have to do as much as we can for Gramma," she told him. "Lord knows she's got all she can manage with the kitchen work."

But eventually he heard Aunt Louisa calling up the staircase. They went down: he was smothered in kisses, and Aunt Louisa asked him: "How's my boy? You're *my* boy, aren't you?" Then Uncle Ivor kissed him, and he shook hands with Mr. Gordon, who was already sitting in Grampa's armchair, where nobody else ever sat. He was plump and pale, and he wore two big diamond rings on one hand and an even bigger sapphire on the other. As he breathed he wheezed slightly; now and then he pulled an enormous yellow silk handkerchief out of his breast pocket and wiped his forehead with it. Donald sat down on the other side of the room and turned the pages of a magazine, from time to time looking up to observe him. He had called Donald "my lad," which sounded very strange, like someone talking in a book. At one point he noticed Donald's attention, and beckoned to him. Donald went and stood beside the armchair while Mr. Gordon reached into his pocket and pulled out a fat watch with a little button near the stem. "Push it," he said. Donald pushed the button, and tiny chimes struck inside the watch. A few minutes later he signaled to him afresh; Donald bounded over to him and pressed the button again. The next time, his mother told him to stop bothering Mr. Gordon.

"But he *asked* me to," objected Donald.

"Sit down right there. We're all going in and have our tree in a little while. Uncle Ivor's going to be Santa Claus."

Presently Uncle Willis came into the room. "Well, everybody, he said, rubbing his hands together, "I think the parlor's warm enough now. How about our tree?"

"It's about time," said Aunt Emilie. She was wearing a red taffeta dress which Donald had heard his mother discussing with his father earlier. "*Most* inappropriate," she had said. "The girl doesn't seem to realize she's living on a farm." Aunt Emilie reached down and took Donald's hand. "Would you care to accompany me, sir?" she said. They walked into the parlor holding hands. The fire in the fireplace roared and crackled.

"Where's Ivor?" said Uncle Greg. "Has everybody got a seat?"

"Here he is," said Uncle Ivor, coming in from the hallway. He had put on an old red knitted skull-cap and a red dressing gown, and he had a wreath of green fluted paper around his neck. "This is all Santa Claus could find," he announced.

Aunt Louisa began to laugh. "Look at your Uncle Ivor," she told Donald. "I am," said Donald. But he was really looking at the tree. It was a tall hemlock that reached to the ceiling, and underneath it was piled the most enormous assortment of packages he had ever seen. "Look at that!" they all cried.

"What *do* you suppose is in them all?" said Aunt Louisa.

"I don't know," he replied.

Uncle Ivor sat down on the floor as near the tree as he could get, and lifting up a large crate he passed it to Uncle Greg, who stood in the middle of the room. "Let's get this out of the way first," he said. Then Uncle Greg intoned: "To Donald from the Folks at Rutland."

While Uncle Ivor went on passing out packages, Donald struggled with his box. He was vaguely aware of the little cries that were being uttered around him: "How lovely! But it's too much!" "Oh, you shouldn't have!" "Why did you do it?" as the others opened their gifts, but he was too preoccupied to notice that most of the exclamations were being addressed to Mr. Gordon, who sat in the window looking very pleased.

It was too good to believe: a fire engine three feet long, with rubber tires and a bell and a siren and three ladders that shot upward automatically when it stopped. Donald looked at it, and for a moment was almost frightened by the power he knew it had to change his world.

"Oh . . . isn't . . . that . . . lovely!" said his mother, her annoyance giving a sharp edge to each word. "Louisa, why did you do it?" Donald glanced up quickly and saw Aunt Louisa indicate Mr. Gordon with a jerk of her head, as if she were saying: "Everything is his fault."

His mother moved along the floor towards the crate and fished out the greeting card. "I want you to keep each card in with the present it came with," she told Donald, "because you'll have a lot of thank-you notes to write tomorrow, and you don't want to get them mixed up. But you can thank Aunt Louisa and Uncle Ivor right now."

He hated to be told to thank a person in that person's presence, as though he were a baby. But he said the words bravely, facing Mr. Gordon: "Thank you so much for the beautiful fire engine."

"There's more there, my lad," beamed Mr. Gordon; the diamonds flashed in the sunlight.

Aunt Emilie was holding out her arm in front of her, looking at her new wrist-watch. Grampa had put on a black silk dressing gown and was smoking a cigar. He looked perfectly content as he turned to Mr. Gordon and said: "Well, you've spoiled us all." But Donald's mother interpreted his phrase as a reproach, and added in explanation: "We're not used to getting such *elaborate* gifts, Mr. Gordon."

Mr. Gordon laughed, and turning to Donald, told him: "You've barely started, my lad. Tell your Uncle Ivor to get on with it."

Now it seemed as though nearly every package was for Donald. He opened them as fast as he could, and was freshly bewildered by the apparition of each new marvel. There were, of course, the handkerchiefs and books and mufflers from the family, but there was also a Swiss music box with little metal records that could be changed; there were roller skates, a large set of lead soldiers, a real accordion, and a toy village with a streetcar system that ran on a battery. As Donald opened each package, the little cries of admiration made by his parents came closer to sounding like groans. Finally his father said, in a voice loud enough for Mr. Gordon to hear him above the general conversation: "It's bad business for one kid to get so much."

Mr. Gordon had heard him. "You were young once yourself," he said airily.

Aunt Emilie was trying on a fur jacket that Uncle Greg had given her. Her face was flushed with excitement; she had just planted a big kiss on Uncle Greg's cheek.

"The little Astor baby got five thousand dollars' worth of toys on its last birthday," she said to Donald's father, running her hand back and forth along the fur.

Donald's father looked at her with narrowed eyes. "That," he said, enunciating very clearly, "is what might be called an *asinine* remark."

Save for the crackling of the fire there was silence for a moment in the room. Those who had not heard knew that something had happened. Uncle Greg looked quickly at Donald's father, and then at Aunt Emilie. Maybe there would be a quarrel, thought Donald, with everyone against his father. The idea delighted him; at the same time he felt guilty, as though it were his doing.

Uncle Ivor was handing him a package. Automatically he untied the ribbon, and pulled out a tan cashmere sweater. "That's Mother's and Daddy's present to you," his mother said quietly. "It's a little big for you now, but I got it big purposely so you could grow into it." The small crisis had passed; they all began to talk again. Donald was relieved and disappointed. "How about christening that bottle of brandy?" cried Uncle Willis.

"You menfolk sit here," Gramma told them. "We've got to to get out into the kitchen."

"I'll bring yours out to you," said Uncle Ivor to Aunt Louisa as she got up.

On her way out of the room Donald's mother bent over and touched his shoulder. "I want you to put every present back into its box just the way it was. After that you carry them all up into our room and stack them carefully in the corner under the window. You hear me?"

She went out. Donald sat a moment; then he jumped up and ran after her to ask if he might save out just one thing—the fire engine, perhaps. She was saying to Gramma: ". . . quite uncalled for. Besides, I don't know how we're *ever* going to get it all back to New York. Owen can take the big things at least with him tomorrow, I suppose."

He stopped running, and felt peace descend upon him. His father was leaving the farm. Then let him take everything with him, fire engine and all; it would not matter. He turned and went back into the parlor, where he meticulously packed the toys into their boxes, put the covers on, and tied them up with lengths of ribbon and string.

"What's all this?" exclaimed Mr. Gordon suddenly, noticing him. "What are you doing?"

"I have to take everything upstairs," said Donald.

His father joined the conversation. "I don't want to find those boxes lying all over the place up there, either. See that you pile 'em neatly. Understand?"

Donald continued to work without looking up.

After a moment Mr. Gordon said under his breath: "Well, I'll be damned." Then to Donald's father: "I've seen some well-behaved kids in my time, but I don't mind telling you I never saw one like *that*. Never."

"Discipline begins in the cradle," said his father shortly.

"It's sinister," murmured Mr. Gordon to himself.

Donald glanced up and saw his father looking at Mr. Gordon with hatred.

In the kitchen his grandmother, his aunts and his mother were busy preparing dinner. Donald sat by the window mashing potatoes. The blue of the sky had disappeared behind one curtain of cloud, uniformly white. "We'll have more snow before night," said Gramma, looking out of the window above the sink.

"Want to smell something good?" Donald's mother asked him. He ran across to the stove and she opened the oven door: the aroma of onions mingled with that of the roasting turkey. "He's coming along beautifully," she announced. She shut the oven door with a bang and hung the pot-holders on their hooks. Then she went into the pantry. Donald followed her. It was very cold in here, and it smelled of pickles and spices. His mother was searching for something along the shelves, among the jars and tin boxes.

"Mother," he said.

"Hmm?" she replied distraughtly, without looking down at him.

"Why does Mr. Gordon live at Uncle Ivor's?"

Now she did look at him, and with an intensity that startled him. "What was that?" she demanded sharply. Then, before he could repeat his question, she went on in a suddenly matter-of-fact voice: "Dear, don't you know that Uncle Ivor's what they call a male nurse? Like Miss Oliver, you remember, who took care of you when you had influenza? Only a man. A man nurse."

"Is Mr. Gordon sick?"

"Yes, he is," she said, lowering her voice to little more than a whisper. "He's a very sick man, but we don't talk about it."

"What's he got?" He was conscious of being purposely childish at the moment, in the hope of learning more. But his mother was already saying: "I don't know, dear. You go

207

back into the kitchen now. It's too cold for you in here. Scoot! Out with you!" He giggled, ran back into the kitchen, satisfied for having definitely established the existence of a mystery.

During dinner his father looked across at him and, with the particular kind of sternness he reserved for remarks which he knew were unwelcome, said: "You haven't been outside yet today, young man. We'll take a walk down the road later."

Aunt Louisa had brought a large glass of brandy to the table with her, and was sipping it along with her food. "It's too cold, Owen," she objected. "He'll catch his death o' cold." Donald knew she was trying to help him, but he wished she had kept quiet. If it became an issue, his father would certainly not forget about the walk.

"Too cold!" scoffed his father. "We have a few basic rules in *our* little family, and one of them is that he has to get some fresh air every day."

"Couldn't you make an exception for Christmas? Just for one day?" demanded Aunt Louisa.

Donald did not dare look up, for fear of seeing the expression on his father's face.

"Listen, Louisa," he said acidly. "I suggest you just stay on your side of the fence, and I'll stay on mine. We'll get along a lot better." Then as an afterthought he snapped: "That all right with you?"

Aunt Louisa leaned across Grampa's plate toward Donald's father and spoke very loud, so that everyone stopped eating. "No, it's not all right with me!" she cried. "All you do is pick on the child from morning till night. It's shameful! I won't sit by and watch my own flesh and blood plagued that way!"

Both Gramma and Donald's father began to speak at once. Gramma was saying, "Louisa," trying to soothe her. Donald's father shouted: "You've never *had* a kid. You don't know the first thing *about* raising kids."

"I know when a man's selfish and plain cussed," Aunt Louisa declared.

"Louisa!" cried Gramma in a tone of surprise and mild reproof. Donald continued to look at his plate.

"Have I ever come up to Rutland and stuck my nose in your affairs and criticized? Have I?" demanded Donald's father.

"Now come on," said Uncle Willis quickly. "Let's not spoil a beautiful Christmas."

"That's right," Grampa said. "We're all happy. Let's not say anything we'll be sorry for later."

But Aunt Louisa would not retreat. She took a fast gulp of brandy and almost choked on it. Then, still leaning toward Donald's father, she went on: "What do you mean, come to Rutland and criticize? What've you got to criticize in Rutland? Something wrong there?"

For an instant Donald's father did not reply. During that instant it was as though everyone felt the need to say something without being able to say it. The one who broke the short silence was Donald's father, using a peculiar, soft voice which Donald recognized immediately as a vicious imitation of Uncle Ivor. "Oh, no! There's nothing wrong in Rutland!"

Suddenly, with two simultaneous motions, Donald's mother slapped her napkin into her plate and pushed her chair back violently. She rose and ran out of the room, slamming the door. No one said anything. Donald sat frozen, unable to look up, unable even to breathe. Then he realized that his father had got up, too, and was on his way out.

"Leave her alone, Owen," said Gramma.

"You keep out of this," his father said. His footsteps made the stairs creak as he went up. No one said anything until Gramma made as if to rise. "I'm going up," she declared.

"For God's sake, Abbie, sit still, " Grampa told her. Gramma cleared her throat, but did not get up.

Aunt Louisa looked very red, and the muscles of her face were twitching. "Hateful," she said in a choked voice. "Just hateful."

"I felt like slapping his face," confided Aunt Emilie. "Did

you hear what he said to me when we were having our presents?"

At a glance from Uncle Greg, Aunt Emilie stopped. "Why, Donald!" she exclaimed brightly, "you've scarcely touched your dinner! Aren't you hungry?"

In his mind's eye he was seeing the bedroom upstairs, where his father was twisting his mother's arm and shaking her to make her look at him. When she wouldn't, he punched her, knocking her down, and kicked her as hard as he could, all over her body. Donald looked up. "Not very," he said.

Without warning Mr. Gordon began to talk, holding his glass in front of him and examining it as he turned it this way and that. "Family quarrels," he sighed. "Same old thing. Reminds me of my boyhood. When I look back on it, it seems to me we never got through a meal without a fight, but I suppose we must have once in a while." He set the glass down. "Well, they're all dead now, thank God."

Donald looked quickly across at Mr. Gordon as if he were seeing him for the first time.

"It's snowing!" cried Gramma triumphantly. "Look, it's snowing again. I knew we'd have more snow before dark." She did not want Mr. Gordon to go on talking.

Aunt Louisa sobbed once, got up, and went out into the kitchen. Uncle Ivor followed her.

"Why, Donald! You've got the wishbone!" cried Aunt Emilie. "Eat the meat off it and we'll hang it up over the stove to dry, and tomorrow we'll wish on it. Wouldn't that be fun?"

He picked it up in his fingers and began to chew on the strips of white meat that clung to it. When he had carefully cleaned it, he got down and went out into the kitchen with it.

The room was very quiet; the tea-kettle simmered on the stove. Outside the window the falling snowflakes looked dark against the whiteness beyond. Aunt Louisa was sitting on the high stool, doubled over, with a crumpled handkerchief in her hand, and Uncle Ivor was bending over her talking in a very low voice. Donald laid the wishbone on the sink shelf and started to tiptoe out, but Uncle Ivor saw him. "How'd you like to go up to the henhouse with me, Donald?" he said. "I've got to find us a dozen eggs to take back to Rutland."

"I'll get my coat," Donald told him, eager to go out before his father came back downstairs.

The path up the hill to the henhouse had been made not by clearing the snow away, but by tramping it down. The new snow was drifting over the track; in some places it already had covered it. When Uncle Ivor went into the henhouse Donald stood still, bending his head back to catch some snowflakes in his mouth. "Come on in and shut the door. You'll let all the heat out," Uncle Ivor told him.

"I'm coming," said Donald. He stepped through the doorway and closed the door. The smell inside was very strong. As Uncle Ivor approached the hens, they set up a low, distrustful murmur.

"Tell me, Donald," said Uncle Ivor as he explored the straw with his hands. "What?" said Donald.

"Does your mother often run to her room and shut the door, the way she did just now?"

"Sometimes."

"Why? Is your father mean to her?"

"Oh," said Donald vaguely, "they have fights." He felt uncomfortable.

"Yes. Well, it's a great pity your father ever got married. It would have been better for everybody if he'd stayed single."

"But then I wouldn't have been born at all," cried Donald, uncertain whether Uncle Ivor was serious or not.

"At least, we *hope* not!" said Uncle Ivor, rolling his eyes and looking silly. Now Donald knew it was a kind of joke, and he laughed. The door was flung open. "Donald!" roared his father.

"What is it?" he said, his voice very feeble.

"Come out here!"

He stumbled toward the door; his father was peering inside uncertainly. "What are you doing in there?" he demanded.

"Helping Uncle Ivor look for eggs."

"Hmmph!" Donald stepped out and his father shut the door. They started to walk along the road in the direction of the Smithson farm. Presently his father fell in behind him and prodded him in the back, saying: "Keep your head up. Chest out! D'you want to get round-shouldered? Before you know it you'll have curvature of the spine."

When they had got out of sight of the house, in a place where the tangle of small trees came to the edge of the road on both sides, his father stopped walking. He looked around, reached down, picked up a handful of the new snow, and rolled it into a hard ball. Then he threw it at a fairly large tree, some distance from the road. It broke, leaving a white mark on the dark trunk. "Let's see you hit it," he told Donald.

A wolf could be waiting here, somewhere back in the still gloom of the woods. It was very important not to make him angry. If his father wanted to take a chance and throw snowballs into the woods, he could, but Donald would not. Then perhaps the wolf would understand that he, at least, was his friend.

"Go on," said his father.

"No. I don't want to."

With mock astonishment his father said: "Oh, you don't?" Then his face became dangerous and his voice cracked like a whip. "Are you going to do what I told you?"

"No." It was the first time he had openly defied him. His father turned very red.

"Listen here, you young whippersnapper!" he cried, his voice tight with anger. "You think you're going to get away with this?" Before Donald knew what was happening, his father had seized him with one hand while he bent over and with the other scooped up as much snow as he could. "We'll settle this little matter right now," he said through his teeth. Suddenly he was rubbing the snow violently over Donald's face, and at the same time that Donald gasped and squirmed, he pushed what was left of it down his neck. As he felt the wet, icy mass sliding down his back, he doubled over. His eyes were squeezed shut; he was certain his father was trying to kill him. With a desperate lunge he bounded free and fell face-downward into the snow.

"Get up," his father said disgustedly. He did not move. If he held his breath long enough he might die.

His father yanked him to his feet. "I've had just about enough of your monkeyshines," he said. Clutching him tightly with both hands, he forced him to hobble ahead of him, back through the twilight to the house.

Donald moved forward, looking at the white road in front of him, his mind empty of thoughts. An unfamiliar feeling had come to him: he was not sorry for himself for being wet and cold, or even resentful at having been mistreated. He felt detached; it was an agreeable, almost voluptuous sensation which he accepted without understanding or questioning it.

As they advanced down the long alley of maple trees in the dusk his father said: "Now you can go and cry in your mother's lap."

"I'm not crying," said Donald loudly, without expression. His father did not answer.

Fortunately the kitchen was empty. He could tell from the sound of the voices in the parlor that Aunt Louisa, Uncle Ivor and Mr. Gordon were getting ready to leave. He ran upstairs to his room and changed his clothes completely. The hole he had breathed in the ice on the windowpane had frozen over thickly again, but the round mark was still visible. As he finished dressing his mother called him. It was completely dark outside. He went downstairs. She was standing in the hallway.

"Oh, you've changed your clothes," she said. "Come out and say good-by to Aunt Louisa and Uncle Ivor. They're in the kitchen." He looked quickly at her face to see if there were signs of her recent tears: her eyes were slightly bloodshot.

Together they went into the kitchen. "Donald wants to say good-by to you," she told Mr. Gordon, steering Donald to Aunt Louisa. "You've given him a wonderful Christmas"—her voice became reproachful—"but it was *much* too much."

The thick beaver collar of Mr. Gordon's overcoat was turned up over his ears, and he had on enormous fur gloves. He smiled and clapped his hands together expectantly; it made a cushioned sound. "Oh, it was a lot of fun," he said. "He reminds me a little of myself, you know, when I was his age. I was a sort of shy and quiet lad, too." Donald felt his mother's hand tighten on his shoulder as she pushed him toward Aunt Louisa. "Mm," she said. "Well, Auntie Louisa, here's somebody who wants to say good-by to you."

Even in the excitement of watching Uncle Willis and Uncle Greg drive the others off in the sleigh, Donald did not miss the fact that his father had not appeared in the kitchen at all. When the sleigh had moved out of sight down the dark road, everyone went into the parlor and Grampa put another log on the fire.

"Where's Owen?" Gramma said in a low voice to Donald's mother.

"He must be upstairs. To tell the truth, I don't care very much where he is."

"Poor child," said Gramma. "Headache a little better?"

"A little." She sighed. "He certainly managed to take all the pleasure out of *my* Christmas."

"A mean shame," said Gramma.

"It was all I could do to look Ivor in the face just now. I mean it."

"I'm sure they all understood," said Gramma soothingly. "Just don't you fret about it. Anyway, Owen'll be gone tomorrow, and you can rest up."

Shortly after Uncle Willis and Uncle Greg got back, Donald's father came downstairs. Supper was eaten in almost complete silence; at no time did his father speak to him or pay him any attention. As soon as the meal was over his mother took him upstairs to bed.

When she had left him, he lay in the dark listening to the sound of the fine snow as the wind drove it against the panes. The wolf was out there in the night, running along paths that no one had ever seen, down the hill and across the meadow, stopping to drink at a deep place in the brook where the ice had not formed. The stiff hairs of his coat had caught the snow; he shook himself and climbed up the bank to where Donald sat waiting for him. Then he lay down beside him, putting his heavy head in Donald's lap. Donald leaned over and buried his face in the shaggy fur of his scruff. After a while they both got up and began to run together, faster and faster, across the fields.

About the Author

PAUL BOWLES was born in New York City in 1911. After a number of years spent in Paris, North Africa, and Latin America, Mr. Bowles returned to North Africa to buy a small house in Tangier, Morocco, and from this base he has traveled to Ceylon, India, and Thailand, at one time even making Ceylon his winter headquarters. The author of four novels, *The Sheltering Sky*, *Let It Come Down*, *The Spider's House*, and *Up Above the World*, Mr. Bowles is the author of another collection of short stories, *The Delicate Prey*. He is also well-known as a composer and, over a period of years, he has gathered for the Library of Congress one of the most extensive collections of recordings of native North African music.